The Ascension of Mary

WILLIAM WEST

Relax. Read. Repeat.

THE ASCENSION OF MARY
By William West
Published by TouchPoint Press
Brookland, AR 72417
www.touchpointpress.com

ISBN: 978-1-952816-88-8

Editor: Kimberly Coghlan
Cover Design: Colbie Myles
Cover Images: Adobe Stock: sad teenage girl by zea_lenanet

Visit the author's website at williamwest.net

First Edition

Printed in the United States of America.

In memory of my sister, Terry Anne West Kelso.

APPARITIONS

ONE - JONAH

I KNOW YOU THINK I'M AN OLD FOOL, ESTHER, but this is important, and I need you to listen to me. I've been sitting on this front porch waiting for two months now. I watched the sky, and I watched the road. I sipped my tea, and I did some more watching, some more waiting. I thought you'd be here by now. Every day has been the same as the one before. I was sure the time to go was getting close. I felt it in these old bones. But then something strange happened. This young girl walked by in front of the house. Oh yes, I know, a lot of young girls live in the neighborhood and pass through here on their way to the other side of the Eisenhower, but this girl was different. I could tell right away. She had a determined way of walking. Something was special about her, and it wasn't long before my suspicions came true. Things began to happen—things that changed the last fifteen years or at least made me think I needed to stick around and help fix things.

Who would've thought that a young, white girl named Mary would be able to change the life of this stubborn, old black man? I mean completely turn it around. And with a profound connection to something beyond explanation or rational understanding. Blind faith in the unknown on my part. Yes, ma'am. Funny thing that was. You remember giving me that lecture? Practically every Sunday it was, explaining your beliefs when I would question mine because I didn't want to go to church. I still see you standing at the front door, so pretty in that lacy blue dress you wore most

Sundays, one eyebrow raised in playful defiance, your arms folded under your ample breasts and that shiny, black purse you saved for special occasions hanging from the crook of one elbow.

I can just hear you. "Some things you just have to have faith in, Jonah, whether you understand them or not." Then you would quote the Bible, Hebrews 11:1. Yes. How could I forget that? "Now faith is the substance of things hoped for, the evidence of things not seen." That's what you would say to me, and that's the only way I can explain it. Mary had that effect on me, and as far as I could tell, something mysterious about that girl made me want to follow my suspicions to the end just to see what she was capable of—especially after I learned who Mary was.

So anyway, I was sitting in my rocker on the front porch, bundled up against a frosty wind blowing out of Chicago like a harsh warning that it would be back next winter. I knew that you would've told me, "Get yourself inside in front of the fireplace," but I was determined to see you again. My sweet Esther.

Flashes of my life kept jumping into my head, like I guess most folks have when it's almost time, gusting around me like the wind, mostly of when I was younger, back when I thought I controlled all things, when I thought I was the center of the universe. We used to sit on the stoop, you and me, and watch the neighborhood like we were hoping for any kind of change to take place, sweep by and summon us away from the same old passage of people, and cars, and growing weeds.

You looked at me and said, "Jonah Culpepper, someday, you are going to be somebody. Your name will be on every marquee of every jazz joint in Chicago."

I laughed at that until my side ached because I hadn't been playing the piano very long then, and as much as I wanted it to come true, that idea was still so far outside the world of this tall, lanky kid from the South Side, I couldn't imagine it ever coming true.

How I got started was quite by accident—and maybe with a little divine intervention, I suppose. I was interested in this special young lady who sang in the choir at the South Side Gospel Church, so I started helping out in the sanctuary while the choir was rehearsing. The choir director was Miss Margaret Turner, and she noticed me sitting in the pew, staring at the choir, and tapping my feet. She couldn't tell I was staring at you. Yes, you were that special young lady who sang so beautifully above all the others. Miss Turner just thought I was interested in the music. She offered to teach me how to play the piano, and of course, I thought why not, that would get me even closer to the choir, which it did. I picked it up real fast and took to it like those keys were a part of my fingers. I started playing with the choir and accompanying solos.

I'll never forget the day Miss Turner introduced us, and I felt your smile melt my heart. Esther Hubbard. I couldn't stop saying your name. We spent a lot of time together in the beginning, practicing and rehearsing, then talking and laughing. What really surprised me was when you told me that you didn't even like singing all that much, that your real love was the violin. The day you first played for me was the day I realized that nothing in this world could take me away from you.

As much as you used to tease me that you knew what I was up to, you must have seen something in me too, Esther Hubbard, because we never saw anyone else after that, and like it was my plan all along, you eventually became my wife. Needless to say, I thought my life was blessed.

It was a time when I couldn't get enough of listening to jazz greats like Oscar Peterson, Fats Waller, and Thelonious Monk. There were others of course—Art Tatum, Bell Evans, Bobby Broom, and Bud Powell to name a few— who helped me, unbeknownst to them, to perfect my style, and before long, I was on my way. I got small gigs all over town and eventually a spot at The Jazz Showcase before landing a regular gig at Andy's. You were able to sit at a table near the stage, so when I played, I felt like I was playing to you, and I was able to put all my love into my music.

I had no shortage of success, and it came easy. My life was everything I had wanted it to be—an exciting career, a beautiful wife, and eventually three wonderful children. I wanted to be a good example for them so I stayed away from drugs and alcohol for the most part because I had seen too many of my friends lose everything to those demons. I had it all until the day tragedy knocked on our door, entered our house where it wasn't wanted—when I was the least prepared for it, and that ungodly presence hit me where it hurt the most.

When tragedy took our children, that was it. I was done. I lost interest in everything, and I mean everything. You got me through the worst of it, and I guess your God had a hand in it too, but I was so caught up in myself that I failed to notice how it all affected you. I must have worn you out clean to the bone. I didn't see how your heart was just as broken as mine, and it just gave out before I could come to my senses and help you. There was nothing left for me except to sit here on this front porch and ask for forgiveness—and wait for the Lord to come and take me.

That's what I thought, anyway.

But that's when Mary appeared, walking in a beam of sunlight that followed her down the sidewalk in front of our house. She stared over at me out of the corners of her eyes, wary as a lamb that had wandered too close to the edge of the forest, finding itself alone and full of prayers that the old, dark wolf, peering at her from over the top of the milkweed bushes wouldn't jump out and make her his dinner.

I didn't know it then, but it was like we were both meant to be in that place at that moment in time, for my part to see a new purpose in my life through Mary, and for her part, well, that just might be the strangest story of all.

She couldn't have been more than fifteen or sixteen, and after I instinctively checked my watch to put this all into some kind of cosmic perspective, and then noticing that the time was 3:30, I figured she was walking home from school or the green line, just coming back from a music lesson. The violin case strapped on her back gave that away, and it must've been why I immediately felt connected to her.

Esther, I still hear you playing your violin just like it was yesterday. I've never heard a sweeter sound than what came out of your violin.

Seems like another life now with your violin and my piano both silenced by tragedy. We hadn't even lived here that long, but we knew we had made the right move. Neither one of us missed falling asleep every night to the sound of gunfire on the streets of Chicago's South Side. In Oak Park, we were relaxed, proud, hopeful, and a little naïve, as we never even thought about what problems might arise from an African-American family moving into an affluent neighborhood of Chicago.

I don't blame Oak Park. Not a bit. That wasn't the problem at all, and it still isn't, not even after the violence that took our son, that same violence we tried to escape. Maybe I was wrong in bringing us here. I accept the blame for that, but there's nothing I can do about it now. Nothing but sit here and wait.

I was beginning to think the time was near when I started hearing a violin playing some of the same music you used to play. I thought that you had found a violin in heaven and were playing for me, so as I wouldn't be afraid to cross over.

So, when Mary turned up the driveway to the house next door, I realized it was her violin I'd been hearing, and I got to thinking that if Mary was a part of the family who had lived in that house, we had another connection besides the music.

I didn't know how I felt about that possibility because it just might bring back a lot of terrible memories and make them all real again. That house had been empty for a while, so I knew that girl must be new to the neighborhood. I never saw that house go up for sale, and I never saw any moving truck bring new neighbors with all of their possessions either, so I have to admit, I was curious, and it wasn't long before I discovered something else about Mary. Like I say, I think she came into my life for a reason, but not just for me. She was meant to make a difference and change the course of time.

Two - Mary

A LOT HAS HAPPENED THIS WEEK, PAPA, and my life is changing so fast, I didn't want to lose track of myself. I talk to Mama about things, and I talk to you. I know you can't answer, so I write down my thoughts about what has happened. I feel I won't get lost if I do that. And I can share my life with you. Anne Frank said, "Parents can only give good advice or put them on the right paths, but the final forming of a person's character lies in their own hands." I've been reading her diary since I found it in some of Mama's things when we started packing to move.

Mama and I finally got to the new house, Papa. I wish you could've been with us. It took us three days to drive across the country from California, and the day we arrived, we were so tired we just fell onto the sofa and stared at our suitcases and all the unopened boxes scattered about on the floor. Mama didn't feel like cooking; we didn't have any food anyway, so she told me to leave everything as it was. "We're going out to eat," she said. "I'm tired of eating roadside fast food."

We went to this restaurant almost around the corner where the funniest thing happened. We encountered this silly-looking lady who approached our table like it didn't matter that we were still eating. She had pink hair and thick eyelashes and a broad smile that never changed when she spoke.

"Oh, Honey, you are *so* pretty," she said. Her cheeks were pink and full of wrinkles that vibrated with every word. Her voice was like a wind-up doll, high and squeaky. She asked Mama if I was her daughter, and without waiting for an answer, she asked, "How did you get such a beautiful, dark complexion when your mother's skin is so creamy?"

It was an odd compliment, almost an insult like there was something mean behind it. Mama always called me Peanut, and she told me it was because my skin was the color of peanut butter spread ever so lightly over a fresh slice of white bread, and maybe with a little peach preserves on top just for sweetness. Mama just smiled and told the lady that she ate a lot of peanuts when she was pregnant, and she punctuated it with her usual silly laugh like she was apologizing for it.

I could tell the woman didn't know if Mama was being serious or not, so she just said "Oh," like the key in her back suddenly stopped turning. The lady walked away, and Mama looked at me and rolled her eyes. I knew it bothered her, but I didn't mind so much because she always made me feel special. But there was something else too. I was Peanut to Mama and Mary to everyone else, so it was like I had a dual identity. If I wanted to, I could create a different personality for each name, and that made my life more interesting, if not more exciting. Without that, my life was dull, and at fourteen years old, that was sad. But then that was before I saw the ghost in my bedroom.

At the breakfast table the next morning, I held up my glass of milk against Mama's arm. "Look, your skin is the color of milk." We both laughed the same silly laugh.

Mama said, "You may *not* call me Milk."

I've always called her Mama. I didn't even know her real name until I went with her to her office one day, and one of the other attorneys called her Rachel. I called her Rachel a couple of times that day until she sat me down and told me that I was the only special person in her life who could call her Mama. Rachel was what all the other people called her. I guess Mama had a dual identity too.

At the breakfast table, she leaned over nose-to-nose with me, and we gazed into each other's eyes, sharing the light, which made our eyes look like emeralds.

"You're a funny bunny," Mama said.

"You're a silly billy," I said.

The clouds moved over the sun, and the color of our eyes changed to the deep green of a pine forest.

"I like it that we're so much alike," I said.

"Me too, Peanut," Mama said.

"I wish my hair was your color though." My hair was the color of coffee, and Mama's hair was more like a strawberry milkshake.

I've always had to imagine what you look like, Papa, because I've never even seen a photo of you. I asked Mama about that one day, and she said she never got a photo of you before you died. I'm sorry I never got to know you. Mama said she'll eventually tell me about you, but that hasn't happened yet. The memory is too painful for her.

"Don't you have any happy memories with my father?" I asked her.

"My happy memories are with you now," she said.

Mama and I moved to a nice, but old, neighborhood in a town called the Village of Oak Park, just west of Chicago. It's early spring now, but scattered piles of snow are still on the ground. Before we moved from California, I did some research about Oak Park and found out that it's famous for being the birthplace of Ernest Hemingway and for having some of the first homes designed by Frank Lloyd Wright. I had to look him up too, and I thought it was interesting that someone could be so famous that people could look you up and read about everything you did. I was also glad that we were moving to a place that was famous for something. Our house is not one of the homes designed by Frank Lloyd Wright, but it's still a nice house and probably too big for just the two of us.

Everything about the house is scary, though. I hear things at night, and I sit up in bed and stare into the shadows and dim light, hoping to identify the source of the sound as something natural like a ticking clock or a cat outside the window. Lights tumble across the walls, which I tell myself come from passing cars on the street even though I don't hear any cars. All this makes me wish we'd never moved to Oak Park. I questioned Mama's judgment for moving us to such a big, old house in such a cold part of the world until I found out why.

✦ ✦ ✦

WE'VE ONLY BEEN IN THIS HOME A FEW DAYS NOW, and we're still unpacking boxes. Mama surprised me with a new cell phone. My complaining about the cold and the noises keeping me up at night must have caused her to worry about my mental health.

"You seem to be a little stressed," she said. "I wanted to do something to make the transition easier for you. Don't think I'm giving you this phone just because you complained so much about not having one when every kid at school in California was walking around texting someone or at least pretending to text someone so they'd look popular. That's superficial."

I think she wanted to justify that in her own mind as well. She had decided the phone was necessary to stay in touch with me and give us both peace of mind. It did take my mind off the anxiety of moving to a new town, at least for a while.

I sent a text message to my friend back in California.

> Just got this new phone, so now we can stay in touch. I'm so happy, but I'm also nervous because I think there's a ghost in my bedroom. I wish you could spend the night like we used to do.

I waited and waited. Her response never appeared, but the noises and lights in my bedroom persisted. Each night, I practice my violin, attempting my best at my two favorite compositions—Meditation and The Swan—before falling asleep with the tune from the last composition still in my head and the lights drifting overhead like a conductor's wand leading me into a dream.

In the dream, I'm performing on stage in front of an adoring, mesmerized audience, and the conductor keeps glancing over at me in sweet approval. On the second night of this dream, I saw the conductor's face clearly as he guided me with each note to perfection, but when the final note was silent, I looked up and he was crying.

"I think this house is haunted," I told Mama.

"This house holds a lot of secrets," Mama said.

She sat me down in the living room, which is dark with old, heavy furniture that we acquired with the house. I avoid this room because it feels sad, even now after Mama told me about the house. We sat beside the fireplace, listening to the popping and hissing from the burning logs, and Mama's eyes became a burning pine forest.

"I grew up in this house," she said.

I felt my eyes get bigger and warmer from the fire. I wanted to ask her why she hadn't told me about the house before, but I waited for Mama's thoughts to spill from the tears filling her eyes, trying to put out the fire from the memories that lay there.

"I lived here with my brother and our parents," she said. "My life was normal then—at least I thought it was. But when I got older, things changed, and I moved away to go to college and never went back."

"Why?" I asked, hoping to fill in some of the gaps Mama was obviously leaving empty.

Mama paused for a minute, staring at the fire, searching for the words in the dancing flames, as a thick strand of her hair fell over her eyes. She didn't move the hair as was her usual habit, and the sadness hid behind it and fell across her cheeks. "My parents and I didn't get along then, and time was never able to fix things between us. When I had you, I realized that you were more important to me than anything. It was just too difficult to go back."

I had so many questions about what happened to make things so bad, why Mama had kept this a secret, and why we had moved back to the house now. I left all these questions to drift about like blowing embers in my head until Mama's sadness wasn't covering her answers. But there was one question that couldn't wait. "What happened to them?" I asked.

"They're all dead now. My brother Paul enlisted in the army and was killed in Afghanistan shortly after he got there. He was only twenty years old. You weren't even a year old then, so you never had a chance to know him. Mama died shortly after that, and my father just recently died. I promise that one day I'll tell you all about them when I can remember the good times and not all the bad."

I began to feel that it wasn't the house but Mama who held all the secrets, and I'd have to wait to learn what those were. I trusted Mama though and felt that she was strong enough to work through this.

When we lived in California, Mama worked as a public defender because she had a passion for helping people who might not otherwise get a fair trial in what she called "our blinded justice system." She had finished college and law school with me on her hip or in a stroller, then day care, and finally a public school close enough where I could walk home on my own. I learned early to take care of myself, and I didn't blame Mama for not being there because when she was, I was always her first priority.

Whenever I felt down or overwhelmed, sitting alone with my head in my hands, heavy with a passive resistance to life, with my loneliness and my lack of friends, Mama was always there like a feather to push back my hair and kiss my forehead. That one caring gesture generated enough strength for me to sweep away all my worries, knowing that it was more important to pass on that strength to others.

Mama rubbed her hands together and held them up to the fire in a halting gesture that gathered the warmth. "Oh goodness me," she said with a sigh, and still addressing the fire, she quickly diverted the conversation, as was her customary strategy in the courtroom when a particular witness examination was not going her way.

She laughed about all the idiosyncrasies of the house, the creeks and groans of the stairs, the howling and whispers of wind in the doors and windows, the phantom footsteps when nothing was there except the tapping pipes or a mouse scurrying about in the attic.

"I've seen flickering lights in my bedroom," I added.

"Probably just a short circuit in this ancient electrical system," Mama explained. "There is really no need to worry, Peanut."

She was trying to comfort me not only about the house but also about the secrets of the past it held. Mama turned away from the fireplace and was looking at me with the strand of hair still covering her eyes, so I reached over and pushed the hair off her face and kissed her on the forehead.

"I won't be scared if you're not," I said.

That night, I practiced arpeggios and double stops and just for fun, an Irish reel called The Hills of Ireland. My head was spinning with the music. I jumped into bed, my fingers still dancing over the notes that lingered in the air as I waited to see if the music was going to stir my dreams. My resolve not to be frightened by the house was extinguished when the lights appeared, and for the first time, I realized that the lights in my bedroom just might be something other than a phantasmagoric display caused by sparking wires or electrical surges.

The lights had waited for the music to end and the darkness to settle. In anticipation, I defiantly gripped the edge of the blanket just under my chin. The lights first appeared from around the closet door, not so much as escaping from the closet as venturing out to play in the darkness. They moved in different directions about the room as if searching for something

to illuminate, never crossing paths or working against each oth
came together on the wall just above my headboard.

I tilted my head backward on the pillow and my eyes as far back as
could to enable a view of the wall. The blanket under my chin trembled in
the grip of my fingers. The light began to change shapes around its edges,
undulating amoeba-like as if contemplating its next move. I considered the
possibility that the light was watching me in the same way I was watching
it. Maybe it was just as afraid. Maybe it was curious or cautious.

The oddest thing was that I didn't scream out for Mama. Nothing made
any sense. The light suddenly and swiftly moved into a triangle shape from the
ceiling down the wall to the bed, then moved across the ceiling as it fanned out
to a cone shape above the bed, its base spotlighting my entire body and
moving up to a dark spot, pulling at it like a black hole, on the ceiling.

Just as quickly, I jerked the blanket up over my head and lay
motionless until I could no longer see the diffused light through the
blanket. The light moved slowly toward the closet and left the room in total
darkness once again. I didn't move until morning.

✦ ✦ ✦

THE END OF SPRING BREAK IS FINALLY HERE, the end of one nervous week of
moving and getting settled, the end of a life I was comfortable with to the
beginning of a new life full of anxiety. I'm glad I can talk to you because
without you, I would have no one, and considering what you are, that
makes me feel very odd.

Spring is different in Chicago because it seems that winter is only
beginning to weaken. Commuters are starting to emerge from behind their
heavy, hooded coats and scarves that are wrapped around their heads
several times to hide their faces, but to me, it's still cold. I never
encountered sub-freezing temperatures in California.

By the time the sun made its way across Lake Michigan and up over
Chicago, and finally, over the house across the street, it entered my
bedroom window on the second story shyly and politely as it brushed away
the dust and slid across my face like a silken scarf letting in the dawn. I
was happy when the sun finally brought some warmth into my room, and

I allowed it to lie on my face and remain there until I remembered this was my first day at school in Oak Park.

I blinked and sat up quickly, looking about my room for any disturbance, frantically examining the walls and floor and furniture for any evidence of what I had witnessed the last three nights. The same dream, the same lights, the same uneasiness like a child's fear of the bogeyman. I had tried to believe what Mama said, that it was just the house. I tried to pretend that it was just haunting nightmares, the result of my anxiety about moving and being in a new, strange house. None of it worked. I had to face this fear head-on.

I waited but nothing happened. I stared at the closet door, building up my courage. I slipped out of bed and tip-toed across the room, then flung open the closet door, not thinking about what I would do if something dangerous confronted me. Feeling emboldened, I shuffled through the clothes hanging in my closet like Scarlet O'Hara madly searching for something to wear. There was nothing unusual. I suddenly felt safe and fell back upon the bed.

From there, I immediately noticed a faint, flickering yellow light in the lamp on the ceiling, and I laughed at my Nightmare on Elm Street behavior. "Oh goodness me." I laughed and laughed.

I took my cell phone from the night table and quickly sent a text to my friend in California.

> First day of school. A little scared. Wish you were here so we could do this together. Last night I thought I saw the ghost in my bedroom. Just a spastic light on the ceiling. Hahahaha.

There was no reply. I stared at the phone, anticipating some sarcastic response about all the popular kids my friend and I thought were so dumb (translation: they were a lot cooler than we were). Remembering the two-hour time difference, I tossed the phone behind me onto the bed and slipped out from under the blanket. I drew the curtains back from over the windows to let in more sunlight.

The house across the street was crouched in the shade of large oak trees, neglected and hiding in the darkness as if sad and abandoned. I hoped spring would bring renewed life to the neighborhood. I turned away and went into the hall.

A faint, timid light emerged from under Mama's bedroom door. I smiled and scurried across the cold floor to the bathroom. I've had the same routine every morning to get myself ready for the day, nothing special to look at, so nothing special to do to myself. If I stare too long in the mirror, I start wishing I looked like Mama. Shower, dry hair, brush hair, after breakfast, come back to brush teeth. Nothing different. When I was done, I went downstairs to the kitchen where Mama was making breakfast.

She was cheerful. "Good morning, Peanut!" There was a little melody in her voice. "Are you ready for this? A new school and new friends. I think it's going to be exciting."

"I don't have any friends. This school won't be any different."

"Not true, Peanut. What about Jessica? She was a good friend."

"But she's in California, and I'm in Chicago."

"Oak Park."

"Whatever. Jessica doesn't talk to me anymore anyway."

"I know it's hard, but you just have to be positive. You're smart and pretty, and everyone who meets you likes you."

"That's not true, Mama."

"Oh, come on, Peanut. Cheer up. This is a new opportunity for both of us. We have to make the best of it."

"I'll try."

"I have my final interview for that job at the Public Defender's Office today, so after school, you'll have to let yourself in the house. Are you going to be okay with that?"

"Sure. I did it in California. I can do it here."

"Don't forget to practice your violin."

I rolled my eyes as I sent one last text to Jessica.

> I thought we were BFFs. I guess forever really doesn't mean forever.

This time there was a reply.

> You need to get a life, Mary.

I felt tired all day and on the verge of crying. A lot happens in the nothing that happens to me. I sensed that others were looking at me, but I refused to return their stares. I could hear their whispers in the hallways when other students passed me and when I sat alone to eat my lunch and when I was introduced by the teacher in each class. I could tell they were not friendly. Only once did I speak, and that was when I had to. My math teacher called on me to see if I wanted to try solving a problem, which had been on a test right before spring break. No one in the class had been able to solve the problem. I guess my pride got the best of me, and I quickly solved the problem at the blackboard to the astonishment of my teacher, but my pride was short-lived as I walked back to my seat and realized in the sneers and angry eyes following me that I should have kept my pride to myself.

My music class is last period because it's a performance class, and those who are lucky enough to get into the orchestra get to rehearse for the next performance. That's what I want, so of course, I was nervous. I was sitting against the wall, clutching my violin, when this bleak-looking, big-boned girl with big blond hair and a big chest—actually everything about her was big—walked straight up to me from across the room and stood where her big knees were almost touching my knees. Yes, I was intimidated. I could feel it, and it made me angry at myself.

She said, "You're new, aren't you?"

I tried to laugh off my anxiety. "You can tell?"

"Yes," she said, staring expressionless down at me. "I'm Camille. I'm the concertmaster in the orchestra, so you have to do what I tell you. Are we clear?"

"Yes."

"I'm also here to help you," she said.

"Really?" I was hoping that didn't come out as too sarcastic, but that's how I was feeling since she was offering to help me just after she had admonished or really threatened me.

"Yes. If you want a seat in the orchestra, you might need some advice. The violin section only has a few open seats, and there are a lot of you newbies who'll be fighting for those seats. We'll see how you work out. Like I said, I might be able to help you."

I thought Camille was going to leave, but she didn't. She kept staring at me like she was waiting for me to say something, I looked up at her and held my hand up as if it held the question, "What?" I didn't say it, though. I just waited.

"What are you anyway?" she finally asked.

Her question was troubling and vague. "Can you be more specific?" I asked.

"You don't look white, you don't look black or Mexican. Are you a mix of something? What are you?"

"My Mama's white. I guess I'm white. I still don't understand. Why does it matter?"

"Don't know. Guess we'll see," she said.

The school day could not have ended any sooner.

I walked home, and by the time I reached the house, I noticed the next-door neighbor sitting on his front porch. I had no desire to talk to anyone but fearing that he had seen me and not wanting to appear rude, I instinctively acted on one of the many lessons by lecture and example Mama had taught me—always be friendly and respectful to everyone unless they give you a reason not to be, and even then, just walk away. I extended my hand in a cautious but polite wave. He nodded to acknowledge me, and for a moment, his eyes pierced the dull afternoon sun and illuminated his dark skin under a blue baseball cap with a large C on the front.

I sensed he was searching for an answer to something he saw in me or something he hoped not to find, when suddenly he nodded a second time. I felt my cheeks flush and the corners of my mouth rise to a half-smile.

I entered my house through the back door as was my habit for years in California so I would not be visible to anyone on the street or in the neighborhood. I immediately locked the door behind me. Home was more than just a safe place. It was a place where I could be myself without criticism or ridicule—the stinging unspoken accusations that left me feeling like an outcast.

In California, I always felt comfortable and relaxed at home, but this one was still too new and different to give me that feeling of belonging and security.

The brief encounter with the man next door had given me a small hope that there might just be someone who likes me, but even that was not enough to calm my nerves. My experiences at school still bothered me like a persistent muscle tic that wouldn't relax. I wished I didn't have to go to school. I wished I could be home-schooled. I wished others would just leave me alone.

I dropped my books and my violin case on the table in the kitchen and grabbed a snack of juice and a carrot, which Mama had left in the refrigerator, her usual habit. I went to the small room next to the kitchen, which had been a dining room when we moved in. Mama converted it into a sitting room to take advantage of the afternoon warmth gathered by the large windows overlooking the backyard. There was a small sofa, a television, and a bookcase filled with books Mama referred to as her imagination library. In the corner, an easel sat next to boxes of art supplies to encourage me to develop my interest in art.

I began to draw a face on the large sketchpad on the easel, and when I had the basic shape I wanted, I took a piece of charcoal and filled in the features of eyes, ears, nose, and mouth, leaving the cheeks for last. I drew a conductor's wand diagonally across the page from the bottom to just beside the right jaw line of the face. I stepped back and stared at the face. It was a nice, gentle-looking face with kind eyes.

If I drew your face, Papa, it would be that face. I covered it with another blank page. I wanted to take my mind off everything that was happening in my life. I turned on the television, and as soon as I sat down on the sofa, the voices distorted into an irritating white noise. The undulating images of people began moving in and out of each other on the stage, and the audience became a sea of bobbing turtles before Dr. Phil's head filled the screen like a giant angry egg.

I turned off the television. Something was wrong with the Wi-Fi. I was disappointed that I had turned it on in the first place. Practicing the violin would at least be more productive and keep me from becoming a crazy person on a crazy afternoon talk show. But the white noise persisted. I waited, and still, it persisted. I shook my head to clear any disturbance in my inner ear. It didn't stop and even grew louder.

I went back to the kitchen where the noise followed me. I was getting more irritated, suspecting that the sound was in the wall between the two rooms. I went toward the front of the house, stopping at the door to the dreaded, dark living room with the heavy furniture that threatened to swallow me if I became too relaxed there.

The sound now came from up the stairs. I realized that I had left my juice on the kitchen table, and I was now holding the carrot like a knife in a firm grip. I slowly ascended the stairs, angling my body and twisting toward the sound as I went. At the top, I realized the sound was coming from the front of the house. I advanced down the hall, my back against the wall, the carrot knifing toward the sound.

It was definitely coming from my bedroom accompanied by a flicker of light under the door. I began to fear that the faulty ceiling fixture had started a fire in my bedroom, but I didn't smell anything burning, and I didn't see any smoke drifting out under the door.

I turned the doorknob in my trembling hand, trying to keep the knob from creaking in the latch. Pushing the door open, I saw a brighter light coming from the ceiling, a swirling aurora of green and red light around the white light of the fixture that was blinking on and off rapidly.

As I stood in the open doorway, staring at the ceiling, the flickering stopped as if it sensed my presence. The fixture was dark, but the light still surrounded it on the ceiling. The edges of the light moved toward me across the ceiling, inch by inch, as my heart began to race. The light began to change its shape into what I thought looked like the conductor's face in my dreams—and the face I had just drawn. I turned and ran down the stairs and out the back door.

I ran as fast as I could. I didn't have a plan or a destination or a safe place to run to. I didn't think about it until I stopped at the bottom of the steps leading to the porch where the old man sat—the man whose dark eyes had connected with my sadness and anger and made me feel better. The old man looked stunned.

"What you in such a hurry for, girl?" he asked.

His words pushed me back slightly, and I removed my foot from the first step and placed it back on the walkway. "There's something in my house."

"Well, I can tell already that there's something wrong. You look like you've just seen a ghost."

"I have." I blurted it out and only then realized how crazy it might sound. "I think I have anyway. Whatever it is scared me."

"A ghost, huh? Why don't you come on up here, girl? I'm tired of straining my neck to see you."

I came up the steps and sat in the rocking chair next to the old man. I stared at him, trying to figure him out. He was bundled in a heavy coat with a blanket over his lap. He had a grey mustache and goatee, which made his face look very thoughtful. "You don't believe me, do you?"

"Now I didn't say that. But let's be frank; ghosts aren't your usual house guests, and very few people, to my knowledge, have ever seen one."

"It's not exactly like the white sheet kind of ghost. In fact, it's more like just a weird light. Mama says it's the faulty ceiling lamp, but I just now saw it, and it wasn't coming from the ceiling lamp."

"Did it follow you over here?" The old man looked around, smiling; his eyes drawing in the light from the afternoon sun.

I narrowed my eyes at him. "No. I think it stays in my bedroom. It's like it can't leave my bedroom."

"Well, that *is* odd. Good for us, I guess. Funny how the previous owners of that house never talked about a ghost."

"My grandparents. They died. Do you think one of them could be the ghost?"

The old man stared at me a long time before speaking again. "I don't know. I didn't know them that well."

"Neither did I," I said, looking away. "I never met them."

"Really?" the old man said, and it wasn't so much a question as a statement of puzzlement, like he was pondering what I had said. "Now that *is* strange. What's your name, girl?"

"Mary. Mary Hester."

"Now I seem to remember that the family who lived in your house had the last name of Kelly. Was that your mother's name before she got married and had you?"

"I don't have a father. I mean I don't think Mama ever got married. It has always been just the two of us."

"Ohhh." He drew the word out like he was letting everything sink in. "Now, that sounds like you've got more to figure out than anything about this ghost."

"Why is that?"

"Just not normal, that's all. But then, neither are ghosts."

"Do you mind if I stay here awhile?" I asked, hoping to change the subject and take my mind off the ghost.

"That's fine, Mary." His long, strong-looking fingers lifted off his blanket and pointed to the rocking chair where I sat. "Do you like that chair? My wife used to sit there. In fact, she loved that chair. I think my wife would be okay with you sitting there, so I guess you can stay as long as you want, but sometimes I don't talk so much, so don't be offended by that. I'm just not a talker."

"You could've fooled me," I said.

The old man gave out a soft chuckle without looking at me, and I laughed along with him. "My name is Jonah," he said.

"Bet you have a whale of a time with that name."

He let out a sharp, loud laugh. "Oh, you're a clever one, Mary."

"Most people don't get my jokes. Your name is from the Bible, isn't it?"

"So is Mary."

"Mama's name is Rachel. I think that's from the Bible too. Isn't that funny?"

"Very."

"Is your wife, uh . . ."

"She passed a few years back. A lot of heartache in these two houses."

"I'm sorry."

"No need. My wife's name was Esther." Jonah watched me like he was waiting for what he had said to sink in and take away the sadness from my face, and when I looked up in surprised discovery, he smiled. "Yep, from the bible," he said. "Now here's the icing on that cake. People called our son Jake, but his given name was Jacob."

My eyes grew as big as two limes, and my jaw dropped even further like I was about to take a bite out of an apple. "That is just too funny." I laughed. "We're all right out of the Bible. I wonder if we're at all like the people in the Bible who had our names first."

"Now, I might be old, but I ain't that old." He laughed. "So, I wouldn't know any of them, but that would be something, wouldn't it?"

"I didn't mean that. Oh, wait," I said, as the sadness returned. "You said your son's name *was* Jacob, not *is*."

"Yeah, he passed many years ago. I guess we all carry around a ghost or two. Maybe you're lucky."

"How am I lucky?"

"You can see yours. Maybe your ghost doesn't want to hurt you. Maybe it just wants to talk to you. Have you thought of that? You could try listening. It might let you know what it wants. Or it might tell you what it's like on the other side."

We both looked back toward the street, not really focusing on anything in particular. The silence gathered awkwardly around us. I was so used to Mama's almost endless chatter that I thought any silence was an indication that something was not right.

"Do I need to leave now?" I asked.

"Only if you want to," Jonah said. "I usually fix myself a glass of tea about now, so if you want, I can fix you one too."

"Yes, please. Thank you."

Then there was more silence, which made me very confused. Suddenly, I heard a faint and familiar humming, which I soon realized was the tune of Massenet's Meditation. Jonah leaned slightly toward me and looked at me out of the corner of his eye. "Was that you playing the violin at night?"

I smiled so big I could feel all my teeth showing. "Yes. You were humming one of the pieces I love to play."

"So I was. So I was." With a deep sigh, Jonah pushed himself out of his rocking chair and let out a muffled groan as he grabbed his lower back. "I think you might need to come help me with that tea, Mary," he said.

I jumped up behind him. "I'll be happy to help, Jonah."

As Jonah made his way to the front door, he said, "You're a very polite young lady, Mary. I like that. I think that just maybe you're a lot like Mary in the Bible."

As the front door closed behind me, I wondered if I had made the right decision, trusting my feelings about Jonah instead of Mama's warnings about letting down my guard with strangers. Jonah headed down the hall, leaving me in that distracted gap of space that tore at my curiosity. Jonah's house was similar to ours in the layout of the rooms, but it was decorated differently and was actually more simplistic and modern than the threatening personality of the house Mama and I inherited.

I wanted to ask Mama if we could redecorate as soon as possible. There was an overwhelming musty odor that indicated a lack of care as if the interior had given up on life. In the front room was a large grand piano hiding under a layer of dust that smothered any life it once might have had.

The sofa against the opposite wall was covered with scattered papers, some of which looked to be music scores. The chair next to the fireplace was surrounded by stacks of newspapers on the floor, and behind the chair, in the corner, was a music stand straining with a large, opened music book.

"The kitchen's back this way, Mary," Jonah said.

Only then did I realize that I had stopped in the doorway to what appeared to be the music room, my mind captured by the suffering silence that stirred in the faint dust-filled air. "I'm sorry," I said, knowing what Mama might say. "I didn't mean to snoop."

"No need to worry about that," he said. "That used to be a very busy room. Now the only thing I do in there is read the Chicago Tribune by the fire." He chuckled as if a pleasant memory had passed through his head. "Funny thing is, sometimes I sit there, and I can hear the music as if it never really left the room."

"That's a beautiful piano," I said.

Jonah came back down the hall and entered the room. "You know what," he said, giving my shoulder a slight tap as he passed, "there's something I want to show you."

He went to a bench in the corner behind the music stand where there were two rectangular boxes. He picked up the box on top and sat it on the sofa. I could tell it was a hard case for a violin.

"You might enjoy this," he said as he opened the box to the most beautiful violin I had ever seen, protected in a nest of red velvet. Jonah chuckled under his breath as I audibly gasped. "This is an Anna Tartari violin."

He pointed to the *f*-hole where I could see *TARTARI* inscribed inside.

"She's a violin maker from Cremona, Italy," Jonah said. "It was a very special violin to Esther. When Esther's violin teacher passed away many years ago, he left this violin to Esther in his will. He said he wanted this violin to be heard in heaven when she played it. Esther always used this violin when she played with the Chicago Symphony."

"She must have loved playing this violin," I said. "I'd love to play with the Chicago Symphony one day."

"She did, she did. And when she played, I'm sure there were a lot of smiles in heaven."

"What a beautiful instrument. It must be worth a fortune."

"I suppose, but even a fortune wouldn't come close to the value of its memory to me. Esther used to play Meditation too, so sweet and gentle, like a bird soaring over a still lake. I always wanted that piece of music to be the last thing I ever heard on this Earth. I always thought it would be Esther to play it for me."

I waited while Jonah tucked away the violin back in its corner. He remained there for a moment with his head down as if saying a small prayer before turning back around.

"How about we get that tea now," I heard him say in a voice with renewed energy that still struggled to shake off some lingering sadness.

I didn't see him come back to where I was standing in front of the sofa. I was staring at a photograph in the bookcase, which was built into the wall. I heard him ask me if I was okay.

"That photograph," I said, pointing to the one I was staring at. "Is that your son?"

"That was his senior year," Jonah said. "He was such a handsome young man. Destined for greatness. It's hard to live with all the sadness and anger that erupts when a tragic thing happens, like what took my Jacob."

"I'm sorry. I didn't mean to make you think about that," I said. "If it would help you to talk about it though, I'd be willing to listen."

Jonah stared at me like what I said was the oddest thing he'd heard anyone say. I started to apologize when he put both of his hands on my shoulders and looked down at me. "You remind me a lot of my Esther. Maybe one day I'll take you up on that offer."

The kitchen was neatly cluttered, with folded grocery bags stacked on a table against one wall. In the corner by the back door was a trash can filled with aluminum plates and cardboard containers for tv dinners. The refrigerator and the microwave were probably the only appliances that had been used in a long time. Jonah pulled out a large jug of tea and took two glasses from a cupboard next to the refrigerator. He filled the glasses with tea and handed them to me. He told me to set them on the table beside the rocking chairs on the porch, He said he would be out in a minute. I was feeling comfortable that I had made the right decision in following him into his house.

I leaned back contentedly, a rag-doll in the rocking chair, my feet two opposing pendulums dangling from the front of the seat, my hands on the front of the armrests to keep from sliding further down. I was relaxed, comfortable, and happy. I hadn't even thought about my morning at school. I attributed that to Jonah and wondered why I had been so reluctant initially to trust him. I didn't feel threatened by him. I never would've climbed the stairs to his porch if that had been a problem.

Instinctively I had followed Mama's caution against strangers, but she had also taught me to treat everyone the same no matter what or how different they were or what race they were. "These are only visible images," Mama said, "like the colors and shapes of a painting. You need to look deeper to discover what the painting is about or how it affects you. It's the same with people."

I did think about the photograph of Jonah's son, Jake, though, and although it was impossible for me to have ever seen that photograph before, Jake's face was the face of the conductor in my dreams and the one I had drawn on my sketchpad.

Jonah came back carrying a plate of cookies, which he set on the table next to the glasses of tea and motioned for me to help myself. He sat back in his rocking chair with another slight groan before reaching over and taking one of the glasses of tea. In the long moment of silence, we enjoyed the blending of simple joys—the bittersweet taste of green tea, the soft and crunchy feel of shortbread, the relaxing movement of the rocking chair, the cool air left by the diminishing sun. Simultaneously, we sighed at the recognition of how important it was not to let these joys pass unnoticed. I stopped thinking about the ghost, and that made me happy. Tilting our heads towards each other, we laughed as we each added this small human connection to the list.

"So, I was wondering," Jonah said. "Do you practice the violin because your Mama wants you to, or do you play because it's natural, like it's a part of your life?"

He tripped me up with that question, and I'm sure the expression on my face gave that away because he smiled like he was waiting patiently for me to decide.

"I guess I never thought about it before," I said. "I've been playing the violin for a long time, it seems like anyway, and it's just something I do."

"You don't need to decide right away," he said. "You're still young. Discovering who we are is the most beautiful part of the trip. When I met my Esther, she was a singer. She had the most beautiful voice I had ever heard, for sure. But when I got to know her, I found out that she played the violin, and that's what she really loved. She passed on that love to a lot of kids. I wish you could have known her."

"She sounds very special," I said.

"Oh, she was," Jonah said. "She was indeed."

I caught a movement behind Jonah as Mama's car passed into the driveway. "That's my mom," I said. "Maybe I should go now."

"You tell her about that ghost now. No need to keep secrets about something like that."

"I promise." I started to leave, but I turned back at the top of the stairs. "Will it be okay if I come back sometime?"

"I think Esther would approve of you sitting in her chair, so it's fine with me."

As I ran down the porch steps, I felt happy at last, despite the news I had to tell Mama. I continued to run until I reached the back door, just as she was stepping inside. "Wait!" I called out as the door was closing.

Mama looked surprised. She could see that I was physically okay, but I could see in her eyes she suspected that something was not right. "Where were you?" she asked.

"I met one of our neighbors."

She stiffened sharply. "Were you at the house across the street?"

"No. I was next door," I said excitedly, not stopping for a breath until I had told her everything. "I saw our neighbor on my way home, and when I got scared at the lights in my bedroom, I ran over there. We were sitting on his front porch. He's really nice. His name is Jonah. I felt safe there."

"Whoa," Mama said in surprise. "That's a lot of information. I'm glad you're okay, though."

Mama had thrown me another curve ball, this time about our neighborhood. "Well, like I said. I felt safe there. But what's the problem with the house across the street?"

"It's just that I never trusted the people who lived there. Sorry. I guess I overreacted. Why don't we go over to Jonah's house so I can thank him? Then we can check your bedroom."

We walked hand in hand next door, but Jonah was no longer sitting on the porch. I let Mama take charge. She knocked on the front door then stepped back with her hands clasped over her heart, a look as if she were praying with her eyes open. Jonah opened the inner door and stared at us through the outer glass door.

"Hi, Jonah," Mama said.

"Rachel," Jonah said.

"It's been a long time," Rachel said.

"Wait," I said. "You two know each other?"

"Jonah has lived here a long time, Peanut."

"Mary is your daughter?" Jonah asked.

"Yes, she is. I wanted to thank you for . . ."

"No need," Jonah interrupted. He turned to me, his image through the glass door swirling like a dark, blurry hologram. "You'll have to get your mother to help you with your ghost the next time." And with that, Jonah closed the door.

We stared at the door in disbelief before turning to leave. I then stared at Mama in confusion, hoping to draw out some explanation. She didn't flinch; she didn't take her eyes off that empty space in front of her as if there the secrets of her past were playing out again.

"What was that all about?" I demanded. "He was so nice before."

"Years ago, Jonah blamed me for the death of his son. I guess after all these years, he still does."

"You didn't . . . did you . . . I mean."

"No. It's a long story, Peanut. I promise I'll tell you."

"These stories you're going to tell me someday are starting to add up."

"Okay. I guess it's time, but first, I think you need to tell me about this ghost."

"I'll do better than that. I'll show you."

I took Mama's hand like she didn't know the way to my bedroom. I didn't want any distractions to take her away from my mission. The door was still open as I had left it in my haste to flee the house. Still standing in the hall, I reached into the dark room and flipped the wall switch. The ceiling light fixture came on, erasing all the dim shadows lingering within its reach. I frowned and turned the switch off. The light went off. I turned the switch on and off repeatedly until giving up with a groan.

"Are you sure?" Mama asked.

"There's something here," I insisted. "And it's scary and weird. I saw it clearly, but now it's hiding like it's playing some game."

"Do you want to sleep in my room until we figure this out?"

"What about the other bedroom?"

"No," she said abruptly. "That room is off-limits." Mama immediately turned and started down the hallway toward her own bedroom.

"That does it," I called after her. "What's going on here? You're starting to scare me more than this house does."

She stopped suddenly as if my words had echoed off the walls and entangled her in their vines. "You're right," she said.

I came forward and took Mama's hand as the phantom vines released their grasp. We descended the stairs to the sunroom, which was now only dimly lit in the reflective light of dusk that came through the trees in the backyard.

Mama sat at an angle toward me and patted my knee. "I thought I was always protecting you from my past so you would have a clean, fresh start, not burdened by things that happened to me. But now that we're back here where it all happened, I'm facing it all again. I think that maybe all along I was also shielding myself from the pain."

One thing Mama and I have in common is pain.

THREE - RACHEL

THE CULPEPPER FAMILY MOVED INTO THE NEIGHBORHOOD when I was seventeen. Jonah was a jazz pianist, and his wife, Esther, was a music teacher at Oak Park and River Forest High School. She also played violin with the Chicago Symphony and gave violin lessons and voice lessons in their home. They moved from the South Side of Chicago to get away from all the gang violence. They had two girls, Olivia and Tameka, and one boy, Jake, who was a little older than me. Olivia and Tameka were both older than me and Jake.

I remember the day they moved in because it was summer, and my mother was in a good mood. She baked some cookies, and together, we went next door to welcome the Culpeppers to the neighborhood. I was nervous about it because even though I knew some black girls from school, they kept to themselves for the most part, and we only interacted on the cheer squad. I say interacted, but it was really more like silently sharing the same space because it seemed like there was this barrier that we weren't supposed to cross. There were so many times I wanted to break down that barrier and say something like "Oh, that's such a cute dress. Where did you get it?" I never was a trend-setter, though. I never was brave enough, and I felt terrible about it. Greeting the Culpeppers was an effort to correct that. But I was nervous about meeting them because I had never been in the home of a black family. I didn't know what to expect.

I was very naïve at seventeen, and now looking back on it, I can see the reasons why—the strict religious influence from my mother, the social mores at a mostly-white school in a relatively affluent suburb of Chicago, and the subtle segregation that existed at school events, holiday celebrations, and even birthday parties. I had been taught right from wrong, but my principles had never been tested because I had never experienced any overt prejudice. I had never questioned why equality of races only existed on paper until that day when I entered the lovely home of Esther and Jonah Culpepper.

My mother had her ups and downs. Some days, she couldn't even get out of bed, and other days, she would clean the house from top to bottom while she sang along with every song on the radio. I didn't know how sick she was until later when her depression took a stranglehold on her life. I only knew when to stay away and when it was safe to be around her.

Through it all, she was a picture of elegance in St. John's dresses and Stuart Weitzman shoes, matching purses, and every wave of her golden hair held in place with a standing weekly appointment at her stylist. She was prideful of her knowledge of Emily Post's guidelines of etiquette, and one thing you always did was welcome a new neighbor with a heartfelt gift. She baked cookies all morning and timed them perfectly to be ready when the appropriate hour for visiting arrived.

Esther answered the door with her daughters standing curiously behind her. We obviously took them by surprise, standing on their porch with two plates full of cookies. The visible expressions on their faces changed from questioning our intentions to mild shock and then to reserved hospitality. Esther invited us in, and the five of us sat around the kitchen table where she placed the plates of cookies. Esther impressed me as a practical and sensible woman—she dressed without pretense; she wore her hair neat and functional for playing and teaching violin and she spoke softly, reflecting a shy acceptance of her life. She was about the same age as my mother but had a natural beauty, which expressed itself without make-up. Esther dusted some lint off the front of her dress before sitting down, and she apologized for not having a formal place to sit.

"We turned our living room into a music room," she said. "There's not much room to move around in there with that big old piano. My husband

Jonah and I are both musicians, and I needed a place for my students."
Esther was very polite.

"You have a lovely home," my mother said.

Olivia and Tameka nibbled at the cookies with extended pinky fingers as they giggled and whispered to each other like I wouldn't be able to figure out that they were making fun of what they perceived as our white noblesse oblige toward their family.

Esther noticed too and admonished them with a look to behave. "Girls? What do you say to our neighbors?"

Olivia and Tameka sang out in unison, "Thank you!" Then they looked at each other and laughed.

I kept quiet except when spoken to and allowed my mother and Esther to guide the conversation—all the usual talk about how many children they had, where they go to school, and what the husbands did for a living. It only took a few minutes before Olivia tugged on Tameka's arm.

"Can we be excused, Mama?" Olivia asked. "I have some work upstairs, and I need Tameka to help me."

"Why don't you be a good host first and show Rachel around the house?" Esther asked. Olivia's eye roll indicated that she was not okay with that, but she still said, "Okay, Mama."

Tameka was staring at me like she wouldn't mind. Olivia kept tugging on Tameka and rolling her head and eyes to demand that Tameka help her out.

"It's okay," I quickly interjected. "I really can't stay that long, anyway. I have a paper to write," which wasn't true.

Olivia and Tameka scurried off, and Esther quickly changed the subject to her hopes that we would be able to come back someday. "I'd like for you to meet Jonah and Jacob. They went to the high school for football tryouts. Jonah is such a typical football dad. That's probably the biggest reason we moved to Oak Park. Jonah wants to make sure that Jacob will be at a good school so he can get noticed for a football scholarship. Jonah already has Jacob playing quarterback for Notre Dame." Esther laughed and gave me a wink.

Esther was a lovely woman, and I knew even then that I would feel comfortable with her welcoming me into their home if I needed to distance myself from my mother's low periods. I didn't meet Jacob until a week later when I came back from cheerleading camp. He was struggling with a lawnmower in the front yard, so I fixed a glass of iced tea and took it out to him, not realizing until I was face to face with him that he might not even be Jacob.

"I'm Rachel," I said. He looked puzzled about why I was presenting myself to him, so I added. "I'm your next-door neighbor." I noticed I was still holding the glass of tea as if I were the one drinking it, so I quickly extended my arm, offering the tea. "I thought you might be thirsty."

He looked down at the glass of iced tea and laughed. "Did you think I was the lawn boy?"

"No. I was hoping you were Jacob."

"Jake," he corrected me. "My mom told me about you." He took the glass and drank it down, then handed the glass back to me. "Thanks," he said. "I wish my sisters would do that, but they're too busy looking in the mirror at themselves to take any notice of me."

Now I was laughing and I couldn't seem to stop, no matter what he said. "Are you going to be our new star quarterback?" I asked.

"Yeah, that's me," he said. His smile was bright but modest, his dark eyes sincere and playful. "How did you know?"

"Your mom told me about you, too. It's good to know who I will be cheering for."

"Oh yeah, you mean like all official with pompoms and everything?"

"Yeah. I'll be the awkward one on the sideline in the ridiculously short skirt."

"Will you bring me some iced tea?"

"Not sure that I can do that, but I can try."

Jake laughed shyly. "I guess I should get back to finishing this."

I smiled behind an awkward half-wave. "Well, welcome to the school, and welcome to the neighborhood."

That was when a carload of guys from the school drove by, and one yelled out the window, "Hey there's our new quarterback." And one on the other side of the car yelled, "Here, catch this," as a beer bottle came flying over the top of the car and smashed against the sidewalk in front of the house, scattering broken glass out over the lawn.

Jake shook his head as the car sped away with squealing tires and a wake of fading laughter. "Yeah, welcome to the neighborhood," he said, and over his shoulder, I could see the old man who lived in the house across the street, standing in his driveway, his arms resting on the bulk of his frame like two heavy wings, and he was smiling at the whole scene. He saw me watching him, and he turned like a big turtle shifting its weight and went back inside his house.

The tears took a few seconds, but there was no holding them back. I tried at first, but I was scared, not for me, but for Jake. And I was embarrassed. I didn't mean to be so selfish about the emotion of what had just happened, to take Jake away from what was rightfully his—to be angry as hell. But he remained so calm. And strong. I didn't know if it was for me or if that was his learned reaction to what he had witnessed all of his life. It didn't matter. He didn't deserve any of it.

Four - Jonah

I TRIED REAL HARD NOT TO LET ON ABOUT ANYTHING, but my suspicious nature was working even harder at getting the best of me. When Mary stopped in front of Jake's photo—you know the one in the music room from his yearbook—I could tell she saw something in his face, almost like he was talking to her through the photo. There was definitely a connection, and she couldn't let go of that.

Sometimes I think that some people have a similar type of energy, almost like a magnetic fingerprint if there could be such a thing. It identifies people who belong together and draws them toward each other, even from great distances. That's what made it so gut-wrenching to turn away Rachel and Mary when they were standing at our doorstep.

Esther, I know you used to tell me that my anger and resentment were going to make me a bitter old man. I should have written down all of your wisdom and saved it for rainy days to remind me of my mistakes before I repeat them. You lived to see me move away from the church because of my resentment toward God for taking our children—and thinking that some of it was because of what I had done.

When you were gone, I began to question God's existence altogether because the one thing that made no sense to me was why God would extend benevolent blessings on some of the worst people in this world and turn around to dole out terrible tragedy on others who made righteousness a part of their lives every single day. And don't give me that God gives us challenges to make us stronger bullshit, pardon my French. We have plenty of challenges just trying to survive this life. We don't need God giving us any more. What is God anyway? That question has been eating away at me ever since the day I found you lying on the floor of our bedroom—when there was nothing I could do to help you.

That was five years to the day from when we got the call about our daughters in that car accident. In my mind, I still see them as they were then— Olivia, our cautious one, getting her master's in microbiology and looking ahead to her doctorate at Stanford. She was destined for a Nobel Prize for discovering a cure for cancer. And Tameka, shy with some, outgoing with others, but a friend to everyone; just graduated from the University of Illinois, getting ready to start medical school, working summers at the free clinic in Chicago, and already talking about working in Kenya for Doctors Without Borders. They were so different, our girls, very competitive, and yet, they got along without a hitch, never argued over boyfriends or clothes, and if need be, they came to each other's defense without missing a beat. It was almost as if they were twins, even though they were almost three years apart.

It's funny how not one of our children ever wanted to pick up a musical instrument or sing in the choir. I guess they figured it was better to make a name for themselves in their own light rather than live in someone else's shadow.

I wish we had never bought Olivia that car. She and Tameka could have taken the train home instead of meeting up to drive back for Christmas break. Those highways in Indiana are always a mess with all those semi-trucks, and the 57 is the worst. All those warning signs over the Dan Ryan couldn't stop that one drunk driver. It was a good thing he died in that accident because I might've killed him for what he did. No parent should ever have to bury a child or face the agony of identifying a child for the coroner's record. I thought I should be the one and save you from further heartache, but that was a mistake.

Now there is nothing but agony and pain gripping the shell that used to be my heart. At least one of us was able to remember Olivia purely as the beautiful woman she was.

I turned to stone, Esther, and well, you just couldn't release enough anger. Sorry, baby, but it was like you had sucked in all the anger in the world and filled your gut with so much of it that your whole body hurt. You yelled at me for sending the girls away to college when you had wanted them to stay near home. I couldn't argue with you. I couldn't tell you that it wouldn't have mattered. They were grown women with strong wills. What happened wasn't my plan.

When Jake was taken from us, I felt a profound change in myself that turned me into a mere reflection of all the darkness, all the sadness, all the loneliness that existed without emotion because those things didn't need emotion to lay on my heart and smother all meaning. I began to play deep, heavy blues, instead of the pulsing jazz I had always loved. But when Olivia was taken, I stopped playing the piano all together. I had no reason to express my loneliness because I didn't have anything inside me anymore. My shell of stone just became harder and crustier like I was observing the world from behind an iron mask. You got me to take off that mask, Esther.

"I met with Pastor Roberson," you said. "He reminded me that we still have Tameka, that we need to pray for her and hold her hand and help her through all of her injuries, both physical and emotional." You held my face in your soft hands and wouldn't let me look away. "We need to remember the good times, Jonah, the good in our children. I need you to hold on to the belief that their short lives were not without purpose."

I was too weak to argue. I just could not understand why God would punish us like that, and then you would go to his church for understanding and a way to move on. I didn't tell you then, but the only thing I was holding on to was the unfinished business surrounding Jake.

Jake showed his talent for sports at an early age, and he wasn't the least bit interested in joining a gang. I asked him one day if anyone had ever tried to get him to join or if he had ever thought about it, and he looked at me as if I had asked him to take his sister to the school prom. "Why would I do that?" he asked. "I want to play in the NFL, not for some prison team." What he said next, though, I would never forget. He said, "The thing is, Dad, I know I probably won't be able to play forever, so I want to have a plan for when I can't play anymore. I was thinking I could either get a coaching job or be a sports announcer for one of the networks. I figured a major in communications would give me a backup plan, you know. Get me prepared for that so I don't end up living on dried-up memories."

He made me a proud dad that day, and of course, he had to finish it in his usual way of making a joke, when he turned and angled his head like he was posing for a yearbook photo.

"And I would hate to deprive the world of this famous smile," he said, and he was right. He had a smile that could melt a whole room full of hearts.

"Just be careful with that thing." I laughed. "It could be dangerous."

Jake laughed too.

I had to put my dad-hat back on, though. "A part of me is being serious, son," I told him. "You're going to encounter some obstacles and temptations, so don't allow anything, especially a girl, to get in the way of your dreams. Your mother told me I was crazy to move the family here, so don't prove her right."

But it was more than just getting us out of the South Side. It was more than just giving us a better life. It was always about finding a real home where we would feel safe and secure and our children could get the best education. When your children are talented, you have to do that. And I admit, where Jake was concerned, I wanted him to get noticed by college scouts, win the Heisman Trophy playing for Notre Dame, get the #1 draft choice in the NFL. Why not dream big? I wanted my kids to achieve, to be the best, and not just live on dreams and what-ifs.

I began to live my whole life at the mercy of that goal, and I feared anything that might stop, defer, deter, or deflect that progress. That's why I was so suspicious when Rachel started coming around. I wasn't here the day she and her mother showed up at the house with cookies.

I admit that when you told me about it, I was defensive. "Sounds like they were feeding the help," I said. "Did she ask you if you'd clean her house?"

"It wasn't anything like that," you said. You put me in my place right away. "They were very nice. It was your daughters who were rude, getting up and leaving the table like they didn't want to be bothered."

"Did they invite us to dinner?"

"Well, no."

"Uh-huh, see. They ain't going to, neither."

"Don't talk like that," you said. "They're not family. I didn't invite them, either. They made the effort, and that's good enough for me. We can get to know them first and see where that goes."

"You're right again, as always," I said and leaned over for a kiss.

"Sometimes I think you start something with me just so you can get a kiss."

"You might be right about that too," I said.

I was still suspicious when I saw Rachel come over into our front yard with a glass of iced tea. Jake didn't need any distractions, and here she was all tall and slender, wearing shorts and this little top that left her shoulders bare and her waist exposed. She was nothing but a distraction. I was about to go down and tell him he needed to finish mowing the lawn when this carload of boys drove by yelling something out the windows, and one of them tossed a beer bottle that broke all over our front yard. I wasn't going to lie down and let trouble ruin my plans, so I went running down there, but it was too late. That car was already gone. I wasn't able to see the license plate from the upstairs window, but I was able to see that it was a black Camaro, and I could hear the loud pipes as it drove away.

Rachel was still there, and she had started picking up the glass and putting it in a neat pile on the sidewalk. I came charging out the front door asking if they got a license plate number, and they were both looking at me like they were more stunned at my reaction than they were about that carload of thugs.

"I think I know who that was, Mr. Culpepper," Rachel said.

I have to admit, she was very polite and respectful, but I was still upset. "Were they friends of yours?" I asked, and I guess my tone was either threatening or accusatory because her eyes got real big.

"No, it's not like that at all," she said, her defenses going up immediately. "I just recognize them from school. They're always up to no good, and they probably just want to see if Jake can take the heat. I think they're just having fun, like hazing a pledge who wants to get into a fraternity. The football team here is sort of like that. I don't think they mean any real harm."

Her last statement really got me, like she was minimizing the ramifications of hate. I must have feared even then that something bad was going to happen. I kept on about needing to do something because they shouldn't get away with it. I must have been yelling because Jake was telling me to calm down. He didn't seem to let it bother him.

"Rachel's right," he said. "They're just some guys from the high school. It's only going to make things worse if we contact their parents or go to the cops."

"What they did wasn't right, though," I argued. "Someone could've gotten hurt."

"They're just trying to scare me, get me to quit the team," he said. "But I'm not going to do that. The best way I can get even is to play the best football I can—and maybe even end up the first-string quarterback before the season starts."

That boy of mine was smarter than me. Even though I knew he was right, I still kept an eye out for any suspicious activity, anything that looked like any of those boys were up to no good. I was gone most every night playing at clubs in Chicago, but when I was home, I always seemed to have one ear listening for any noise I didn't recognize. I was driving myself crazy running to look out windows or walking around the house to check for anything unusual.

You noticed what I was doing after a while, and you looked at me with your hands on your hips. "You're acting like a fool, Jonah," you said. "Have you gotten yourself into some kind of trouble with someone at the club?"

I didn't lie to you. I never could lie to you. "It's not like that, baby," I said. "I guess it's just an old habit from living on the South Side." I couldn't tell you what was really bothering me.

I saw that same car again a few nights after that first time when I was coming home from the club. It was parked at the end of our block, sitting in the dark just outside the reach of the light from the streetlamp. It was like seeing the devil. I drove on by and parked in our driveway where I could still see it. I stayed in the car, waiting for something to happen. I didn't know what. I waited for the scuffling of shoes on the pavement, for laughter, needless sinful laughter, or voices whispering about getting away before the cops arrived.

I got out of the car eventually and walked down to where the car was parked. I looked without being too obvious, wanting to find someone hunkered down on the seat, but I didn't see anyone. I walked to the corner and crossed the street, and that was when I heard voices coming from one of the houses across from ours. Three boys chattered their way up the sidewalk then crossed the street and stood behind the car laughing and urging one of them to do it before he got into the car.

One boy then bent over and vomited half on the grass and half on the curb. He stood up and wiped his mouth on his sleeve before getting into the backseat of the car. They never saw me standing in the darkness. They never knew I had heard their voices echoing in the stillness, telling the world how drunk they were and how they weren't going to talk about what they had done. One boy said he felt kind of guilty about it, but none of them ever said exactly what it was. The boy who owned the car pointed at the other two and made them swear that they would never reveal it to anyone.

FIVE - MARY

TEARS WERE STREAMING DOWN MAMA'S CHEEKS as she stared into the shadows under the window, and I realized that she wouldn't be able to continue.

"We can talk about it some other time," I said. "I didn't realize that day was going to be such a scary day to remember."

She seemed relieved, and yet, her lips remained slightly parted as if they still held the words to describe memories that her gently-shuttered eyelids were not ready to release.

"It wasn't that day so much as what came later," she said, dabbing at the tears on her cheek with the back of her hand. "To remember any part of it is to remember all of it."

I changed the subject, sort of. "That guy across the street sounds kind of creepy. Do you think he still lives there?"

"I don't know," Mama said, catching the last tears from the corners of her eyes. "I haven't seen him since we moved in. We can ask Jonah. Maybe he knows. I will try not to drop any other surprises on you." Mama's fleeting smile was apologetic and vulnerable, and when her eyes found mine, I could tell she meant to keep her promise. "As for the extra bedroom upstairs, that used to be Paul's bedroom years ago. We were very close, so I was quite upset when I found out that he was killed in Afghanistan. I don't think my parents changed anything in his room, so one of these days,

I'll have to go in there and do that. I'm just not ready to tackle all of the past right now. It holds some memories that I'm just not ready to face. I know that's my problem, and I need to be a big girl about it, so maybe one day we can go into it together. We can clean it out and make it into a music room for you. That would help me move past those memories. I need to learn to deal with all of it."

"It would be nice if we could be friends with Jonah," I said. "He was nice to me, and I felt very safe with him."

"I'll speak with him," she said. Mama's expression changed suddenly and she reached across the table and grabbed my hand. "I forgot to tell you my good news. I got the job at the Public Defender's Office. I start next week."

I had no doubts that Mama would get the job, but to help take her mind off the sadness, I jumped with excitement and declared that we should celebrate.

"Celebrate? How do we do that?" she asked. "Should we go out for pizza? Oh, wait, silly me, I can make a pizza right here, and it will be even better than Lou Malnati's."

"Who?"

"Lou, oh never mind. He invented the Chicago deep dish."

"You can invent a pizza?"

"Of, course. You can invent anything. What shall we invent? How about a magic pill that will make us happy forever?"

"I think we already have that," I said and leaned into Mama's encircling arms.

"Yes, we certainly do," she said.

Mama opened the refrigerator wide and started pulling out tomatoes and mushrooms and onion and cheese and garlic and spinach and a jar of artichoke hearts for the pizza. Then she pulled out a large flatbread, which she said she had been saving for a special occasion just like this. We both laughed that same silly laugh, and I was happy because Mama was happy, and I didn't want it to end.

I began moving furniture in the sun room and thumbing through a box of CDs next to the stereo. The one that captured my attention was titled "Fallen" by a group called Evanescence. The entire cover was filled with the mysterious, almost spooky face of a young woman with dark, cat eyes.

I started the CD, and ethereal music filled the room. Each song title struck a personal note with me on some level, such as *Haunted*, and some not so pleasant to think about such as *Everybody's Fool* and *Going Under*. One song captured my interest—*My Immortal*—a title that I had no immediate connection with, but that's the one I liked immediately with its classical overtones and longing, searching lyrics. I turned up the volume, losing myself in a flowing movement until I heard what sounded like soft crying in the background. I turned down the volume and realized it was coming from the kitchen.

I went to the doorway. Mama was standing in front of a butcher block full of vegetables with a large knife in her hand and dabbing at her eyes with the back of her other hand. "Mom?" I asked. "Are you okay?"

"I'll be okay, Peanut," she said.

"I can tell it's not the onion."

"No. It's the song just now. It made me remember something from a long time ago. Your father and I danced to that song. We were very much in love."

"I'm sorry. I didn't know."

"It's okay. I'm sorry. I don't want my sadness to reflect my memories of your father. Maybe that's why I never talked about him."

"Really?" This was the second time that day that I had created a beautiful sadness, once with Jonah and then with Mama. I needed to know if they had something to do with my dreams. "I need you to look at something," I said.

I went to the easel and raised the cover sheet over the face I had drawn. Mama drew in a breath and quickly covered her mouth. "Oh my, did you draw that, Peanut?"

"Yes, this afternoon."

"That's Jake," Mama said, and she couldn't stop staring at the drawing.

"That's what I thought," I said.

"That's such a perfect likeness, but why did you draw a picture of Jake?"

"When I was at Jonah's house, I saw a photo of him, but that was *after* I had drawn this face. But that's not all. I drew it because it was the face I saw in my dreams."

"There must be some explanation. I must've shown you a photo of

Jake years ago, and I just forgot. And for you to draw that from memory now shows that you have such a wonderful artistic talent."

I ignored her compliment because I figured all parents would lush over their children's accomplishments even if a professional eye would see only a meager and crude effort. "You never showed me any photos from your past. Not Jake, or your family, or even my father," I said.

Mama closed her eyes and took in a deep breath. The words she was about to say obviously required some gathering of courage as if she were about to leap from a plane for her first parachute jump or run blind run through a mine field. She didn't know if it would be disastrous or exhilarating.

"Peanut, Jake *was* your father."

I must have stared at Mama for a long time without any type of response, verbal or otherwise, which I was perfectly capable of.

I watched Mama tilt her head and look at me like I had just stopped breathing. "Are you all right?" she asked.

"Just trying to take it all in," I said. My hands came up like I was about to catch a ball thrown at me, but it wasn't a ball; it was my history in a nutshell. "I have lived for fourteen years without a father, and when I finally find out who my father is, I also find out that even though he is dead, he's not really dead because his ghost is living in my bedroom, and I don't know if *it* . . . if . . . *he* wants to hurt me or help me."

"Peanut, there's no such thing as ghosts."

"Then what is that in my bedroom?"

"I don't know. This move has been so traumatic for you. I didn't realize."

"And that means Jonah is my grandfather." I started to cry.

"Oh Peanut, I'm so sorry. This is so much for you to take in. I was going to tell you. I really was. But little by little. Your visit with Jonah threw me for a loop."

Then we were both crying and hugging each other, our chests heaving softly against each other, sharing the memories, real or imagined.

Six - Rachel

Jake had the most beautiful voice. It was deep, like a man's voice, like distant thunder. It made you pay attention. And when he sang, the sky opened up to an endless view of clear, crisp imagination. I discovered it when he was home alone, shooting baskets on his driveway court. Since the driveways run up together between our houses, I could see him clearly from the back of our house. He didn't know I was listening, and I didn't interrupt him until he was through, when he took a mental break between songs.

I came out of the backdoor, and he turned around when the door creaked as it closed behind me. He just stood there looking at me and dribbling the basketball like it was an extension of his arm. I had this habit of tilting my head when I felt I was at an impasse with someone. It was my gauntlet, which I would throw down to allow the other person to make the next move. When he saw that, he smiled big, without saying a thing, which I figured was his gauntlet, so I did the same.

"Taking a break from football?" I asked.

"I needed to take my mind off it for a while."

"Which one are you better at?"

"Don't know. They're like apples and oranges."

"I'm pretty good at basketball myself," I said, making it sound like a real challenge.

"Really?"

"You could find out if you're willing to risk your reputation in some one-on-one."

"Something tells me I better take you seriously. If I win though, then you have to show me some of your cheerleading moves."

"Fair enough, but if I win, you have to sing me a song."

Jake laughed loud enough to shake the basketball net. He was always so easygoing. I loved to hear his laugh, and I tried all the time to get him to laugh just so I could selfishly enjoy it. But I loved his singing even more. He told me that he only sang when his parents were not around because they were very self-conscious about him and his sisters not wanting to follow a career in music. None of them wanted to learn to play an instrument. He feared that his mother might try to push him into the school choir if she ever heard him sing.

He admitted that he *did* like to sing, but sports were always a big deal to his dad, and luckily, he was good at just about every sport, so he figured that would be a career that he would have to put in little effort to be successful.

He did sing a song for me that day, but only after I did a cheer for him because, of course, he won our game, hands down. I think I did make one basket, and even that surprised me. It's very possible that he let me make that one.

So anyway, I was performing a cheer and couldn't keep a straight face with him standing there with his arms folded across his chest like he was judging me, but when he started laughing, I dropped the cheer and started dancing around him in a circle and singing this hip hop song, *The Way You Move*, by OutKast. I was rapping the Andre 3000 part:

Boom, boom, boom,
Ready for action, nip it in the bud,
We never relaxin,' OutKast is everlastin',

I was still circling around Jake when he surprised me and started singing Sleepy Brown's part:

I like the way you move,
I like the way you move,

So, it didn't matter how well I was rapping anyway because Jake was being so charming. At that point, he had me mesmerized. I got mixed up and couldn't remember all the lyrics, so I was laughing at myself when he started singing a song called *Like You*, which I recognized because it was by two rappers named Bow Wow and Ciara. He was doing all these hand movements and moving around like he was on stage,

Now I done been with different kind of girls
Like I done seen em all but ain't none of them at all like you

So I started singing the Ciara part and dancing in this fantasy zone that he had created.

I ain't never had nobody show me
all the things that you can show me,
And the special way I feel when you hold me
We gone always be together baby,
that's what you told me
And I believe it . . ..

So that was how we got started, and I don't know why we were so attracted to each other. I found his spirit the most attractive of all. We didn't get serious right away, though. We started studying together, and during our breaks, we would turn on some music and dance if we were energetic enough, or we would go outside and play basketball if it was warm enough. I wasn't sure if Jake felt the same way about me, so I wasn't going to rush anything.

One day, there was a change in both of us, which started when I grabbed his football and asked him to show me how to throw a spiral. First, he showed me how to grip the ball, and when he put his hand over mine on the ball, I felt the sense of his energy flow right up my arm. I tried to ignore it and deny what I felt, but that just made me overcompensate with my silly laugh, mostly at my own awkwardness.

We threw the ball back and forth, and I finally caught one with a little more grace. Through his contagious laugh, he said I should try out for the team, which made me determined to show him up, so I ran at him like I was going for the goal. My fake almost worked, but he still caught me, and I went down right on top of him. I was embarrassed and laughing and apologizing, still lying on top of him until I buried my face on his shoulder and whispered into his ear.

"I don't want to get up," I said.

"I don't want you to either," he said.

That's when I told him how I felt because I was that sure of his sincerity. "I'm attracted to you," I said, "and I'm telling you that because I trust you."

"I'm attracted to you too," he said. "It's scary, though."

"Why is it scary?" I asked.

"Our race differences," he said. "The way people at school will react when it gets around. I've been fighting my feelings because I don't want to create problems for you."

I knew he was being totally honest with me. He could've just taken advantage of me. "I've thought about it too," I said. "I've never had much controversy in my life, but I think I can deal with it if you're there with me."

I rolled over, and we lay there for the longest time side by side on our backs in his backyard with our hands touching and our fingers like blades of grass fluttering against each other in a breeze. We talked about the challenges we might have to face being friends in a world closed to that sort of thing, and after a while, our fingers were weaving in and out, testing to see how they fit together, interlacing, and eventually finding that perfect fit like when two pieces of a puzzle find each other and your heart leaps with silly excitement. That simple act sealed our pact against the world that day, and I couldn't help but smile at the sky when suddenly, we were holding hands.

"You didn't tell me about the song," Mary said. "*My Immortal.* Even though there is sadness, I want to know."

"He was my immortal. He still is." I laughed. I couldn't help it. It was a memory laugh, soft and tender, and I felt it escape from a shiver of pleasant reminiscence. "We danced to that song at Homecoming. I felt like I was dancing inside him, a part of him, and I told him that I didn't want that song to come true for us, but it did. Not then, but later. I knew that night was going to be special—was going to be the one I would always remember."

I stopped because suddenly I remembered something I had forgotten about that night. Mary could see that change in the way I was looking at her, not really seeing her, but seeing something else.

"What?" she asked. "What is it?"

"I just remembered something that happened as we were leaving the dance. It was so childish and could have been a terrible end to a beautiful night."

"Is that when my father was . . . ?" Mary looked frightened.

"No, no, it was nothing like that," I said. "We were walking through the parking lot. My hand was inside Jake's arm, and I was looking up at him and smiling so big at everything he said because he was being so sweet and attentive, you know, with compliments about my hair, my dress, how beautiful I looked. Everything he said was perfect, and I had the biggest smile on my face, my cheeks were hurting. I didn't see the other boys at first. Suddenly, he put his hand over my hand, and I could tell something was wrong. His eyes had narrowed toward this group of boys leaning against a black car. It was the same group who had driven by the house and tossed that beer bottle onto Jake's yard.

"They were all on the football team, and one of them, his name was Rainy McBride, was the quarterback Jake had beat out for the first-string team. Rainy had always had this habit of taunting everyone by saying he was going to rain down on them, and it seemed like he was always in trouble or looking for trouble. We both looked away, hoping that nothing would happen, but my heart was pounding, and I thought we were going to pass by them without an incident until one of them whistled. Then came the cat calls.

"'Look at the pretty couple. Pretty boy with the pretty cheerleader.'

"'Must be why you don't ever come out drinking with us.'

"I gripped Jake's arm tighter and whispered, 'Just ignore them. They're probably drunk,' but his pride got the better of him. He waved at them and smiled.

"I wished he would have left it at that, but then he said, 'Thanks, boys.' It was pleasant enough, but I could tell he was being sarcastic, and maybe they could too, or maybe they were just looking for an excuse to start something.

"Then Rainy called out, 'Who are you calling boy, boy?'

"That did it. Jake slipped away from my arm and walked toward them. 'I was just being nice,' he said, 'but obviously one of you has a problem. Or maybe all of you do.'

"That's when Rainy stepped forward almost chest to chest with Jake and said, 'Now you don't want to hurt that passing arm of yours, do you? We still have some games left to play.'

"'And you would be happy to step in, wouldn't you?' Jake asked. 'Unless of course if your face was too banged up to call plays.'

"A crowd was starting to gather. No one was trying to stop it because everyone wanted to see a fight. I looked around hoping to find a teacher in the crowd. I was surprised that no teacher was in the parking lot for security since fights always seemed to happen at parties and dances. But I did see Tracey Button, this big, awkward kid, who was making his way through the crowd a head above everyone. Tracey played center on the football team and had few friends. Jake told me once that Tracey was his only friend on the team, which was good since it was Tracey who could make Jake look good or bad depending on how he hiked the ball.

"Tracey just pushed everyone aside and walked right up to Jake and Rainy, towering over both of them. Most of what he said was directed at Rainy and the other boys standing behind Rainy. 'Looks like someone is having a party here and forgot to invite me,' he said. 'That pisses me off, so I might just bust of few heads. It could be here, or it could be on the football field. Your choice. I know you guys ain't my friends, but that don't bother me cause I don't want to be your friend, not if you act like this. Whatever problem exists here, it's time to get over it.'

"There was a scattering of applause in the crowd, and an equal number of groans, but everyone quickly disappeared. That wasn't the end of it, though. They didn't get over it, and that was the tragedy."

I looked at Mary, hoping to be drawn out of the sadness. Our smiles emerged, magnetized and drawn to each other until our noses were touching and we were laughing at our silliness, which is what I needed. I felt good again. On the outside. Outside, not wanting it to mix with what was going on inside where hurt and sadness never left, inside where a strange blend of love and sadness cradled the memory of that one night that was so beautiful, a night I will never have again.

That night, holding and being held and feeling him inside me, I wanted him to stay inside me forever. I now know it was then that Mary was conceived—because that was the only time. Both of us wanted it to be special, saying good-night at the front door, tip-toeing up to my room and opening the window so Jake could climb in from the trellis on the front of the house, pulling him and closing the window, but not before I noticed a light go off in the house across the street.

"I wish I could be in love like that," Mary said. "It's so beautiful."

"You will. You have a lot of love to give, and the right guy will be very lucky to receive it. You're here because of that night—and because of a lot of love."

"I can't wait," she said.

"I can."

SEVEN - JONAH

FOR A FEW DAYS AFTER THAT VISIT FROM MARY AND RACHEL, I stopped sitting on the front porch and moved my stubborn ass to the back porch where I thought I could find some peace and quiet and just maybe a speedy and safe passage.

You should know that I miss you more with each day that goes by, Esther, each day that you are no longer here with your soft hips for me to lay my head on while we listen to the crickets and you stroking what's left of my hair.

Didn't take long for me to realize my mistake, staring at the side of the garage and a scattered collection of weeds creeping out of the ground like fingers pushing what was left of the snow into the sunlight. I didn't feel you again until I moved back to the front porch. I found an old cigar, the kind I used to smoke, but I couldn't find my knife to cut the end off, so I had to bite off the end. I know I gave that knife to Jake for his seventeenth birthday when I decided to give up cigars. It might still be in all of his stuff, which I never had the strength to go through. I didn't think one more cigar would hurt me. If anything, I thought it might hurry me along.

Sitting in this rocker and puffing on that nasty old stogie and remembering the days when some of the guys would come over to jam or just sit and sip on some Woodford Reserve and talk about what we would do if we ever had a lot of money, got me to thinking about those days when waking up was a joy. All those guys are gone now—Buzz died when something popped in his brain. Willie Z from AIDS. Tubbs got himself murdered just driving down the street. Sticks spent his last days hooked up to an oxygen tank until the emphysema finally took him, and poor Curley, with no dignity left, OD'd on the bathroom floor of The Backdoor Club with the needle still in his arm. If I told that to a stranger, he'd probably say I was the lucky one. People don't realize that what you can't see, what you don't know about, is the worst kind of hurt.

My hurt still gets me angry, to this day. I think about that car and how it kept appearing on our street, from that first day when it spit that beer bottle out onto our front lawn to the first time I saw that car parked down the street, and then every other time after. It taunted me with its presence on the street and in my dreams.

I didn't realize how much it was still with me until it took shape in the smoke from my cigar that drifted out over the porch along with the shadows and shapes of those boys jumping out of that car like they owned the world and strutting down the sidewalk, each step snapping on the concrete like a challenge to anyone to tell them they didn't belong here. I saw them go to that house across the street when they didn't know I was sitting here watching them. That was right before I left for Andy's Jazz Club that Saturday night when Jake went out to a movie with Rachel—and we never saw him alive again.

I started to relive that terrible night when suddenly Mary came walking out of the smoke from my cigar. I must have been so lost in my thoughts that I didn't see her come up the front walk to the porch. She was standing almost right in front of me, very defiant in her stillness, in her refusal to move until she received some conscious level of recognition from me. I saw every bit of Tameka's stubborn attitude absorbed into this little girl's essence.

"Are you okay?" she asked, narrowing her eyes at me to add without words that I better be or I'll be in trouble.

"Of course," I said. "Why wouldn't I be?"

"I haven't seen you in a few days, so I thought you might be sick."

"It was nice of you to ask," I said, "but I don't think I'm leaving this world anytime soon. Believe me, I've tried, but the Lord just doesn't seem to want to take me right now."

"Well then," she said—and this is where her obstinance really showed through. "I'm not going to let you avoid me." Simultaneously with that reprimand, her right foot lifted slightly and stamped the porch boards in one fluid motion.

Oh, how I remember Tameka doing that very same thing when she wouldn't let up until she got her way. I had to let that thought pass and several others as well before I answered. In the meantime, I raised my eyebrows and gently stroked the stubble of beard on my cheek in a measured contemplation of her declaration.

"In that case," I said, letting a smile cascade over my goatee, knowing for sure, it would explode in laughter if I tried to restrain it. I didn't want her to get the wrong idea. "I promise that I'll never do that. And I suppose since it has been a few days, we have some catching up to do."

"I don't understand. You said you were trying to leave this world. Why would you want to do that?"

"My wife is gone. My kids are gone. Family is everything, so I have nothing left."

"I think you do," she said.

"What's that," I said.

"That's my secret." She smiled.

"Oh, really?" I said. She was starting to make me laugh.

"I'll tell you when I get back," she said. She turned to leave but stopped at the top of the steps like she forgot something and looked back at me. "You'll still be here, right?"

I gave her a serious nod. "Right," I said.

Then she was off, just like a little bird flying back to the nest to make sure it was still there. I waited patiently, laughing inside. But that shadow of Tameka was still on the porch.

"Where have you been, Daddy?"

I tried to look away, but I couldn't. "Please don't do that to me," I said. "There is no measure of the emptiness you left behind. You and your sister. And Jake. And your Mama. I am hurt. I am haunted. It was my job to protect all of you, but I didn't. I couldn't. I failed you. I can't do this anymore."

"Don't cry, Daddy. I'm not gone. I still need you. You help me through this, and I'll make you pancakes. Remember when me and Livia made you pancakes? We knew how much you like chocolate chip pancakes."

"Oh, girl, you're the best. You and Livia both. Always taking care of me. But don't tell your Mama. She doesn't want me getting fat."

"We can dance after. You remember the father-daughter dance when you took me and Livia together?"

"I'll never forget."

"I didn't know you could dance like that. Everyone in the gym crowded around in a big circle and watched us. I was so proud."

"Me too, baby girl. I have always been proud of you."

I could see us, as clear as if I was there, and I could feel them in my arms, holding Tameka and Olivia, the glitter around their eyes sparkling from the spinning glass globe overhead. We were dancing to some slow ballad.

"That's beautiful," I said. "Very sad but nice. Who's singing that?"

They both laughed at me, and in unison squealed, "That's Mariah! Daddy! *Thank God I Found You*! It's not sad; it's beautiful."

"Maybe we're not hearing the same song. I know Mariah, and that's not Mariah."

Together they laughed almost drunkenly. Echoing. Brought me back.

A shrill, irritating laugh broke the still air and cut a path from our porch to the house across the street. Two boys, maybe from the high school, were cruising on skateboards down the sidewalk. They stopped in front of that house and kicked their boards up. Holding them like drawn swords against the ground, they stared back across the street into that cut path.

Mary tightroped up the steps, holding in one hand a plate of cookies and in the other her cellphone that was playing the song I had heard. It wasn't Mariah Carey.

"I'm back," she sang out.

My mind was playing tricks. "What is that song?"

"Do you like it? That's *My Immortal*. It's by a band called Evanescence. It's ancient, came out way before I was born, but I like it. My mom said that she and my dad used to dance to this song."

"Is that right?" I noticed the two boys were gone. I didn't see if they had gone into that house or skated on down the street. I haven't seen anyone go in or out of that house in years, not since, but I've seen lights go on and off. There was a son who moved away. Could be he's back.

"You seem far away," Mary said. "Are you sure you're okay?"

"I'm sure, child. You wait here now while I get some tea to go with that plate of cookies you're holding."

She waited, squirming in your old rocker, anxious to tell me her secret, which I'm sure I already knew. I wasn't really ready for tea, but it was a good excuse to get up and take a break, collect my sanity, make sure that what I was looking at was really what it was.

Tameka had been so real, it scared me. I had never hallucinated like that before. I was well aware that I've felt angry, and sad, and remorseful, and lonely, and even nostalgic, but I've never seen anyone so vividly before, even when I tried to drown all of those feelings in the bottle. It was new. It came from somewhere beyond what I was familiar with.

This was nothing like Mary's ghost. She saw something, but whatever she saw didn't affect her or come from something wrong with her. Seeing Tameka was all in my head, but she was still here, and that was something totally different.

I held out my hands and looked down at them, expecting to see a trembling mass of snakes, but my fingers were calm and rhythmic as I willed them to move, to prove that my brain was still functioning as it should, connected and in control. They were just as I had seen them countless times before when I was warming up just before starting a set at Andy's Jazz Club. But there was no heart or desire left for them to feel the music and share it with anyone.

The only thing now that was keeping this old heart beating was that child sitting on my front porch, waiting to tell me what I had hoped one day would be one of my children bursting at the seams with the news of our growing family and my official passage into old age. I grabbed two glasses of tea and went back to the porch.

EIGHT - MARY

I DIDN'T DREAM MY DREAM FOR A FEW DAYS. I didn't see Jonah on his front porch either, but I wasn't going to let him hide from me. I decided to give it some time. Mama and I had conversations in the kitchen as she prepared dinner or in the little media room off the kitchen where we ate, conversations about her job or my classes at school. The conversations were more casual than if she had decided to sit me down and continue her story. I could tell she wasn't ready for that yet, but I wasn't going to let that hide from me either. I already had enough information collected in my head to create a memory about my family's past, but many chapters were missing, and I had a feeling that they were a big part of why Mama and I were back in this house.

I wanted to remember you, Papa, as if I had been there to share your life, or more importantly, for you to share mine.

I imagined that you were there with us when I told Mama about a friend I had made in my music class. Her name was Camille. We got off to a rocky start, but we both played the violin, and she was concertmaster in the school orchestra, so I was excited that she was going to help me with my audition for a seat. She gave me her phone number and told me to text her anytime I needed any advice.

I imagined you sitting in my bedroom each night while I practiced my violin, and you would always smile with great pride. The violin had always soothed me and made me feel accomplished at something. I was always pushing my repertoire and my technique, hoping that one day I would be able to play well enough to solo, just like in my dreams. I struggled through a Rachmaninoff concerto, wishing I still had my violin teacher in California to help me. I switched to the Brahms lullaby. I preferred the harder pieces like the violin concerto in D major, but I was content with ending on a sleepy, satisfied note. I fell asleep almost immediately, and I wasn't worried about my ghost because I figured, as Jonah had said, it might not want to hurt me. It certainly had plenty of chances to do that already. I felt safe.

There were no lights to guide me into sleep or terrify me with morphing faces. It was confusing, and I lay in bed staring at the faulty ceiling lamp and wondering what could be the trigger that draws the light ghost from the closet. There was really no one to turn to for an answer to that question, and I fell asleep trying to come up with an answer.

That's when I had the dream again with all the same images until the end when the conductor looked at me approvingly before leaning over like he was going to shake my hand, but instead, he poked me in the gut with his baton, which felt more like a fist. I woke up with a painful knot in my stomach as if I had swallowed a grapefruit whole. I lay awake the rest of the night flailing about in the bed, trying to find a position comfortable enough to ease the pain.

I was swimming in Jello, and the struggle was tiring. It suddenly occurred to me that I was getting my period, and I managed to make my way like a wounded bird to the bathroom. There was no blood, but I inserted a tampon anyway just in case it came later. I took a pill for the pain and went back to bed, finding the only comfort came when I curled up in a fetal position, and I tried to imagine myself floating. I remembered this from Mama's lecture when I first started getting my period. This mental yoga, as she called it, was the only thing that worked, and I finally drifted off to sleep.

By morning, the pain had subsided. I wanted to tell Mama about my ghost and the pain in my stomach that seemed so connected to the dream I had. She wasn't in the kitchen or any of the other rooms downstairs. I started back up the stairs when I heard her voice, like a soft wind through a cave, call my name. I went to her bedroom and opened the door slowly, just enough to see her bed. Several layers of sheets and blankets held her shape, facing away from the door. It shifted slightly to where I could see her profile through her tousled hair that fringed the pillow.

"Peanut, I'm don't feel well this morning. Will you be able to fix yourself some breakfast?"

"I'll be fine, mom. Do you think you have the flu?"

"No. It's not that. I have cramps and a sharp pain in my back. I think I just need to rest."

She had beat me to it. I had wanted to tell her about my dream and its connection to the pain I felt. I wanted her to tell me it was probably something I ate that gave me the stomach ache and could have even caused the dream to end the way it did. I wanted her to make me feel better with her logical explanations for all the weird experiences I had, but that didn't happen. Instead, she needed me. I wanted to shout at her that I was having real problems. I wanted to demand her attention. I wanted to be the brat. I had to take a moment to exhale all of my selfishness in one dark cloud before entering the room.

I walked to the side of the bed and noticed her breathing was slow and shallow, producing the same soft wind that had carried her voice to me through a cave. It was now strained and full of needles, making her eyelids flutter with each reach into her chest. I started to take her hand, but her fingers were trembling and frightful.

"Are you sure you'll be okay?" I asked. "I can stay home if you need me."

Through her trembling, with her eyes still closed, she nodded. "I'll be fine, Peanut."

I had never seen Mama hurting with such crippling pain before. I was worried, but I oddly expressed my worry with impatience and anger. I was sullen and moody all day at school. I didn't want to look at anyone. I didn't want to talk to anyone because no one deserved my attention when the only person I wanted to give it to was at home alone, in pain. I had almost made it through the day without a problem until my music class when I was warming up my fingers on my violin, playing through arpeggios, almost attacking them with a ferocity I wanted to release before it came out in tears.

"Whoa, girl, you need to relax," a voice came from behind, breaking my concentration.

I turned, almost whipping around. Camille was smiling, not just smiling, but smiling at me, the kind of smile that was more a smirk than a smile.

"You're going to break a string playing like that," she said.

I just stared at her, possibly for longer than I should. "I don't feel well," I said. "You're right." I needed to leave the room before the tension shattered the surface of my forced and imagined calm. I placed my violin and bow on a bench and headed for the bathroom.

"Wow, must have gotten your period," she said, loud enough for the whole room to hear, loud enough for the whole room to erupt with laughter as I placed my hand over my mouth and hurried down the hall, escaping behind the closed door just in time before my tears singed my face in angry sobs of hurt and worry.

I was unable to comprehend why this was happening, what I had done or who I was that would invoke such ridicule. I splashed cold water on my face, clenched my fists against the porcelain, bit my lower lip, anything to fight back the remnants of my tears. When I was convinced I could hold myself together, I went back to the music room and picked up my violin.

Mr. Drummond called my name as I entered the room, and I was relieved that I had not missed my audition. He was looking down at the music when I began to play. We both heard it after only a few bars. He held up his hand at the same moment I stopped playing.

"I'm sorry," I said.

"I'm glad you heard it too," he said. "But next time, make sure your instrument is tuned before you play. Could you imagine if this had been a recital, or a symphony performance, ruined by one out-of-tune string?"

"I thought it was," I said. "Tuned that is. It won't happen again."

"No. Not if you ever want to be in the orchestra."

He made it very clear. No matter how I felt, no matter what terrible tragedy had inflicted my life, I needed to be prepared. No mistakes. I could only think about what might have happened. I was sure my violin was still in tune. I should have checked it, yes, but still, something had happened.

My only answer was Camille. I sat back on a bench against the wall and began tightening the peg on the one string that had been loosened. Across the room, Camille was still smiling at me.

On my way home, I noticed Jonah had returned to his place on his front porch. I immediately went up onto his porch and waited for him to notice me. He seemed to be lost in his own thoughts. I put myself at ease by demanding that he talk to me because I knew he wouldn't refuse. I told him I needed to check on Mama, and I made him promise not to leave before I returned. Just being with him for a few minutes had cheered me up.

Mama was not anywhere in the house, and her car was not in the garage. I thought she started feeling better and went to work. I didn't even think to call her. That's how *not* used to my cell phone I was. I did like to use it to play music, and I had downloaded some of the songs she had loved. I checked around the house before I left. There were no strange noises in the house, so I went back to Jonah's house.

This time, I brought some cookies to eat with the tea he always made. He had an odd look on his face when I got there, and I assumed he had been thinking about something I had interrupted. He went inside to get the tea, and I waited until he returned.

Jonah took a long sip of tea like it stirred something in his head. "Are you the only musician in your family?" he asked.

"I guess," I said. "I never thought about it before. Mama doesn't play any instrument, and I didn't know anyone else in my family. Except . . ."

"What's that?"

"Mama said that my father had a beautiful voice, and she loved to hear him sing."

"Really? Your father?"

"Yes. Jake. Your son."

"Is that right?" He paused. "You know what that makes us then?"

"You're my grandpa!" I couldn't restrain my voice from sliding up an octave as I exclaimed that discovery.

"I guess you're right about that then."

He smiled real big.

I got up and hugged him tight around the neck. I didn't want to let go.

"You got to be easy with these old bones, Mary. But it sure does feel good to get that hug."

"I thought Mama was going to talk to you about it. I'm sorry if I jumped the gun."

"I'm not. I suspected as much when you looked at that photo of your daddy in the house the other day. I'm glad you're okay with it. It's nice to have family."

"Yes. I agree." This time I took a long sip of tea before I asked what had been bothering me ever since I saw his dusty piano. "Why don't you play anymore?"

"It's a long story. I just don't have the passion like I used to. It's a part of my past now."

"That's kind of sad. Since we talked last, I realized that music *is* a part of who I am. It helps me express how I am feeling when I'm sad or angry or happy. I thought all musicians were the same way."

"You're very wise for your age, Mary."

I told Jonah about the dream I had last night, and of course, he said it was probably something I ate, which could have caused the dream and given me a stomach ache as well. I concluded there had to be an adult conspiracy or a manual of set answers to deal with child and teenage problems.

I told him about my trouble in music class, and of course, he told me there was a lesson for me to learn because everyone is allowed one mistake. Make the same mistake twice, and I would be all by myself in the sympathy department. As far as revenge goes—and he was really adamant about this, he said, "Don't ever follow that path because it'll lead down a darker path of regret. You don't have any proof of Camille or anyone else tampering with your violin. If it was Camille, I figure she was just jealous and maybe even a little threatened by you, so the best thing you can do is just try even harder to be the best violinist you can be."

It's funny how sometimes—and often enough to be a significant moment in my life, a conversation or a series of changes in my life led to one big moment—or the possibility of a big moment.

"I just thought of something," Jonah said. He scratched the side of his face when he said this, which I came to understand was the most demonstrative display of excitement he ever made about anything. "My Esther used to talk about a contest that she encouraged her students to enter."

"Oh, I don't know," I said because contests made me nervous. "I have so much happening right now. I don't think I have any time for anything else."

"This wouldn't demand any extra of your time. All you'd have to do is keep practicing and improving just like you do now."

"What's the contest part, though?"

"I'll have to do some research on that to find out when it is and how to enter. From what I remember, though, after you enter, you're given a day and time to audition, and that's it. You might be called back for a second audition, but the winner gets to play with the Chicago Symphony in a chair next to the concertmaster, or possibly a solo. What do you think?"

"I could give it a try, but I don't think I'm near good enough to play with the Chicago Symphony. And I don't have a teacher to help me."

"I think you *are* good enough, or you *can* be if you put your mind to it. You have to think big if big dreams are ever going to come true. I'll make a deal with you. If you give it your best, I'll be your teacher, at least until your mother finds you a better one."

So, there I was facing a choice with this opportunity, and I had to decide if I was going to let this moment be a conundrum or an epiphany.

NINE - RACHEL

THAT SILLY GIRL OF MINE. SHE WAS SITTING ON Jonah's porch when I got home. I don't think she saw me drive up. She was so engaged in conversation with Jonah, the miracle of their word images was all she saw. I could see it in the glow of her eyes as I ascended the front steps, feeling like a mouse tiptoeing past a fox's den. They were talking about music and auditioning for a position in the orchestra, which I assumed was the high-school orchestra, only later to find out that Jonah had told Mary about a prestigious position with the Chicago Symphony for which his wife, Esther, Mary's grandmother, had been a judge. Mary's excitement was in the squeal of her voice, but so was the restrained worry and realization of her young age, which kept her from literally leaping out of her chair and dancing around the porch.

As I took the last step onto the porch, Jonah noticed me standing there, and then Mary turned with instant exuberance of the need for me to join their conversation. I didn't want to spoil her mood; it was rare lately to see her so excited.

"We were talking about Mary's music," Jonah said.

"I could tell," I said. I looked at Mary. "Is that all?"

"He knows," Mary said. "I'm sorry."

"It's okay, Peanut." I turned back to Jonah. "Is it okay with you?"

He nodded with a sadness in his eyes that saw what I had seen since Mary was born. "I couldn't have asked for a better granddaughter," he said.

"I miss Jake too," I said. "I miss him every day."

"My heart turned to stone, Rachel."

"I was hoping Mary could change that. Half of Mary is Jake. And every day I see a lot of Jake in her."

"I see it too. Mary has made a good start with changing things," Jonah said. "One of these days, you and I will have to sit down and talk."

"That would be nice," I said.

Mary jumped impatiently. "Jonah offered to help me with my violin."

"I still remember a thing or two about performance and a little about the violin from Esther. I make no guarantees, though."

I had so much to say, but I couldn't find the words or the place to start. My mind was racing, crowded with love and history and hope, all held together with tears of sadness I held inside. I could only smile and hope I was able to express my thoughts through my smile.

"Thank you for bringing Mary back here," Jonah said. "I hope you're going to stay awhile."

"Of course, why wouldn't we?" I asked. I didn't catch his meaning right away.

"Well, a lot has happened since you left. In this house and in *your* house. I didn't know if you wanted to live with the memory of that. I figured you probably made a life for yourself somewhere else, and maybe selling that house is the way to bury all the ugliness of the past. I'm sure you could get a pretty penny for that house now."

"Some things are worth more to me than money," I said. "I'm sorry I couldn't come back until now."

That girl of mine. In one day, she had started the conversation I wanted to have for the last fifteen years. She was my miracle child. I'm afraid for her, and that was the conversation I needed to have with her. I didn't want to end the conversation with Jonah; I didn't want him to think I was avoiding him, but I had to talk to Mary. She must have sensed that because suddenly she jumped up and down, apologizing for not asking how I was feeling.

"I'm okay," I said. "But I'm a little tired. I hope Jonah will understand if we take a raincheck." I turned toward Jonah as if to apologize for talking about him in the third person. He looked puzzled like I had just walked out on a party he had given just for me, so I added, "We would be thrilled if you would come over for dinner tonight."

"That would be nice," he said matter-of-factly. "I don't want to be the one who is weighted down holding grudges, especially now that we have a connection standing here right in front of us." He looked at Mary as if examining her for clues of a conspiracy to defraud him. "But there has been some time since we saw each other. I have some questions about why it took so long for you to come back here with Mary. And that would be just the beginning. So, you can change your mind about that invitation if you want to."

"Not a chance," I said.

Mary chimed in. "No, not a chance!"

Mary and I stood there a moment, both of us smiling steadfastly to seal our joint declaration. When I turned to leave the porch, I caught a movement or a fleeting change in the shapes of shadow and light. It came from across the street, enough to draw my attention, and in that moment, I saw the curtain in one window being drawn closed. The memory of that house rushed back at me like a fist in my stomach. I slipped on the step and nearly fell, catching myself quickly on the thick stone railing to regain my composure, ignoring the sharp pain that grabbed at my lower back, and letting out a high-pitched laughing howl before anyone had time to fear that I had hurt myself.

Inside I was a different person—a train wreck full of dust and smoke. I don't know why I kept putting off dealing with these important matters—the house across the street, Paul's old bedroom, my old bedroom, why I was forced to leave home, why I stayed with Mary in California, why I never returned until now, why I finally did return when the only reason was locked up and silently growing inside of me. I'm not sure why I kept putting off talking about all of it. It bothered me to do it—to allow all these unresolved issues to knock about in my head like billiard balls ricocheting off the rails and off each other, but I did it anyway. Maybe I was hoping they would all get resolved on their own, or just evaporate, lose their importance, and go away altogether. Silly.

That slight little movement in the curtain was nothing more than a hummingbird's darting appearance before it stops in the air, suspended on invisible beating wings, to examine a flower. I was that flower, and the memory staring at me was the rapid beating of the last fifteen years that brought me to this present moment.

The priority of where to start was inside me, clearly, physically—a tumor growing in my stomach, which told my oncologist to tell me to get my affairs in order because even the best prognosis is one year. I'd been able to hide it from Mary until now. I knew she'd start asking questions, and she'd figure out that something wasn't right. This morning's bedridden episode of pain was the beginning of what I would find harder and harder to hide from Mary's inquisitive and demanding nature. I still dreaded telling her, but I *needed* to tell her. That was in my plan from the beginning, when the cancer was discovered, when we still lived in California.

The house sat empty for a while after my dad died. It was the great symbol of my life, of the greatness that is always suddenly taken away. I acquired the house in probate, and for weeks, I picked up the legal documents like a novel and read them over and over again until finally, it dawned on me that the house would be my beginning and my end. The only relative Mary would have left would be Jonah. My mission was clear— to encourage a bond between Mary and Jonah, a lasting bond that he could not deny, which he would have to accept as his responsibility as her grandfather to take her in and see that she would have the life I had hoped I would be able to give her.

"You recovered really fast, mom," Mary said. "When I saw you this morning, you looked like you were dying."

"I am, Peanut," I said. The words came out before I could even think of how I was going to respond.

"What?"

"That was kind of abrupt. I'm sorry."

"I don't understand. What are you saying?" The shock of tragedy flared with welling tears that slipped down Mary's face.

I grabbed her hands and held on. "Let's sit down so I can explain."

"This isn't happening," Mary said. Defiance was emerging in the words that fluttered over her trembling lips.

"Actually, it has been for some time, and this is exactly why I didn't tell you, at first." I told Mary how my cancer was discovered and why I kept it a secret, hoping I would be able to defeat it and never have to worry her. I explained my plan to move back to this house and see her bond with Jonah so she would have support and love even if I wasn't around. It was not an easy thing to talk about, even at this perfect moment, and by the time I was through, we both were crying.

"I don't understand why this is happening to you, to us. You don't deserve this." Mary squeezed me harder with each word. "I won't let this happen! It's just not fair!" She backed away and stared at me. "Where is it? Is it in your stomach? Is that why you were in pain this morning? Where is it?" Her voice rose defiantly. "Is it here?" She placed her hand on my stomach, and I felt her trembling desire to push the cancer out of me.

I could tell that she wanted to reach inside me and grab the tumor and pull it out. Mary's eyes were closed, and the intensity in her face pushed down through her arm and hand into my stomach.

She screamed. "You leave my mom! You are not wanted here! You leave now!"

I grabbed Mary's shoulders and pulled her to me. With one hand behind her head, I held her face against my chest until her sobs and shaking slowly dissipated. "Mary, I don't want to live my life in anguish. We could be in a terrible accident tomorrow, and our lives could be changed forever, or worse. I want our lives to be full of happiness, and I want you to know that I love you every day, unconditionally. We have to learn to put this out of our minds and make each day one to be proud of."

"It's not going to be easy," Mary said.

"Nothing is," I said. "But that will just make life even more precious."

Mary looked up at me through green pools that broke from the corners and streamed down into her smile, and I knew she understood what I said. I felt her arms grow a little tighter around my waist, and the sensation of her embrace smoothed the pain that had been in my back since the night before, smoothed it until it disappeared.

"Anyway, there's always a chance I can beat this thing," I said, hoping Mary would believe my words, which were very different than the oncologist's.

"Would you make me a promise?" Mary asked.

"Of course, Peanut."

"From now on, would you include me? I mean, let me know so I can help, so we can fight this together."

"I don't want to fail you. I don't want you to ever think that I put you second before anything, so yes; we will fight this together."

The doorbell rang, and just like that, we both shifted to another mood. How convenient it would be to have a subconscious bell that would sense when our moods needed changing. Your world is falling apart with grief and sadness, and you're about to collapse from the weight of it when ding, the bell releases you from the pain so you can be a mother to your daughter, or you can attend a cocktail party and laugh at meaningless jokes, or you can think clearly enough to deliver a moving closing statement to a jury where the life of an innocent person hangs in the balance. I had been doing that for the last few months, but without the bell to drive away the undercurrent of gnawing, negative emotions. This time, I had Mary to hold onto. Literally. I grabbed her hand and pretended that all the problems had slipped away as we almost skipped to the front door where Jonah awaited. He had changed clothes. He had put on a hat to walk next door to our house. He was adorable.

We almost overpowered him with our exuberance, Mary grabbing his arm and pulling him inside, and I taking his other hand in mine.

"Come in, come in," I said, my voice singing in hyperbolic tones, which I quickly realized was my way of hiding the undercurrent of pain.

"I hope I'm not too early," Jonah said.

"Not at all," I said. "I can throw on a big pot of spaghetti if that's okay with you."

"That would be perfect," Jonah said. "In fact, I was hoping Mary could play something for me while we waited."

We all agreed that would be perfect, so Mary raced upstairs to get her violin as I escorted Jonah to the living room. I apologized to Jonah if it all seemed old and dark, this room that Mary calls the scary room because I haven't had a chance to change anything since we moved in. Jonah explained that it didn't matter to him as he had only been in the house that one time before so long ago when the circumstances were very different and his focus was not on any home decor or furnishings. I felt us starting to move toward the truth of that time when we both heard Mary scream.

TEN - JONAH

WELL, IT'S OFFICIAL, BABY. YOU A GRANDMOTHER. Of course, we missed the first fourteen years of her life, but I'm not going to dwell on that. Her being here now makes up for it. She's definitely Jake's, but the funny thing is, she embodies all three of our children in different ways. She's beautiful, stubborn, and sharp as one of Buddy Guy's guitar licks. Can't say as I can separate any of our kids from those qualities. The mystery is why Rachel stayed away with Mary for so long. It wouldn't have brought Jake back, but just maybe everything else would be different. I aim to find out. And why did she choose to come back now?

Rachel said she loved Jake, still does. She seemed sincere, so I guess that was one more thing I was wrong about, thinking she might be one of those white girls you hear about who are mystified by a man with black skin. Her parents didn't want anything to do with us. They made that perfectly clear after that day Rachel's mother brought those cookies over. I thought Rachel was being a typical, defiant teenager, doing what she knew would upset her parents.

Her old man coming over here, knocking on our front door until the hinges rattled, to tell me to keep Jake away from his daughter with the oddest combination of calm and defiance like he was giving me instruction about something he thought I wouldn't understand. I was taken aback for sure, him being a doctor and all, and there I was, feeling my muscles tensing up, but taking a deep breath on the inside to give myself a moment to fully receive his subtle racism. I gave him the biggest smile I could find—obviously a fake, sarcastic, demeaning smile—and I said, "If my son's friendship with your daughter bothers you, then it seems to me that you are the one with the problem, not me." And I could tell his wife put him up to it because I had heard her the night before yelling at him to be a man and get some control over Rachel.

Her brother was already gone by then. Joined the army, Jake said, and shipped out to Afghanistan. Told Jake he had to get out of that house and make a new start because of things he had done, which he couldn't talk about. That was a crazy family for sure, and I didn't want Jake mixed up in that any more than Rachel's father wanted her dating Jake, but I knew Jake had a good head on his shoulders, so I trusted him. I didn't need to go storming over to their house and get my head shot off, knowing they could get away with it just by telling the cops they were afraid I was going to rob them.

The funny thing was, when I had my say and stood there defiantly in our doorway, Rachel's father started to shake a little like a sail that lost its wind, his lower lip quivering and his eyes darting back and forth with no real purpose. He finally looked back up at me and said, "You know, you're right. I had no business coming over here like I did. I'm sure our kids know what they're doing. Please accept my apologies." He didn't wait for an answer. He just turned and left, and I never talked to him again. Not even after Jake was killed in their house.

Rachel knows what happened back then; I'm sure of it, and I suspect she was laying low for the last fifteen years. Everybody who knew anything about it is either dead or moved away now, except me. Until now anyway. It has been tearing me up, wanting to find out what happened on that terrible night—and her part in it. I've tried to forget the past, but what I did won't let me. I was hoping that if I knew, then I could finally relax and enjoy the experience of having a granddaughter.

Rachel invited me over to their place for dinner, and I saw that as an opportunity to win this battle going on in my head. I can see you now, tilting your head with a sly look of those sparkling brown eyes. "To settle your ambivalence? Is that what you mean, dear?" You always had a way of reminding me not to go running my mouth if I wanted to find answers or get something done.

I showed up at their house with a friendly smile, and this time, it was sincere. I could tell right away that I was early because there were no smells of dinner cooking. I do miss your cooking, baby. Their house was clean but still wearing a musty coat of curtains and an old smell in the sofa, which no amount of cleaning can get rid of. I suspected Rachel's father, much like myself, had neglected the house after Rachel's mother died. I hate to say it, but we were alike in other ways as well, and no amount of cleaning can erase the sadness in our homes.

Rachel and Mary were trying, consciously or not, by greeting me with unexpected joy. Only a couple of hours had passed, but they met me at the door like a couple of kids at Christmas and I was Santa Claus. That was confusing since they both looked like they had been crying.

I mentioned it would be nice if Mary played her violin, and she dashed upstairs without one complaint, very different from our girls who had a fresh complaint ready for anything we asked them to do. It was always challenging to teach Tameka and Olivia adult responsibility when it came to little things like cleaning their rooms, but oddly enough, they had an abundance of responsibility built in when it came to the big things like grades and pursuing goals. God, I miss them like a phantom limb that I keep feeling.

Rachel and I were starting a conversation in their living room, and I thought I might get a chance to ask a question about her relationship with Jake when Mary let out a scream that shook the house. My first thought was that she had seen a mouse. We waited to hear some sign that she was okay, but there was only that single scream and then silence.

We both went running up the stairs. I was following Rachel since she was faster than me, and I wouldn't know which way to turn when we got to the top. Rachel slowed down as we approached the open door to Mary's bedroom. And Rachel called out, "Peanut, are you all right?"

There was no answer.

Then the strangest phenomenon I had ever seen occurred.

Mary was lying on the floor with a bluish silver light around her. It appeared to be underneath her as well, holding her up off the floor, cradling her— or, I know it sounds strange, but it looked like it had caught her and prevented her from hitting the floor. The light started to fade under her; then it came back as we approached Mary. Without warning, the light was all around us, flickering and waving like an aurora, and the ceiling lamp above us began to flicker and buzz.

Mary jolted upright. Rachel knelt down and grabbed Mary's hands.

"Peanut?" Leaning to look into Mary's eyes, Rachel's voice grew frantic. "What is it? What happened?"

Mary moaned softly.

"Your hands are so cold. I think we need to get you to a doctor."

Rachel looked back around at me.

"We can carry her down to your car," I said. "There's a hospital real close on Park."

"I feel dizzy," Mary muttered.

I don't think Mary or Rachel noticed that the light was swirling all around us. It was warm and kinetic. I suddenly felt I had enough energy to lift Mary, which is what I did. Rachel hurried ahead, and the light left us at the door to Mary's bedroom.

In the car, Mary continued to ramble incoherently. All I could make out were bits and pieces. When we reached Loyola Health Center on Park Street, Mary was able to walk in on her own. She insisted.

I was sitting in the lobby, hands on my knees, staring at them because they wouldn't stop shaking when a voice full of apprehension made me look up. "Mr. Culpepper?" A dark-haired young woman wearing a white smock with a stethoscope hanging from a side pocket was smiling down at me. She leaned into her words but seemed prepared to move on to another person. I was likely, from initial appearance, not be the person she was seeking.

"Yes, that's me," I said.

"Oh," was all she said at first as she shook her head as if to shake off all the doubts she had. "I'm sorry. I'm Dr. Eve Kowalcyzk. I'm treating Mary Hester." We shook hands. "Her mother, Rachel, said I could talk to you about what happened."

"Yes, of course," I said.

"And how are you related to Mary?"

"I'm her grandfather." I was stunned by how quickly it came out as if I was referring to someone else. I realized it was me, and I had someone who needed me. What could have been a burden suddenly made my hands stop wringing. "Is Mary going to be okay?"

"Yes, yes," she said. "But I have some questions about how this happened. Did you see anything that would help us understand? We don't want to overlook anything."

"I wasn't with her, so I didn't see what happened. I can tell you what I saw after, when her mother and I heard her scream."

"That would be helpful."

"It didn't take us long to get up to her bedroom. Maybe ten seconds. Mary was lying on her back, and there was a strange light all around her. It was eerie, a blue or silver light, or both; it was moving in the air around her. I can't explain it any more than that. I thought maybe she had shocked herself and the light was some electric charge lingering in the air. There was a lot of energy in that room, colors and crackling noises in the ceiling. Mary was unconscious when we got to her. She wasn't moving. It was just for maybe a second or two, and then she bolted upright as if someone had pushed her. Even stranger though was what she said in the car on the way here. She was rambling incoherently, but I thought I heard the word tornado, or something about a tornado—looked like a tornado or appeared like a tornado—I'm not sure which. I just figured the shock of it had made her delirious. We wanted to make sure she was physically okay."

"I can assure you that she's getting the best of care. My initial examination didn't show any problems, but we're going to keep her for a little while longer just to make sure. If you don't mind waiting."

I didn't tell the doctor what I saw or thought I saw, with Mary floating on that light, cradled, or levitating like it was going to carry her somewhere. It was scary, like some Stephen King thing, but I couldn't tell the doctor that; I knew she'd immediately think I was some kind of fool, or for sure, she'd get in my face and try to smell my breath for alcohol. I couldn't risk that. So, I waited. Waited in silence, watching the anguish of others who were also waiting, for what, to hear bad news and hoping it wasn't the worst news.

I had been here before. I remember an ambulance backed into the emergency parking bay, and a rush of attending nurses swarmed around the door in a haze of muffled shouting to get the patient onto a gurney and wheeled into the emergency room. One nurse was already squeezing a ventilation bag into the patient's mouth, a black man it appeared lying motionless—except for listing side to side on the jostling gurney—under the blood-soaked sheet. And I don't know if I actually saw that or hallucinated it from my memory of Jake being rushed into the hospital emergency room fifteen years ago. I wasn't allowed in then either, to see him, talk to him, help him, pray for him, hold his hand. A police officer talked to us first, before any doctor let us know what was happening to Jake. He took our information, asked for some identification, clipped my driver's license to his notepad, and while he wrote, noted out loud, "Hmm, you live right next door to where this happened." That was all he said, all he could say before he passed it off to the detective to talk to us later. At least he apologized. Funny, I don't remember if he was black or white. It didn't matter. He was nice. You used to tell me that politeness isn't a characteristic of race. Your wisdom was never lost on me.

Mary and Rachel came back into the lobby, Mary leaning into a hug under Rachel's arm. They were both smiling, which was a relief. I stood up, and Mary transferred her hug to me.

"Thank you, Jonah," Mary said. She shifted back to Rachel, glancing up into her mother's adoring eyes, searching for approval, then looking back at me. "Is it okay that I call you Jonah?"

"Jonah is fine," I said. "As long as you're all right. You gave us quite a scare, child." I looked at Rachel, and she seemed to know what I was going to ask but wanted to wait until we were alone.

ELEVEN - MARY

DR. KOWALCYZK SAID, "YOU MIGHT JUST HAVE A severe case of anxiety and maybe even a little chest cold. I heard some congestion when I listened to your lungs."

Dr. Kowalcyzk was nice. Her stethoscope was cold. I wish I had your opinion, Papa.

"Do you think that's why she fainted?" Mama asked.

"She probably got a little light-headed running up the stairs too fast. I suggest you make sure she drinks plenty of water."

Mama explained it all to Jonah as we headed back home, everything except the last part.

"There is one more thing I wanted to ask you, Mary. Have you been experiencing any headaches or other pains anywhere?"

"Just a little pain in my stomach this morning," I said, "or really a little lower, if you know what I mean." I felt like I slipped up when I told her that.

She had to poke and prod me some more. "When was your last period?" she asked. "Do you remember?"

"I'm not sure," I told her. "But I don't think it has anything to do with that."

"If the pain had been sharp and more localized, it might have been appendicitis. I feel certain we can eliminate that. Did it feel more widespread like indigestion?"

I didn't know how to answer. It was both, and yet, it was neither. "I woke up this morning feeling like I had eaten something rotten. It was like someone punched me in the stomach. The pain is gone now."

"I want to be thorough," she said. "I'm not going to hurt you." She put my legs up in these stirrups like I was riding a horse backward and examined between my legs with a strange-looking instrument. I was glad Mama was there to hold my hand through the discomfort and embarrassment of that.

Dr. Kowalcyzk wanted to talk to Jonah. Did she think he had something to do with the pain? Did she think he had hurt me? That's crazy. Dr. Kowalcyzk came back after talking to Jonah and said she still came to the same conclusion.

Anxiety. I know better, though. I know what I saw, and I know that ghost is real. At least I was smart enough not to tell Dr. Kowalcyzk about the ghost. I had been so caught up in the events of the day, and they *were* significant, but I had forgotten all about the ghost until I came face to face with it in my room. It doesn't have a body, not like I have a body anyway. It's all energy—light and electricity, and it can take different shapes that sometimes look like a face. I may be the only one who can see a face because I can look at clouds and see unicorns and castles and elephants with wings.

So, when I was just about to pick up my violin off my dresser, the ghost appeared out of the closet like a tornado, and it swept around me quickly. That was when I felt the punch. It made me dizzy and weak in the knees. I was startled and tried to grab for the bed, but I lost my balance and went down. I think that's when I screamed, but I didn't hit the floor, or the floor felt like marshmallows. It was soft and pillowy. I could have been floating. I remember the sensation of a shallow ocean surf washing over me and leaving my skin cool and tingly. I was relaxed, falling deeper and deeper into the storied past of many lives passing in front of me so quickly that suddenly, I felt I was being left behind. I couldn't keep up. I reached out for a hand, someone calling me, reaching back for me when I was lifted up and into Mama's arms. If you're the ghost, Papa, I wish you could tell me.

Going back to the house after seeing the doctor made me nervous. I had no idea what was going to happen next. But at the same time, I felt safe, so I knew I had to see this thing through to the end. In the car, I sat quietly in the backseat, staring at the blur of houses and cars and people, a vast migration of change and thought and emotion, of private lives, some with purpose, some without, pushing and pulling, sometimes just to get by. I began to feel very small and insignificant, much like staring at a sky full of stars and feeling afraid that there is no purpose because everything is so much bigger than me.

The ghost made me feel important. I had something no one else had. That got me thinking about the ghost. The fact that it didn't talk did not surprise me. Let's be honest; a ghost doesn't have a body, a mouth, or lungs. It can't breathe, so the act of talking is just not going to happen. It doesn't have eyes, so how can it see me? It doesn't have ears, so how can it hear me? There is no brain, so how can it think? What could it possibly remember?

I looked at what it did have: light, color, electricity. And with all of those things, it had a current that could hold sound, the sound of our voices—our different voices, and the sound of music—the music from my violin. I concluded that a ghost, my ghost, is much like a robot. It can only work with what has been put into its circuits, its waves of energy. It can't make up new stuff, no thought process, no emotion. Or does it?

If you're the ghost, Papa, then maybe the ghost does care for me. Maybe it can hold a memory in those wavelengths and communicate in its own way. If a cell phone can send my voice out to someone on the other side of the world, then my ghost can be just as miraculous. If the universe can pass through my body, then so can my ghost, and just maybe along the way, it can mingle with my energy, the wavelengths in my brain, my voice, my music.

I did know that even the smartest scientist in the world doesn't know everything about the universe—and certainly not everything about my brain. What we know because of science is only a tiny particle of knowledge compared to what may still be out there to learn. I couldn't wait to get home and play my violin for my ghost. I was ready to start a conversation.

I left Mama and Jonah downstairs. I told them I was fine. Mama said she would call me when dinner was ready. I wasn't hungry. I was too full of purpose, of motivation, of kinetic energy. I needed to release it into my violin. I needed to communicate with my ghost. I swung the door wide with one sweeping motion and stood in the doorway to make sure it was safe. I had rationalized that it was, but still, I wanted to make sure. My room was quiet, with no flickering lights, no buzzing or chattering circuits of electricity. I was ready to prove that I could do this, if not for my ghost, then for myself. I wasn't going to let the Camilles of the world get the best of me.

I dug out the hardest piece of music I could find from my stack of sheet music I had yet to learn. Caprice 24, composer Niccolo Paganini. I knew this was far above my playing level, but I refused to be intimidated by the difficulty.

My first time through was rough—missed notes, fragmented phrasing, scattered timing, and poor bow control. I tried again and again, each time getting more frustrated and confused. I wanted to scream, but I didn't want to start that all over again. I gently placed my violin in the case and threw myself onto the bed, face down on the pillow. I cried, pressing the pillow against my face to muffle my deep sobs. I cried until my chest hurt from the erratic release of the pain. I stopped suddenly and rolled over to stare at the ceiling, and I breathed in a slow, deep rhythm to gain control of myself.

I began to feel betrayed and abandoned. Mama was slowly slipping away, fading into my past. Soon I would be alone, the one person I could trust, the one person who cared for me when others didn't care at all, the one person who may not even know how important she is to me, would be gone. The hurt and fear of the unknown, what lay ahead for me, was what was bothering me, was what angered me, and I couldn't think of anything else until I realized those were the most childish, selfish thoughts I had ever had. Yes, I needed Mama, but she needed me more. She needed me to help her fight off this awful thing that was trying to take her away from me.

I heard Mama and Jonah talking downstairs, their voices muffled through the walls. I slipped off the bed and tiptoed to the stairs where their voices drifted up to the landing. I sat down to listen in the middle of a conversation about doctors and appointments and hospitals. I thought at first that they were talking about me until I noticed they hadn't mentioned my name or Dr. Kowalcyzk.

Mama's voice was softening, not in hushed tones, but more from the recounting of a memory with stifled emotions. I leaned closer to the edge when I detected her words drawing in on her breath, holding back tears on long extended vowels, and swallowing words with long-held secrets. She was talking about you, the one person who connected all three of us. She was telling Jonah that she frequently talks to you as if you were in the room with her. Your vivid memory appeared at moments she couldn't explain, but most of the memories were about the times you spent together—and they always made her feel the same way she felt back then, almost giddy with happiness. She laughed at the times when this would happen around others who would be caught off guard by her sudden exuberance, in the courtroom once when the judge actually stopped the proceedings to ask if she was okay, and she had to apologize and explain that she was just having a really good day.

The memories weren't always good though. She dreaded when the memory of that night would come back to her, and she would cry uncontrollably. As she talked, I felt myself drifting, finding it hard to stay with the words, to keep my eyes from closing, my own thoughts from swimming in my head. The last thing I thought of was the pill the nurse at the hospital gave me to help me relax.

TWELVE - RACHEL

I OWED JONAH AN APOLOGY. WE CAME BACK from the hospital, and I invited him in. I still needed to feed him. Mary went upstairs; she didn't feel like eating, but then I heard her playing her violin, and I thought she might get hungry later, so I put on a pot of water to boil for pasta, and I fixed two quick salads for me and Jonah. I had one bottle of red wine, which I put on the table.

"We can open that and let it breathe," Jonah said, "but I'll wait to have a glass with the spaghetti."

We sat at the kitchen table and ate the salads. We were both quiet at first except for small talk, the usual unimportant chatter, but I had to ask Jonah something. I didn't know how, and I was nervous about the answer.

"Mary told me that you never mentioned anything about Olivia and Tameka. I haven't seen them, so I was just wondering . . . if it's none of my business, I won't ask again."

"About five years after you moved away, Olivia and Tameka were in a car accident. Tameka survived, but Olivia did not. Tameka recovered, finished her studies, and graduated medical school. Not long after that, she fell on a patch of ice and hit her head. She was in a coma at Shirley Ryan Hospital for a while and sort of woke up from that, but she remains in a vegetative state. That's how she has been for the past year."

"I'm so sorry," I said. "I don't know if you were aware, but Tameka and

I became friends. I never told her or anyone else about Mary after my own family made it so hard on me."

"You're right. I had no idea you were friends."

"My mother was ill for a very long time. Bi-polar disorder. She would go into rages, and it was best to stay away from her. During one particularly difficult one, I snuck out and went to your house. Jake wasn't home yet from football practice. Tameka must have been home for the weekend because she answered the door and was kind enough to let me in. We went to her bedroom and started talking. We played a card game on her bed, and before you know it, we were giggling and gossiping about everyone at school. That was the first of many great times we had together."

"I never knew," Jonah said. "She kept it a secret, for some reason."

I heard the water boiling on the stove and got up to put the spaghetti in. "I'm sorry the marinara sauce is out of a jar. It has mushrooms, if that's okay."

"That sounds perfect, Rachel," Jonah said. "Nothing fancy for me. This salad is good. Just what I needed and probably the first healthy meal I've had in a long time."

"I wanted to thank you for being here and helping get Mary to the hospital," I said, stirring the pasta and watching it swirl in the water much like the thoughts in my head.

"I was glad to help. I'm glad Mary is going to be okay. It's nice to have a granddaughter to worry about. Thank you for inviting me over. Without you doing that, my stubborn side probably would have kept me angry. I'm sorry for showing my anger when you and Mary came over to the house that first day. I shouldn't hold on to the past like that. I could've missed knowing Mary altogether."

That was a breakthrough, definitely a watershed moment. I thought it was the right time to face all that I had avoided, to come clean with myself—as well as Jonah. He deserved an explanation, and I was the only one who could give him one. I fumbled over my words and danced around it for a while, getting up to drain the pasta, thanking him again for helping with Mary and getting us to the hospital, adding the pasta and sauce to each plate, thanking him for agreeing to help Mary with her violin and the preparation for the Symphony competition.

There was a clear break when I heard a screech and a groan. I pointed toward the ceiling and noticed that Jonah too had heard the awkward notes coming from Mary's violin. We laughed it off. I poured the wine in the glasses and thanked Jonah for being so accepting of Mary and amenable to our presence back in the house. Jonah got up to get the glasses of wine as I brought the plates to the table with a huge sigh, thinking that Jonah had every right to be upset after what happened so long ago, fifteen years of not knowing.

"Rachel," Jonah finally interrupted my ramblings. "Is there something you want to tell me?"

I took another deep breath and let it out like a thick wind in the trees. "There's a lot I want to tell you, Jonah. I don't know where to start."

"How about you start with what brought you back here? You didn't have to—come back that is. You could have sold this old house and made out like a bandit. You didn't have to come back knowing that all the past was still here."

"I did. I needed to, and I wanted to." As I sat down, I began to open up. The presence of food on the table and the comforting flavors of the sauce and the wine helped clear the air for the difficult conversation. We talked as we ate. "Yes, it's been a lot of years, and I want to make up for that. But I didn't stay away because of you. You're right about the past, though. That's why I stayed away, but now, life has kind of caught up with me, and I need to correct some things, not just for you and me, but for Mary too.

"Before I start though, I wanted to say that I'm sorry beyond words for all that happened. I've tried to think of what I would say to you, and each time, in my mind, I return to that day, and I am so overcome with grief that I can't think, I can't speak, I can't stop shaking, helplessly shaking just like that night when I held Jake in my arms as he was slipping away. I don't know why I couldn't move. I think it was my father who called for an ambulance, and I remember Olivia and Tameka suddenly rushing in and finding us."

"I remember hearing their screams. I had just come home from the club. I probably said some things to you that now I regret. It was a dark night for all of us. A darkness that has never left me."

"That night was not just a one-night stand for me—or for Jake. We were taking things very slowly, but we were also making plans for the future. We wanted to be together, but we didn't want to compromise. We had goals, and we were determined to do it all. I wanted to be a lawyer, and I think he would have been proud of me that I achieved that goal. Jake wanted to play professional football, but he wanted to do other things, too. He told me you and he had talked about that. He loved you very much. I could tell by the way he talked about you. He didn't want to disappoint you. That might be why we kept our relationship a secret. That, and my family, who turned out to be worse than I ever expected. Jake didn't know I was pregnant. In fact, I didn't even know on that horrible night. He only knew that we had a hard road ahead of us."

"I didn't know how the two of you felt about each other. If I had, things might've been different. I just feared that you would come between Jake and his dreams, my dreams. I guess I realize now that his dreams were different, bigger, but not wrong."

"I didn't ask for all that trouble. I didn't bring trouble into our families, but I didn't know how to stop it either."

"I don't think anyone can stop that kind of trouble. It's deeply ingrained in people. When I would rail about racism, my Esther used to quote Dr. King to me. She believed as he believed: 'Darkness cannot drive out darkness; only light can do that. Hate cannot drive out hate; only love can do that.' Maybe you have to be truly good at heart to believe that. My Esther was. I think I'm just realistic. I know that people aren't born evil; they're taught to be evil, and they choose to be evil because they are filled with hate. I have known people who could borrow a few bucks from you and then slit your throat to take the rest of what you have.

"Sometimes things happen in our lives that change us and make us want to do something that we know is evil, but we do it anyway. When I saw Jake, all covered in his own blood, being wheeled into the emergency room, I was overwhelmed with fear and sadness that such a thing could happen in a world of good people. When the doctor told me Jake was dead, all I could think about was killing the person who was responsible."

"To this day, I still don't know who that was," I said. "Some said it was Rainy McBride, the boy who got into a fight with Jake that night when we were walking to the train from the movie theater. But they never found the gun, and when that boy died, the truth died with him. The police blamed his death on Jake, said he died from injuries he got in the fight with Jake. I know that can't be, Jonah. You were there. You saw the fight, or at least the end of it. Jake didn't do anything to that boy to cause his death. Jake didn't start the fight. He was just defending himself. Jake had a good heart."

"Thank you, Rachel."

"Before the shots rang out that night, we were having so much fun. I'm very thankful for that, and I'll always remember Jake's laughter as we were dancing in my bedroom. My parents were used to me playing music in my room at night, but we still tried to be quiet so we wouldn't wake them up. We couldn't get enough of each other. We didn't want to say goodnight. We said goodnight at the front door in case anyone was waiting and listening. Then Jake snuck up the trellis and climbed through my window. We didn't want the night to come between us.

"We were dancing, and Jake was spinning me around when suddenly he just fell on the floor. I thought he was joking at first until I saw his face and heard a terrible, painful noise come from somewhere inside him when I put my hand on his chest. Whoever drove by the house and fired those shots into the room must have known what they were doing, and I'll never forget the sounds, the deafening sounds that ended all our dreams."

"Thank you, Rachel, for answering all the questions I had about that night."

I heard a creak in the boards on the stairway followed by a soft moan. We both heard it, and it lifted us out of our chairs. I apologized to Jonah as we went to see what it was. Jonah was following me, both of us anxious that something else had happened to Mary. We found Mary asleep on the stairs, stirring to find comfort where there was none. Jonah helped me one more time, carrying Mary to her bedroom and laying her in the bed. Mary muttered, groaned, and pulled at the blanket as I slid it up over her. She twisted until she was settled and finally content.

Jonah thumbed toward the door and whispered, "I better go now."

"Wait," I whispered. "There's something I want to show you." I don't know why this suddenly came into my head, but I wanted Jonah to feel the connection Mary has to Jake. I took Jonah's hand, and we crept downstairs to the sunroom next to the kitchen. I turned the pages back on the easel to reveal Mary's drawing of Jake, and I watched with my hands over my mouth as Jonah's eyes grew big, as if embracing his son in their vision.

"Mary drew that without ever seeing a photo of her father. She said it was a face she saw in her dreams."

"Oh my," Jonah said. "I do think there is something very special about Mary, your daughter, Jake's daughter, my granddaughter. She is a wonder, and we need to protect her."

I knew what he meant, and I felt it too, possibly for a different reason, which Jonah was not aware of yet. I felt my tears flowing into my fingers still covering my mouth. Jonah put his arm around my shoulder, and we walked to the front door.

"Life is full of surprises," he said. "I can't say that I feel blessed, but I think that just maybe God is apologizing for some of the past."

When Jonah turned to say goodbye, I embraced him and hoped he would receive my gesture as a thankful daughter. I felt his arms around me and his hand against the back of my head.

"I'm glad that I live right next door," he said, looking up toward the stairs, then back at me.

"Me too," I said. "Me too."

He left me feeling good, which made me feel strong. It was a good day, but before it was done, I wanted to tackle one more lingering problem. I wanted to confront the ghost of my mother, which had been in my thoughts for the last fifteen years. To do that, I knew I would have to enter Paul's bedroom, the one I told Mary was off-limits.

Paul had always been my guardian, my protector, my shield against our mother's tirades on her bad days. I was surprised when he and Jake hit it off so easily. It was on one of those cool, crisp days in late fall when Jake and I were goofing around at his house. He was trying to practice shooting hoops, and I was getting in his way when Paul appeared at the fringe of the driveway, with his arms crossed like he was about to reprimand me. Jake and I were both on the defensive immediately, waiting without a word for Paul to say something.

"You know that no one can be my little sister's friend unless I say so," Paul said.

Jake dribbled the ball once and slapped it between his hands, "Is that so?"

My heart was skipping beats.

"Yeah. So, here's the deal," Paul said. "You beat me at a game of one on one, and you'll get my permission to hang out with my sister."

Suddenly I knew Paul was pulling his leg, or at least I hoped so. Jake was not so sure, or at least that's the way he sounded.

"You're on," he said.

Paul was tall and lanky. He was a year ahead of me and played guard on the basketball team and was good enough to get his jersey retired on the wall of the gym the year he graduated, so I was hoping he wouldn't beat Jake too badly. They went at it right away, dribbling vigorously, right to left hand and back, between the legs and behind the back, pounding the court with fakes, speed, and direction changes, jump shots from far away and stretching under the basket, hooting and pointing at each other, laughing and challenging each other. Finally, Paul stopped at the free-throw line, dribbling slowly.

"Seems to me we're tied," he said. "I have to admit; you're the best I've seen in a long while."

"I don't like to brag," Jake said.

"How about this," Paul said. "Whoever misses first from the free throw loses?"

Jake smiled. I could tell he was confident. And Paul was too. I knew my brother because we had grown up together, huddled together when our mother was on a rampage around the house, shared our likes and dislikes, and revealed secrets about our desires and crushes that would never come true. With Jake, it was different. I had known him only a short time, but I already felt that I knew him better than anyone. I could see inside his smile, inside his eyes, inside his mind, and what I saw made me feel special.

Paul took the first shot, arching the ball up high over the driveway toward the garage then down like it knew exactly where it was going, guided by some sixth sense inside the ball, as it slipped untouched through the rim and barely disturbed the net with a soft, hushed breath.

"I think you've done this before." Jake laughed as he stepped to the line and like a rifle shot, sent the ball straight at the basket, hitting the back of the rim hard and down into the net with a bang.

Paul took the ball and dribbled at the line for a long time before sending it straight at the backboard where it hit just above the rim and bounced back hard over the basket. His head tilted with a big smile, and he extended his arms and palms to the sky. "Looks like you win, brother."

That day, when they shook hands with a brotherly pat on the back marked the realization for me that my life was going in the right direction. I always suspected Paul missed that shot on purpose, and I suspect Jake knew it too, but we never talked about it. Jake and Paul became fast friends and practiced basketball almost daily. Occasionally, I would join in, but most of the time I would let them play while I sat on the back steps and watched or read a book.

One terrible time, Eddie wandered over from across the street. He was the same age as Paul, but they never really got along. Eddie kind of sauntered up the driveway like he had just gotten home, but I suspect he was watching us for a long time before getting the nerve to come over.

Eddie pointed at Paul. "Hey, buddy, you want some real competition to play against?"

"Not sure what you mean," Paul said. "Jake here is a natural, and actually he's better than me."

"That so," Eddie said; then he looked over at me. "You ain't having much fun, Rachel. How about you and me go to a movie?"

I guess I looked at Eddie kind of funny for a long time because he got a mad look on his face. "I don't think so, Eddie. I'm not that bored," I said.

Then he did get mad. "Okay, I see what you people are really like now," he said. "A little advice. Better watch yourself."

With that, he left. I got up and walked up to Jake and put my arms around him. "That guy is not a friend of ours," I said.

Paul came over and put his arms around both of us, and Jake started squirming to get away until we were all laughing.

When Paul didn't have any plans, he would ride the green line with us and go into Chicago to hang out at shops and restaurants on the Magnificent Mile. Sometimes, Tameka would come with us too, when she was home from school.

One time, Paul apologized to Jake. "I hope you don't mind my tagging along, but our mother is on the warpath."

"It's fine by me," Jake said. "What happened to get your mother mad?"

"It's not that," Paul said. "She's sick."

I was surprised that Paul let out our family secret, but I was also relieved that Jake would know.

"Somedays she's happy as a lark, singing non-stop and full of energy. Other days, she's a hornet's nest, full of anger and spite. She mostly yells at our dad because we know better than to hang around when she starts tearing around the house. The only time there is any peace is when she's in the basement and can't get out of bed."

"That's a little scary," Jake said, calmly. "Is she seeing a doctor?"

"Oh yeah. She has medication but getting her to take it is another problem altogether. We've learned to protect each other."

I wish Paul could have stayed. He missed the worst part, and he didn't live long enough to see his niece. He couldn't have known I was pregnant. Jake certainly didn't. Paul joined the army and left for Afghanistan before Jake was killed. He came into my room one night and smoked a joint while I sat on the bed. He said his life had been reduced to a small box. I thought he meant that he felt boxed in, that his life was small and meaningless. He wouldn't tell me what he meant. He just said he had to leave because he couldn't face what was inside. He couldn't face dealing with our parents any longer, either. Between the two, he knew he had to make a life for himself somewhere else, somewhere he could correct the mistakes in his past.

The year was 2004. 9/11 was still very much on his mind, and he thought he could honor those who died that day and put honor in his life by doing something honorable. The next morning, he was gone.

I needed Paul when I found out that I was pregnant and our mother went berserk. I don't know where all of her hate came from. She had a good life, and when she was feeling good, she could be so nice to others, no matter who they were or the color of their skin, or their religious beliefs and background. Her good moods were like a drug that evaporated all the hate.

The night Jake died was different, though. She and my dad rushed into my bedroom while I held Jake as he struggled for breath. I could feel the blood soaking the back of his shirt, and I could see the blood in his mouth as he tried to talk. Mama's voice still clangs in my ear like a cathedral bell. "What is he doing in your bedroom? What is he doing in your bedroom? What is he doing in your bedroom?"

Now I remember that my dad left the room. He must have been the one who called for the ambulance. There was banging, loud banging on the front door, and Mama's voice shattering the air in my room, but above all that, I heard Jake's shallow breathing and felt his heart struggling.

For two weeks after that, I couldn't eat—I didn't want to eat, and my skin got even paler, and I was vomiting even when there was nothing inside me. My father eventually took me to the doctor, and that's when I found out I was pregnant. He must have called Mama because she was waiting for us when we got home, and she tore into me as soon as I entered the house. Her words pounded against my head and slipped down my chest to squeeze my heart into a small, unmoving stone.

What should have been a joyous moment had become a signal for the end of our relationship. I can still see the red flare in her eyes burning in her distorted face and singed on her words of hate that she screamed at me.

"You have ruined my life! You have embarrassed the family! You have turned against God!"

Her God. We stopped speaking to each other. At least for a while, until one day at dinner, she sprang the news on me.

"I made an appointment for you, and I have arranged to go with you."

"For what?" I asked.

"Why to get an abortion, of course."

I think that was one of her good days because she wasn't yelling at me when she told me that. It was just a matter of fact, almost pridefully, that she was going to help me with this terrible thing. I should have let it go and just snuck out of the house and left for good when she said that, but I didn't.

"I'm keeping the baby," I said. "I never ever thought about doing what you're suggesting. Jake is a part of me, and I want a part of him to be alive."

I think that night her good days and bad days blended, and she lost control of all of it.

"You have completely lost your mind!" She yelled at me first, then started pleading, but at the same time demanding. "You are too young to bring a child into the world. You have your whole life ahead of you. And this isn't just any child. You will have a *black* child. Think of the problems you will have the rest of your life."

She didn't use any openly racist words, but the message was clear enough. I cried myself to sleep that night listening to her screaming at my father that they would have to send me away until this was over. I don't know what she expected to happen to make it over, but what did happen changed everything and came soon enough.

Three months passed. I was able to finish school and graduate with special dispensation to complete my studies remotely. I started wearing loose clothing to cover where I was starting to show so Mama wouldn't be reminded daily of her ruined life. I stopped seeing my friends from school, and they stopped calling me. No one came by to see me.

No one came to the house at all until the two men in military uniforms rang our front door. I was standing at the front window in my bedroom, and I noticed the car pull up in front of the house. They tried to close the car doors quietly, but it was still loud. Their footsteps on the walkway to the house were loud. Their voices were loud, even though they were almost whispering when they told her that Paul had been killed in action. He hadn't been in Afghanistan very long. He was praised by the two men as a hero as they gave her a small box that held the purple heart medal, which was all we had left of him. She carried that small box around with her for the next week. I couldn't help but think that Paul might have known or prophesied his own future.

All of this was playing out in my head as I climbed the stairs and peeked in on Mary first to watch her, satisfied that she was sleeping unfettered and calm with a gentle rising and falling of the blanket that lay undisturbed on top of her; then I walked slowly and soundlessly down the hall, feeling a force in my mind and at my back that felt like it was pulling my whole body from approaching the bedroom that used to be Paul's.

I didn't want to face this, but I knew I had to. I turned the knob on the door to Paul's bedroom, hoping to find something else to help me remember him, hoping to find something to help me forget that day or the day after when I went looking for mother to apologize to her, to talk to her, to hold her and tell her that I loved her. I searched the house and found her purse and keys so I knew she hadn't left. I knocked softly on the door to the basement bedroom. There was no answer, so I slowly opened the door, expecting to find her asleep, but the room was empty. I went to Paul's bedroom, and that's where I found her.

I put that out of my mind as I went back to Paul's bedroom to face the past. I turned the knob and pushed open the door, feeling the dank air take me back again. Fifteen years had not passed. I was still searching and wanting to apologize when I saw my mother sitting in a chair in the corner with a plastic bag over her head, tied with a thin rope around her neck and the other end of the rope tied at the back of the chair. On the table next to her was a bottle of vodka and an empty pill bottle. She had put a lot of thought into her death, and she left with a clear head and a purpose, dressed in one of her nicest dresses with matching shoes, and a thoughtful application of make-up that made her look pretty with her hands folded neatly in her lap as if posing for a photo when she fell asleep.

As I stood in the doorway, I saw her clearly, her shuttered eyes through the plastic never to twinkle with delight on those good days, so full of energy and promise. I walked slowly to the chair and held out my hand to touch her as I had done that day, hoping she would stir and open her eyes and laugh, but my hand went through her and felt nothing. My legs were shaking and I needed to sit, but I could not bring myself to sit in that chair. I looked around the room for another chair, and when I looked back, she was gone.

It took me a long time to realize that she was hurting, and that's why she couldn't talk to me; she was feeling a deep pain that would not heal, and she had found her only escape. On the table next to the chair where the vodka had been, there was the small black box that the two men had given her. Inside the box was a purple heart, and for a moment, as it lay in the palm of my hand, I thought I felt it beating.

THIRTEEN - JONAH

I WENT TO SEE TAMEKA TODAY, ESTHER. I was looking at her, and through all of her stillness, I was able to see how beautiful she is. She looks so much like you, and I don't remember a day when you didn't look as beautiful as that first day I saw you on the pulpit singing your heart out to God. Of course, that was before that same God destroyed our family irreparably.

God has a plan. That's what the pastor said, and so many others, trying to console us, trying to find meaning in why such terrible things happen in this world. They were empty words to me. Words can't fix anyone's life, but somehow Mary could. She succeeded where all those words failed. She brought me back, out of the abyss, much like you did many years ago, until you were gone too, and I sank back down as quick as riverbank sand pulling at my legs.

So, I'm confused as ever now. I've been on this roller coaster ride of joy and grief. I don't know how much more I can take. That's why I need your help. I need a little more time, so I hope you didn't come here for me today. I mean, suddenly, I'm not ready to go, so if you have the time, then it would be nice if you could sit here with me awhile and listen to my rambling. Step in anytime if you have any answers.

You see, what I'm afraid of is my life happening all over again—riding high on the feeling of success with my music, the love in our relationship, and the promise of our children, only to have it taken away. I won't be able to tolerate that kind of pain again. I figure that's why I stopped going to see Tameka. The doctors kept telling me that there was very little hope. We put all of our love into her after she survived the crash that took Olivia.

Tameka was our doctor, Esther. That was what she always wanted, and I'm sorry you didn't get to see her dreams come true. She was so beautiful, I thought my heart would burst with pride every time she came by the house. Then in an instant, everything was taken away again. I couldn't take looking at her so lifeless, not recognizing anything or anyone.

But then she came to me yesterday and asked me why I stopped. I got to tell you; that scared me. I started thinking that maybe she is still in there behind her blank stare, wanting to get out, wanting to be normal again. I sat with her and held her hand and read to her. She always had a novel in her hand, so I stopped in the hospital gift shop and bought a paperback of Toni Morrison's *Beloved*. That might have been a mistake because I sat there reading through tears that wouldn't stop, in anguish over the idea that a mother would take the life of her own child, even if she had the best of reasons. But it also made me realize that we are haunted by the ghosts of our mistakes.

I want to make up for my mistakes, and I get the feeling that Mary needs me. Her mother says she needs me. How can I tell them no? How can I look selfishly away?

I see that look in your eyes. I've seen it so many times before when you were trying to strengthen my will, erase my self-doubt, encourage me to do the right thing. That's what you're doing now, isn't it? Telling me that I should follow this through to the end, to help our granddaughter.

I'm beginning to feel that all of my grief has been selfish. All of the joy in my life was so suddenly taken away, and I was angry that Jake and Olivia were not given the chance to fulfill their dreams because their dreams were my dreams, our dreams, and they could have had children, and we could have grown old together in joyous celebration of our loving family. That was all taken away from us, and someone was responsible. I don't mean God this time. I mean a real person whose actions resulted in the death of our children, and the hope of our grandchildren. And I thought for so many years that Rachel was a part of that. So, you can imagine my surprise when I found out that Jake and Rachel, despite all my worries about her ruining his chances of success, had given us that one spark of hope. And it pains me that you're not able to share our grandchild with me because *she* will be our eternal life.

She told me that she has a ghost living in her bedroom. At first, I humored her because I thought it was just her fear of the dark or being in that big, old house all by herself—that her imagination got the best of her, but after seeing her being held up off the floor by a strange light, I'm not sure that her ghost isn't the real thing.

Rachel showed me a sketch of a face that Mary drew. It's a face she saw in her dreams, and she told her mother it's the face of her ghost. It's Jake's face. I'm sure of it. She drew it without knowing her father. She drew it without seeing any photo of him. I don't understand it, but I need to see it through. She's not crazy. If she's crazy, then I'm crazy. When she laughs, I hear Tameka. When she talks about the future, I hear Olivia. When she smiles, I see Jake. When she plays the violin, I hear you. Where did she get all those traits of people she never knew? She is the embodiment of something important, and I can't help but wonder if she's the key to understanding the mysterious life that exists beyond this life. If there is such a thing, then I imagine you already know about it.

There is one more thing that I never told you about, never told anyone, but I fear that your God probably already knows about it because I know, and I've lived with the feeling of guilt about it all of these years.

The night Jake died, I was playing at the club. I took a break between sets just like I always do, and I was standing outside with some of the guys while they smoked when I saw Jake and Rachel. They had gone to a movie in Streeterville and decided to walk to the green line at State and Lake, so they walked right by the club. I don't know if I saw them first or if I saw that black car first, but I took notice when it pulled up and stopped at the curb. It must have been close to midnight. I don't know how those boys knew where they could find Jake, but they did, and they all jumped out of the car and confronted him right there on the sidewalk.

I could hear it all from where I was standing, and it wasn't pretty. There were words I don't like to repeat, words that make my blood boil, but the jest of it was that they were telling Jake that he should keep to his own kind, that he had no right being with a white girl, that he was making it where no one was going to want to be with her when she was done with him. And that boy was pointing his finger at Jake, almost like he was pushing it into Jake's chest. I got there in time to see it all clearly, but not soon enough before Jake unwound like a spring snapping loose or a cork popping out of a champagne bottle.

His fist hit that boy in the side of the head, sharp and neat, and the boy staggered back away from Jake, and his legs were giving way underneath him when his buddies caught him, or he would have fallen like a sack of marbles to the pavement. Some of his buddies were stepping forward to retaliate right when I got there and jumped into the mix. They all backed off then, still pointing their fingers at Jake, and they helped the one Jake hit back to the car and left, but not before they sneered back at us with a few more racists remarks.

I knew it was the same group who had thrown that beer bottle in our front yard, and I could see this escalating, even though Jake had put an abrupt end to this one battle. I turned and glared at Rachel, knowing that she knew who those boys were, thinking that she might have been a part of it by telling them where they could find her with Jake to have a little fun. She was stunned, speechless, and shaking like she had just been pulled from the ice on Lake Michigan.

Jake was looking at me like I had just fallen out of the sky. "Dad? What are you doing here?

I pointed back toward the club. "I work right there, Jake. Just a lucky coincidence that I was taking a break."

"We're fine, dad." Jake put his arm around Rachel's shoulders. "We were on our way home. I know those guys. They're jerks, yes, but there's nothing to worry about."

"Right, son. So, you punched that boy upside the head for no reason at all."

I had a lot to say to Jake about his judgment of character, about his naiveté of human behavior. I just stood there and looked at him and looked at Rachel. I wanted to protect them; I wanted to get angry at them. I didn't like this world that would put my son in danger for no reason other than the color of his skin. But Rachel was a white girl, and she couldn't possibly comprehend what it was like to be on the receiving end of racism. She looked frightened, but I couldn't tell if she was sincere. All this was going through my head, and I wanted to stop them and shelter them. But I was also angry, and I was not ready to fully trust Rachel.

Someone called me back because my break was over. I gave my son a hug and left, thinking that I would talk to him about it in the morning, but I didn't get that chance because that was the last time I could have told him all the things I wanted to say.

Fully anticipating the time that I'd have that conversation with Jake, possibly even that same night, as I was able to leave the club early due to another band that was booked for the late spot, I was mulling over all the key issues of trust and acquired hate that has no conscience and no rational thought. I thought about the wariness of human behavior, which is far better received when the worst is expected, and not only are there no surprises when that happens, but you are much better prepared to receive it and react to it appropriately. I was confident that I'd be able to meet Jake coming in from his date, the surprise on his face when he saw me standing there with a smile and a hand on his shoulder to guide him to the kitchen table with no excuses and no pleadings of "Dad, stop worrying, I got this."

I came off the Eisenhower just about half past midnight and drove up Austin to Randolph. That's when I saw a car turning from Taylor onto Randolph at such a high rate of speed that it skidded around the turn, and the back tire hit the curb on Randolph before it sped off and disappeared. I was sure it was that same black car that kept appearing like an apparition of doom.

This time, it was nothing less. And the rest of that night was nothing less than a nightmare. We've talked about this, I know, more times than I care to count, seeing the blur of shadows in the streetlights that turned out to be Olivia and Tameka running next door as I drove up Taylor toward the house, getting out of the car in the chilled air, grabbing my jacket from the backseat because the temperature was dropping fast. I was wondering why I had seen, or thought I saw, the girls and not Jake running next door. Then I heard screams muffled by the walls of that house and up their stairs behind our girls, seeing Jake lying on the floor in Rachel's arms, holding Jake's hand while we waited for the ambulance, thinking all the while as I have thought a million times since if only I had been there just a minute earlier, if I had not stopped at the club to check the calendar and say goodnight to the guys in the band, if I had only talked to Jake and warned him when I had the chance. What if the headlights of my car could have shined into that black car and made those boys have second thoughts about what they were going to do? I knew that someone in that black car had shot up that house, and if I had stopped it then, I wouldn't have had to watch my son being wheeled into the emergency room under a red sheet that was soaking up the last drops of his life.

My grief was always mixed with anger, and it still is. I was able to contain it until the doctor told us to stop hoping. It was eating away at the emptiness I felt, replacing the emptiness with revenge. When we got home, there was a letter on the kitchen table from Norte Dame University. Jake was accepted into the football program with a full scholarship.

I wanted to find that car before the police did. I knew I should've waited until after Jake's funeral until the pain in my chest started to subside until Olivia and Tameka went back to school downstate until we stopped sitting in the dark and staring silently at the emptiness that would never be filled. I knew I should have waited and regained some rational common sense, but I didn't.

I told you I needed to clear my head. I drove around until I found that black car. I waited for that boy to come back to his car, and I confronted him about shooting Jake.

Waiting had given me time to think and looking at him I realized that taking revenge with this boy's life was not going to bring my son back to me. I could only hope that he would live the rest of his life in a small gray room with nothing to do but think about what he had done to ruin so many lives. I never told anyone I went looking for that boy or that I talked to him because the next morning his parents found him dead in his bed.

The police came to our house with the news that there was nothing else they could do because it seemed that when Jake had punched this boy, the punch caused a traumatic brain injury, which caused his death. They didn't find a gun in the boy's car, and they never did find the gun that killed Jake, but they suspected that this boy was involved in causing Jake's death.

They didn't know if he was the one who fired the bullets that went through the wall and struck Jake, or if he just drove the car, but they weren't able to prove any of it. Neither boy probably intended to kill the other, but it was a tragedy nonetheless, for both families. The police didn't say anything about the fact that none of it would have happened if those boys had just left Jake alone.

Rachel told me that she was the one who told the police about what had happened earlier that night, and that's how the police had connected that boy to Jake in the first place.

So, there is good and bad with Rachel and Mary suddenly moving back here, bringing all the past back with them, but also bringing Jake back in a way, and Olivia and Tameka too because Mary is so much like them. I feel like I have my children back with me, so I want to help this child, our grandchild, succeed and learn to play the violin as sweet as you could. I suspect keeping my mind on that will be hard because there's still a part of me that wants to leave this world to be with you again, but just maybe there's a reason why I'm still here, and if that reason is to help Mary, then I need to do that before I move on. If that's okay with you. I hope you understand.

I owe it to Jake, but there's something else too. I'm hoping that if I can do this one last thing, then I can redeem myself from what I have done, what I still can't talk about even to this day, but just maybe, finally, I will be at peace.

MIRACLES

FOURTEEN - MARY

I LOOK AT MAMA DIFFERENTLY SINCE SHE told me she has cancer. She is no longer the person who will always be here with me through all the setbacks, the heartache, the loneliness, the disappointments, for her to help me or for me to help her; and she will no longer be here to share the joy, the fun, the accomplishments, the pride, the hope; all of the emotions that lurk around corners or slip into dreams.

Now, I don't know what the future holds for us. In fact, there might not be an *us*. I see her differently. She is my mother who is dying. I look at her now to find any changes in her appearance—her hair, her skin, her eyes, and I listen for changes in her voice. I'm relieved when I look at her because I don't see any changes. I can't say that I'm happy because I still fear that it's only a matter of time before I'll start to see changes, but right now, I'm just relieved.

I hug her every chance I get, and secretly, I tell the cancer to go away. I will the cancer away with all of my strength, all of my mind, all of my prayers. I don't know if it'll work, but I want to believe that it will.

I don't talk about my ghost anymore, even though it comes to me just about every night before I fall asleep. I don't talk about the room that was her brother's room, or the house across the street. These things upset Mama. I don't want her to have bad thoughts, only good thoughts, good feelings that will help drive away the cancer. So, I practice my violin. I slide the bow over the strings to achieve the most precise clarity I can, and I play with only one thing in mind—not to win a contest, no, only to make Mama feel good.

My plan began about a week ago when I went to Jonah's house for my first lesson. I was humming the tune I wanted to play for Jonah, Paganini's Caprice 24, the one I wanted Jonah to help me perfect. There wasn't much time, but I wanted to conquer it; I felt it would be the one to get me noticed. There was a voice over my own inner voice, and I stopped short of the house when I heard Jonah talking to someone.

Clearly, he was asking questions and repeating the answers, but I never heard the other person answer. I was on the side of the house where I could see through the stone railing of the porch. Jonah was leaning his head toward the other chair, toward Esther's chair, but no one was sitting in the chair. If he was talking to himself, did that mean he was crazy? And what if he actually saw someone in the chair? Esther's chair. But that would mean I'm crazy too.

That's what that would mean, Papa, because I do the same thing when I tell you about everything that happens in my life. Maybe there's no difference. Or maybe it means that craziness runs in our family. At least Jonah's not scary, not the way Mama describes how her mother was.

I've heard Mama talking to someone in the middle of the night. I could never hear completely what she was saying, but I knew that no one was in the house with her. Once I did hear her say, "I miss you still" and "I have never stopped loving you." Just to make sure, I stuck my head around the corner of her bedroom door and said, "Who were you talking to?" She was sitting in her reading chair, looking at a piece of paper, which she quickly slipped between the pages of her book and closed it. "Oh, sorry, Peanut," she said. "I guess I was reading aloud." I knew she wasn't. I will never forget that because it sort of scared me then, and now, looking back on my eavesdropping, I know she was talking to you.

I heard her last night when she thought I was asleep, but I woke up when she opened the door to my bedroom to check on me. She went down the hall, not to her bedroom, but to the one she would not allow me to enter, the one that used to be her brother's bedroom. I heard her gasp, soft and pale, not alarming, and then her voice drifted slowly on choked-back tears. I thought she was talking to you again because she said things like,

"Why did you have to leave us that way?" and "Why wouldn't you let us get you the help you needed?" *Us?* Why say us? And what help was she talking about?

I knew then that she couldn't be talking to you because from what she told me, you didn't leave her, and you didn't need any help with anything. She thought you were perfect. I forgot to ask her about it in the morning, but also, a part of me didn't want to talk about anything that would make her feel sad. We were both running late, and she was happy. There was no time for a serious conversation that would change everyone's mood. It didn't matter. I had forgotten about it until I was headed to Jonah's house, but I wasn't going to let it go if whoever it was made her express such anguish. I needed to know everything that happened in our house, things that had shaped Mama—and were possibly affecting her even now.

I went around the corner and up the steps to Jonah's porch. He looked at me and looked at my violin case hanging firmly by my side.

"I was just thinking about you, child," Jonah said.

"Are you still going to help me prepare for that contest?"

I glanced at Esther's empty rocking chair, but I decided not to ask Jonah about his conversation. Those conversations, like mine or Mama's, should always be private. I didn't ask him about the last thing I clearly heard him say as I came up the steps either—his yearning voice that scared me because he said he still wanted to die.

"I was sitting here waiting for you, so what you say we get started?"

He smiled real big and groaned as he stood up. We went to the music room, and he walked in like he knew exactly what he was doing, but I stopped in the doorway and didn't take another step. "We need to clean this place up. Where are we going to practice?" I asked.

"You only need a place to stand to play the violin."

"But what if you need to show me something? Don't we need to clean off the piano in case you need to show me the correct tempo?"

"I don't play the piano anymore, Mary. I told you that. We'll be just fine without it."

"I want to play Paganini's Caprice 24."

"Really? Another piece that Esther loved to play, and she told me she always imagined herself in a concert hall when she played it. Have you ever played it before?"

"No, but I think it's a piece that can win a contest. It's difficult, but that's what makes it special."

"Maybe it's too difficult. If you had to play it tomorrow, would you be able to play it perfectly?"

"No."

"Then that one needs to wait."

"I thought you said you would help me."

"I am. Listen. First, you need to qualify for the contest. You don't need a difficult piece for that. Whatever you choose, you just need to play it perfectly. We can practice the Caprice for the contest, and that will give you time to perfect it."

"Do you really think I can do this?"

"I've heard you play, Mary, and from what I heard, yes, I believe you *can* do this. But what I think doesn't matter. It's what you believe that matters. If you believe you can do this, then you will. So let me hear you play something you know, and let's work on making it perfect."

"One of my favorites is Saint-Saens, The Swan."

"I love that one. It reminds me of Meditation."

Jonah's simple insight gave me relief. With just a few words, he made me feel relaxed and confident. That was the beginning. I played the piece through to the end while he sat in his stuffed chair, not moving, not looking at me, his eyes absorbing the notes that filled the room as he pondered the melody printed in the air above him.

"This is beautiful," he said, and after a long pause while I waited because I could tell he was feeling what he wanted to say. "This is a long legato movement, right?"

I nodded.

"There shouldn't be any pauses or stops of the bow. All the notes flow together."

I waited. He moved his hand in the air like he was painting a picture with his long fingers.

"Think of the swan appearing to float on the surface of the water, its graceful movement turning with no interruptions, its head lowered on its curved neck like the gentle curve of your wrist over the bow, gliding back and forth without any noticeable stop at the tip or the frog. Your fingers should drift softly on the strings with no break in the transition from one note to the next. Think of what propels the swan, under the water, invisible to our view above the water, its feet gently shift the water back and the swan forward. This is the vibrato of your fingers as they feel the pulsing of the notes.

"How do you know so much about the violin?"

"I guess Esther is more a part of me than I realized. I never had anyone to talk to about music for a long time until now."

"My music teacher in California never explained it to me the way you did. It seems so easy, and yet, it's still a lot to think about."

"But it must all come together because anything beautiful is made up of many parts. Once your muscle memory learns the parts, you won't have to think about them; you'll just feel the music. What you have played is beautiful, but I want to be moved to tears. You can do this. I know you can."

Jonah had challenged me. Over the next few days, I played The Swan as many times as I could, sometimes feeling exhausted and angry and afraid that I would get sick of it and never achieve what Jonah had described. But then, like a miracle, I began to feel the music as if I *were* the music. I felt what Saint-Saens must have felt when he composed the movement, and I was honoring him by transforming his written notes into a musical image.

As I stood in front of the room, Mr. Drummond was preoccupied with shuffling papers at his desk. Most of the students were looking down, probably at cell phones in their laps, while some who expected little more than a beginning student effort—wanting it to be over with so they could get back to their cell phones—were sending humored glances my way, and of course, the one intimidating glare from Camille, who obviously wanted nothing less than my total humiliation.

I took a slow, hardly detectable deep breath, closed my eyes, and began. I felt the music flow through me, felt the lake beneath the soft feathers on my belly, felt the gentle breeze on my face lowered gracefully to meet and be a part of my movement through the music. When I was done, only then did I open my eyes. Several students stared silently with open mouths. Camille's face was buried in her hands, and when I turned toward Mr. Drummond, he was touching the back of one finger to just below his right eye to capture what I suspected was a tear. When he stood and began to applaud, I smiled until my cheeks hurt. I couldn't help it. I was proud of myself. I sat quietly while other students played their pieces. I wanted to shout, I wanted to sing out loud, I wanted to dance. I did none of those things. I couldn't do that when Mama was dying.

Mr. Drummond called me aside when the bell rang, and he waited for the classroom to empty before he told me why. He had made a decision, and he wanted me to know before he made the announcement to the class. "Welcome to the orchestra," he said.

That same huge grin returned to my face.

"You played beautifully today," he said. "In fact, I don't think I've heard The Swan played any better."

"Thank you," I said. I was barely able to muster the air in my lungs to get out the words.

"You and Camille are the best two violinists this year, so this was a hard decision. I'm going to stick my neck out and say that you probably have the potential to be even better than Camille, but I'm going to give the first chair to Camille because she's a senior and has been with me much longer. I'm giving you the second chair. I hope you understand."

A tiny bit of sadness crept into a lump in my throat. "I understand," I said.

"I have a feeling that next year, the first chair will be yours. There is one other thing, and I hope this will make up for my decision. I'm nominating the two of you for the Chicago Orchestra student intern prize. Do you know what that is?"

"I've heard of it," I said.

"It's a contest. You play for the judges in a recital setting, and the winner gets to solo with the orchestra. If you practice hard, this might be yours. This will be a great honor and just may be the beginning of great things for your future."

"Thank you, Mr. Drummond," I said, remembering Mama's advice to always be polite. "It's a great honor."

"Also, I would like to coach you if you need any extra help. No charge."

"I do have a teacher, but I don't think he'll mind."

I left the room feeling good about what I had done, but the urge to sing and dance was gone.

FIFTEEN - RACHEL

AFTER I SAW MY MOTHER—THE MEMORY OF MY MOTHER—in Paul's room, I started seeing others. Hallucinations. I suspected the cancer had metastasized to my brain. I didn't think it could be anything else. No delusions. I was well aware of Elizabeth Kubler-Ross and the five stages of grief. I had studied *On Death and Dying* in college. I was drawn to it because there had been so much death in my life. Everyone I had grown up with, everyone who had made this house a home was gone. The good with the bad was normal for me, and suddenly, I had nowhere to turn for a sympathetic ear. The realization of being alone was shocking. I wanted to cling to Mary even more.

I had seen Jake almost every day since the day he died in my arms, before the paramedics brought him back, gave him a heartbeat again, and gave me hope only to have it taken away so I would experience his dying all over again. His eyes. I've seen his eyes staring into mine, asking why this was happening to him, searching for an answer, longing for something to stop it, and finally fear, which was something I had never seen there before. I pushed away the hurt of that memory and pulled back the look in his eyes that stirred at the warmth of his heart. His loving eyes. I felt his hands drift slowly down to the small of my back and over my hips. I loved the tender strength in his hands as he pulled me to him and I spread my legs to accept him.

Sometimes I would wake in my bed, gripping my knees almost at my sides so the only sensation I felt would be Jake inside of me. Then the loneliness would wrap around me and curl me into a ball and lay my tears on the pillow.

I saw Paul in our driveway one morning as I left for work. He was shooting baskets, and he didn't care that the net was torn that the hoop was rusty, that the backboard was peeling paint. He had a big smile on his face. He was looking at me and winking as he shot the ball blindly over his shoulder, and I watched it go into the basket. He ran past me and around in front of the garage door, rising up to the basket, his body rotating to face me as he lifted the ball over his head and into the basket. I didn't see it go in this time because everything was clouded by a blast of smoke that startled me, and Paul disappeared.

This flash of smoke instantly reminded me of the coroner's report, which accompanied Paul's body when it was returned to my parents. The report had detailed more than the two soldiers who had come to the house. They only told my parents that Paul had died in combat. The report characterized Paul's death with one simple statement, filling in the blank space next to Cause of Death. It read "Severe trauma from multiple perforations of the extremities as a result of the detonation of an explosive device." I wasn't able to finish reading the report. I didn't want to know how he suffered. I wanted to know what he was doing when it happened. At Paul's funeral, I introduced myself to every soldier I saw until I finally located Sergeant Garrett McMaster.

"Paul was my brother," I told him.

"I was Paul's commanding officer," he said. "You should be very proud of Paul."

"I am," I said. "I always have been. Paul joined the army because he wanted to do something important. He wanted to be in Afghanistan. We were very close, but Paul had a life separate from mine. I need to know what he was doing, what being in the army meant to him."

Sergeant McMaster went into great detail about why they were in Afghanistan, how they got to know the people living there, and how it became more than just a reaction to 9/11.

"Several of the guys in my unit wanted to help the people living there. Help them make their lives better. Sometimes though, we had to do things that put us in extreme danger. We were searching homes for Taliban sympathizers when a booby trap exploded right when Paul entered the front door."

Sergeant McMaster paused, and his eyes glazed over as if concealing what he had seen, what he was seeing again as he described it to me.

"Paul had a good heart," he said. "He loved helping the people in Afghanistan. He told me that he met a young woman, and wanted to marry her, but they had to keep it a secret because her family was very religious, and they would probably kill her if they knew she was seeing a man outside their faith. He had applied for papers to take her back to the States when his tour was over. The only favor he ever asked was that I make sure she received his benefits if something happened to him. Our chaplain married them in a secret ceremony so he'd be able to help her either way."

"What happened to her?" I asked.

"I brought her back when we brought Paul back. I figured it was the least I could do for Paul and for her. She was frightened that her family might find out what she had done. She still feared for her life. I accompanied her to a mosque in New York. I thought she could get some help there. She told them her name was Hend Amry, which wasn't her real name. She had heard of an Arab woman with that name who was famous for defending Arabic interests. She looked up the name and read that it meant to hold brave power. She told the people at the mosque that her family had been murdered by the Taliban, which wasn't true either, but she needed to protect her identity so no one would find her. I left her there and didn't see her after that."

I didn't see Sergeant McMaster after that either, at least not for a long time. We buried Paul that day, and when we got home, my mother went into Paul's bedroom and killed herself. I was pregnant. I wanted to find my brother's wife, but I didn't have the means to travel to New York. I wrote a letter instead. I never heard back.

I saw my father recently while I was working. Very poor timing on my part to be hallucinating in the middle of a trial, but there he was, sitting in the jury box with a newspaper folded and tucked neatly under his arm, and wearing the same expression he wore on the day he learned that Paul had been killed, and on the day of Paul's funeral, and when he came up behind me in Paul's bedroom where my mother was sitting in a chair with a plastic bag over her head, and on the day I told him and my mother that I was pregnant with Jake's baby. Now that I think of it, he wore that same expression every day of his life. He never cried; he never smiled or laughed or enjoyed life. I thought he was like every other dad, always working, always tired at night, his face buried in the Tribune.

He was a pediatrician, taking care of other people's children during the day, and ignoring his own at night. Looking back, I can see that he was burned out and needed the solitude to recharge, gain enough energy to make it through another day. He couldn't afford to need help because there was no one at home to fulfill his needs. My conception was probably the last intimate moment he had with my mother.

As her mental health declined, the further he slipped into his dark, emotional cave, seeking refuge in his reading chair by the fireplace and coming out only for dinner or when my mother would storm in and confront him. He always remained calm when she was raging throughout the house, in a good mood or bad; he was calm when she was depressed and incapacitated, leaving us to fend for ourselves with leftovers or cold cereal for dinner.

He must have been grateful the day she decided to kill herself, and like every other decision she made, he didn't stand in her way. The one time I thought I might have seen tears well up in his eyes was the day when he calmly told me that he and my mother had agreed that I should go live with his sister in California where I would be taken care of until I could make it on my own. He didn't even mention the baby that was on the way, but I knew that this was the real reason he wanted me out of the house. I would be an embarrassment, something he would have to explain. It was easier to pretend I no longer existed.

He did this to carry out one of my mother's last wishes, a posthumous success on her part, which left him a totally broken man. I suspected that was what the tears were about because they never broke the surface of his lower eyelid; they never fell; he never gave them to me. It's not like he didn't care about me, at least in an obligatory way. He always sent his sister money for expenses and some extra for me, so he must have cared, or maybe it was just guilt since he never communicated with me either before or after Mary was born.

He was never sick, and I am grateful for that. He died of a massive stroke, never made it to a hospital, and never required assisted living or hospice care. His guilt was assuaged in a will, which either slipped his mind to change or was left as is on purpose, leaving me the only recipient of my childhood home and all of his financial assets, for which I was also grateful. I was determined to use them to help Mary.

My most confusing hallucination was when I saw Mary when she was a grown woman, maybe early thirties, my age now. I don't know if I was dreaming or if it was a self-induced vision that had crept into my head because I wanted to see what she would be like, what kind of person she would grow into. She was beautiful, tall, and willowy in a satin, salmon-hued gown, her hair in a French braid that fell like a ribbon over one shoulder, stunning to behold, and if that wasn't enough to attract the stares of everyone in the room when she entered, she had a smile, Jake's smile, that magnetized the hearts of everyone she met. She was the center of attention, the subject of conversations, the envy of all around her.

She had done something. She must have performed. A man in a tuxedo escorted her through the crowd. Waiters brought her champagne in Waterford flutes. Her eyes stole all the light from the crystal glasses. Those in orbit around her embraced every word she spoke, wanting to absorb any element of her magic, her success. I was overcome with pride as I watched her from above, feeling a tear escape over my cheek and fall to her shoulder. She looked up and smiled. Did she know I was watching her?

I wanted to follow her through the years. I wanted to know her thoughts. Her adult thoughts. She always did seem so mature to me, way beyond her years. Probably the product of an only child with a single parent. She got all the attention, always in the company of adult conversations. Absorbing everything in the courtroom on days she came with me when there was no school. Asking such intelligent questions of my colleagues during recess. "Wouldn't that hearsay evidence from the prosecution witness be exculpatory for the defendant? Yes, he told her he hated the victim, and he had motive, but how could he have murdered the victim if he was in a drug treatment center at the time of the murder?" Jaws dropped. Investigators rushed out to place phone calls. Why didn't we think of that? I regret that I will miss our conversations, those pride-filled moments.

I realized my life was incomplete because everyone I had loved was taken from me, and I wanted to know why. I wanted to feel them again; I wanted to know that everything was going to be okay.

I had gone to a new doctor in Chicago, recommended by my doctor in California, who didn't skip a beat to begin therapy. Her name was Dr. Sweet, but she didn't sugarcoat anything.

"It's not going to be easy," she said. "It looks like what you had in California was a low-grade chemical treatment. We're going to do more tests to pinpoint the tumor. If we can, we'll start with radiation, but on the other end of the spectrum, you might need large doses of chemotherapy."

What I needed was larger doses of Mary. I wanted to home school her, but I knew I had to work. I couldn't be with her, even though, with the estate left to me, I could have quit my job and smothered her selfishly with attention. She was going to need the money so she wouldn't be a financial burden to Jonah with the small things like food and clothing or the large things like college. So, I decided to keep working.

All this organizing for my big finale was such an odd experience, and even stranger was the calm that came over me, going through the motions of extending my life as long as I could, but still resigned to the fact that I would no longer be a part of my daughter's life, or even my own. The cancer had already taken over my life. What little control I had left, I began to take advantage of.

I told Jonah everything, and he accepted it rather well. He agreed to accompany me to the doctor and drive me home. I told Mary's school that she would not be there on the day of my next treatment. Admission to an outpatient room at Mercy Hospital was seamless, and the three of us waited in uncomfortable silence. Jonah sat in the armchair thumbing through the magazines from the wall rack, while Mary sat at a desk with her homework, glancing up at me and smiling occasionally.

I expected the treatment to be routine but exhausting, and that's why I invited Jonah, so he could drive me back home. Dr. Sweet had prepared me with a detailed review of what to expect, so I was not prepared for the multitude of surprises I received that day.

A nurse entered the room and reviewed the chart to make sure we agreed on why I was there. She checked my vitals, told me an X-ray tech would be in soon, and left. The X-ray tech was a tall young man from Ghana, who escorted me to Radiology while I chatted nervously to pass the time.

"I detect a bit of an accent," I said. "Where are you from?"

"I am from Ghana," he said. "I have been in this country only a few years."

"I hope you like it," I said. "Is this what you did in Ghana?"

"Yes," he said, adjusting my arms so he could take the picture he wanted. "I hope one day to get a medical degree and specialize in orthopedics and sports medicine."

"Your family must be very proud of you," I said trying to hold still.

"My family is back in Ghana. I have not seen them since I moved here. I am afraid to go back and visit until I become a U.S. citizen so I will be able to return here without any problems." He went behind the screen and took the picture, then returned to the table. "What I really want is to bring my family here."

It was only then that I noticed the sadness in his voice. When he brought me back to the room, I wished him luck. He leaned toward me and wished me good luck too as he gave me a quick hug. That made me realize that he must have known all along why I was there. He never asked, which was probably a good thing.

The first surprise was when Dr. Sweet arrived. She reminded me of my mother on a good day, tall and slender with rustic red hair that seemed to spray a fine mist of freckles across the pale landscape of her face and arms. Her smile was bright and reassuring. A young woman who wore a hijab that framed her golden skin accompanied Dr. Sweet and waited patiently to the side. She held a large brown envelope in one hand and a clipboard in the other. I was comforted by the atmosphere they emitted and the fact that the three of us were approximately the same age. After I introduced Mary and Jonah, Dr. Sweet introduced the young woman behind her as the radiation oncologist, Dr. Amry.

"Amry?" I repeated. My gaze immediately moved from her eager smile to the name tag on her lab coat, and I read it aloud with the air of discovery, "Dr. Hend Amry?"

We stared at each other as a visible sense of recognition passed over each of us. She quickly looked down at her chart, then back up in stunned amazement. "Oh my gosh," she said. "Rachel Kelly, Paul's sister?"

"Yes!" Unable to restrain my excitement, I think I squealed. I slid down from the patient's gurney and held out my arms to encompass her. We held each other for a long moment before I stepped back to look again at her in what I hoped she received as a favorable stare. "You are so pretty, exactly what I imagined you to look like, knowing that my brother was very selective."

"Thank you," she said. "And I do see a lot of Paul in you. I remember him so clearly, even today."

Turning to Dr. Sweet, I said, "I'm sorry. This must seem very awkward, but Dr. Amry is my late brother's wife, and we have never met until now."

"That's amazing," Dr. Sweet said. "You two must have a lot to talk about."

"This is a surprise I never expected." I was finally able to introduce Mary and Jonah, and I swelled with pride as I identified them as my family.

Dr. Amry and Jonah greeted each other politely, and I could tell from their restraint that each of them had many questions for the other to clarify the obvious discrepancy of this family's history. But Dr. Amry averted her attention to Mary and said, "I have a son who might be your age. What are you, about fifteen?"

"Yes," Mary said. "Almost." Her head turned abruptly as if she were avoiding a pesky fly buzzing about. She didn't understand what was happening, and for a moment I didn't either.

The second surprise. I grabbed Mary's arm for support. "Wait. Are you saying?"

"Yes," Dr. Amry smiled. "His name is Harun. It is the Arabic version of Aaron, which was Paul's middle name."

"Oh my God, Mary! He's Paul's son. You have a cousin." I couldn't restrain myself at that point, and I reached out to give Dr. Amry another hug. Suddenly the feeling of being alone in the world was gone as my family had almost doubled in size in the span of a few minutes.

"I have another surprise for you," Dr. Amry said. She pulled an X-ray from the large envelope she had been holding.

The third. This one stunned me.

"This is the most recent X-ray of the tumor," she said as she pushed the film under the clips on a light board. She pointed to a spot in a milky part of the film. "This is where the tumor was located in your last X-ray."

"I'm sorry," I said. "I don't see it."

"That's because it's not there anymore." Dr. Amry was standing with her arms held up to display the emptiness in her palms.

I was speechless, my mind muddling through what she just said to grasp the reality of it. I heard Mary squeal loudly, and I felt her grab my hand and squeeze hard. "What?" I eventually said.

"It's gone!" Mary squealed again, this time as if she were standing down the hallway and needed my attention. "The cancer is gone!"

"Exactly," Dr. Amry said, smiling at Mary.

Dr. Sweet was smiling too with wide eyes that raised her eyebrows high up into the soft curl of her strawberry bangs. "We can't figure it out, but it's true," she said.

"I can figure it out," Mary said boldly. "I wished it away. I hugged you and told it to leave. And it did. It's that simple."

The fourth surprise washed over the room with the stunning array of a deep, red sunrise. Mary was actually standing with her hands on her hips like Fearless Girl in front of the Wall Street charging bull. I glanced at the others in the room, praying that they would not think my daughter was a lunatic. They could have humored her or brushed her aside gently with an offhand scientific reason why her revelation would be impossible. They could have made her feel small and insignificant.

"Well, maybe that's what your mother needed," Dr. Amry said.

"Sounds like a miracle to me," Jonah said. "And trust me; that is a word that has never come out of my mouth until now."

"Well, it certainly calls for a celebration," I said, placing my arm around Mary. With my free hand, I took Dr. Amry's hand in mine. "Can you join us? I want to catch up on your life. If that's okay with you."

"I would love that," she said. "I still have rounds here, but I can meet you later."

Dr. Sweet interjected that we should wait a few minutes while she coordinated my paperwork, but she added that she would like to see me with follow-up appointments to monitor my health. Reality check. I didn't want that to let me down, though. I didn't want to question how or why this was happening. I just wanted to enjoy my time, or extra time, that had been given to me. I wanted to embrace the moments with Mary—and now my extended family, to create good memories that would survive long after me.

On the way out, we passed the nurses station, which was not the usual scramble of nurses, each checking the charts and computer records for their assigned patients. The nurses were standing in a huddle of whispered chatter. Odd, but not unusual until, walking away, I overheard, one of the nurses say, "You should ask her to touch you. Maybe you'll feel better," which was received by restrained laughter.

At that moment, I decided that Mary was the one who had cured me.

SIXTEEN - JONAH

IT WAS THE MOST REMARKABLE THING, ESTHER, seeing that child step up to set the record straight about this strange phenomenon of Rachel's disappearing tumor. If I had not been there to witness it, I probably would have reacted with skepticism, maybe even brushed it off as a silly coincidence because of the impossibility on the face of it, or even the absurdity.

But then why do some people believe that Jesus healed the sick just because it says so in the Bible. I wish you were here to talk to me about that. I can't remember what you would have said, or if you would have believed. My memory isn't as good as it used to be about some things. I'm sure that blind faith would be a part of it, though. That's what I was telling you about Mary.

Rachel offered to take everyone out for a nice lunch, and she wanted to go to the Signature Room. She wanted to surprise Mary so she didn't tell her where we were going or anything about it. We took the red line from Chinatown up to Chicago Ave and walked through the Magnificent Mile over to the Hancock, then up to the 95th floor.

Did you feel me up there? I felt a little closer to heaven. The whole meal, I kept drifting in and out of the memory of our 25th anniversary. The only other time I had been there. Chicago looks a whole lot prettier from up there. But not as pretty as you looked that day. Happier times, baby.

And as much as I was thinking about you, I did pick up on some interesting conversation. First between Rachel and Mary, before Dr. Amry arrived.

We were all staring out the window at the landscape of the Lake Michigan shoreline where it curled around Lincoln Park and up toward Wrigley Field. I saw us sitting under a blanket in the upper deck watching the Cubs lose another one but enjoying every moment and cheering them on as if they were winning because winning didn't matter to us or any of the other loyal Cubs fans who were there to enjoy the beer and the brisk air while we waited patiently for the comeback when the Cubs would take it all. To everyone's surprise, they did just that in 2016. I wish you could have been here then so we could have gone to one more game.

Mary started talking, and I only heard bits and pieces at first, until my mind came back to the table.

"You remember that day, don't you?" Mary asked. "The day you told me you had cancer and I hugged you and told the cancer to leave your body?"

"Of course I do, Peanut," Rachel said.

"Well, that was the same day I went upstairs to get my violin and fainted, and you guys took me to the hospital."

"Who could forget," Rachel said. "It was very scary."

"I didn't faint because of anxiety or because I ran up the stairs too quickly. I fainted because the ghost swept me up and took the cancer, which I had taken from you when I hugged you. That's how it happened. I'm sure of it."

Rachel lifted Mary's hair out of her eyes and kissed her on the forehead. "You are more special to me than ever, Peanut," she said. "I always knew I couldn't live without you, and now, I know how true that is."

Mary looked at me. "What do you think, Jonah?"

Our children would have never asked me that question, even as adults. It made me realize how mature this child was. She was authentic, the real thing.

"I never believed in miracles before," I said, "but I do now." I avoided the issue of her ghost as I figured Rachel had done as well.

Mary didn't need to say anything. The smile on her face said it all.

"Anything so wonderful and mysterious has to be a miracle," Rachel said. She too was beaming with joy, and Mary received her mother's smile by looping her hand inside Rachel's arm and placing her head against Rachel's shoulder. The love they shared was very obvious. I was starting to feel a little like an outsider and missing the love of my own family when Rachel reached across the table and took my hand.

"Thank you, Jonah, for being here," she said. "It means a lot to me."

"To us," Mary interjected.

I admit it, Esther. I had to choke back a tear, and I hope you don't mind, but I realized then that they were my family.

Dr. Amry arrived soon after that. This was quite a day of discovery, and my mind was having trouble keeping up with all of it, or maybe I just kept getting stuck on how much I wished you were still with me to share it. That was the one thing everyone at the table had in common—a void where once someone of great significance had existed in our lives.

Dr. Amry immediately asked everyone to address her as Hend. She laughed that no one would be able to pronounce her real name, and she went on to explain why she changed her name, and that even now, fifteen years after she arrived in the U.S., she still fears for her life. Falling in love with an American was taboo for her father, and shaming the family was the worst crime she could have committed.

"Is that why you always wear a scarf?" Mary asked. "So no one will recognize you?"

"Oh no, Mary," Hend said. "I am still a Muslim, and this is called a hijab. It is a traditional head covering to express modesty and devotion to family. I guess I don't have to wear it, but I choose to because this is who I am."

"Well, it's very beautiful," Mary said. "And so are you."

"Oh my," Hend said. "Thank you, Mary. I would like to give you the same compliment, and it's not because you gave me one. You really are very pretty."

We all agreed, and laughed, and toasted to beauty as Mary dropped her head onto her crossed arms on the table.

"I am so glad we found each other after all this time," Rachel said. "It seems like a coincidence that was meant to be."

"I came to Chicago looking for you, Rachel, but I gave up after so many years."

"You mean you got my letter?"

"Yes," Hend said. "But it apparently took a while to get to me after it was delivered to another mosque in New York. I hid the letter at first, thinking it might be a trick so my family could locate me. I eventually found someone to bring me here. I wanted to see where Paul was from. By then, I was very pregnant. Another young woman I met at the mosque said she knew a man at Columbia who had just graduated from medical school, and she thought he might be returning to Chicago where his family lives. Almost everyone in his family is a doctor. My friend told me not to worry about him because he was very honorable, and he was Jewish. We both had a huge laugh about that, not that he was Jewish, but that the circumstances of a Muslim woman traveling with a Jewish man had the potential for some interesting conversation.

"My friend was a writer, and she thought that would make a great romantic comedy. But she was right about him. He even asked if I wanted to stay at his family's home until I got settled. I ended up taking him up on that, and I stayed while they helped me get through medical school. I was their housekeeper for many years, and now I rent the apartment above their garage. They call it their Ohana. They have a second home in Hawaii, so they have assimilated some of the language. It's nice enough, but there are times when it feels cramped. My son would really like some privacy. I feel I can never repay them for all they have done."

"Did you ever talk to my father?"

"I used the return address on your letter to locate where you lived in Oak Park, and I stood on your front porch talking to your father. He did not invite me in, and he would not tell me where you moved to. I told him I was Paul's wife, and he looked at me from head to toe. It was a long, scrutinizing pause. He never changed his expression, but I could tell as he stared at my pregnant belly that he thought I just wanted money. Your father told me he couldn't help me."

"That sounds like him," Rachel said.

"He did not appear to be very happy," Hend said.

"He wasn't," Rachel said. "He died a few months ago, so Mary and I moved back. We now live in that same big, old house by ourselves."

"I'm sorry if I created any troubles for you," Hend said.

"You didn't," Rachel said. "My father chose his life, and he died alone, but that's what he wanted. We all have to live with what we make of our lives. Mary never knew him, but she has Jonah now." Rachel looked over at me and winked. "Jonah is Mary's grandfather, and lucky for us, he lives right next door. I wish you could have known Mary's father. He died before Mary was born. I know you would have liked him."

"You must miss him," Hend said. "I know I feel very broken without Paul."

"I still feel that a part of me is missing," Rachel said.

Silence fell like a feather over the table as I stared out the window high above Chicago, seeing only your reflection in the glass as if you were sitting across the table from me. Without turning away from the window, I said, "It's not an easy life when we still cling to those who have been taken from us."

"Funny, the four of us sitting here," Mary said, "even with all of our broken parts, we still fit together. I guess that's what makes a family."

"You are one very wise young lady," Hend said.

"She's smarter than me." I laughed. It felt good to laugh.

"That gives me an idea," Rachel said. "You should move in with us. We have an extra bedroom."

"That might be difficult with my son," Hend said.

I don't know why I said this, but I did, without thinking. "I have two extra bedrooms, and like Rachel said, I live right next door." I regretted it as soon as I said it, not that I didn't like her; it was just that it might introduce a big change in my life that I wasn't ready for.

"You're not going to get rid of me," Mary said. She was staring at me with that same stubborn defiance that Tameka always had when she wanted to get her way. Then Mary tilted her head to draw her mother's attention. "We also have that room in the basement," she said.

Rachel jumped in her seat. "Oh, yes! I almost forgot about that. We never go down there, but it's a nice space. We can fix it up, and it will be quite cozy for your son."

"That's a very generous offer from both of you," Hend said. "I have to ask . . . is Paul's room being used? I think I would like to see it, even after all this time."

"Mary and I have our own rooms," Rachel said. "You would be welcome to stay there as long as you like. It will be so nice to have you around. And I think Paul would feel good about you staying in his old room." Rachel reached across that table and took Hend's hand. That was just the physical connection to what I suspected was an even stronger connection of their hearts and souls, which I could see in their eyes.

And Mary will never know how grateful I was that she had come to my rescue. I was enjoying the special connection that was developing between us, and I didn't want to lose that.

SEVENTEEN - MARY

I DON'T KNOW WHY ALL GOOD THINGS HAVE TO come to an end so abruptly. I wonder if Anne Frank ever felt that way. Is it a fate we all have to deal with—the challenges of life to test our will, our strength, our weakness as humans? Or is there really some supreme being setting all of this up, controlling all things, giving and taking, handing down judgments, fulfilling some dreams but not others, watching over some, and tossing aside others? I can't believe that. There's too much sadness in the world, too much grief. When someone walks away from an airplane crash, the only survivor, and says, "I feel so blessed. God was watching over me," this miracle doesn't speak very highly of the decision to allow all the others on the plane to perish—good people, bad people, babies who haven't even had a chance to decide if they want to be good or bad. Was it a miracle that cured Mama's cancer? And if I did it, if *I* cured her, then what power do I have?

My mind was swimming with questions and very few answers when we arrived home to discover a broken window in the back door, food from the refrigerator out on the countertops, random doors and drawers left open, contents of tabletops swept onto the floor, and my shattered violin at the foot of the stairs. The neck was broken and separated from the body. The bridge was crushed on top of the splintered body, the pieces held together only by the strings, the bow snapped in half and stuffed in a planter box by the front door.

I couldn't move, paralyzed with emptiness, and as I stared at my broken violin through thick, flowing tears, I could only think that this had been done by someone who had clearly *chosen* to be evil.

I didn't even think about the contest until later, after the police had come and taken a report and after we had cleaned up the mess and set about "moving on." Mama had said that was the only way to deal with it. Nothing appeared to have been stolen. Most of the mess was in my room where everything was turned upside down with no sense of purpose. I was relieved when I found my diary on the bed. But my heart sank when I realized that whoever was here had read some of the pages.

The oddest thing was a small puddle on the floor by the bed and a tracking of drops from the puddle out the bedroom door and down the hall. The last drops were at the top of the staircase. The policeman said it smelled like urine to him, and he let out a small chuckle as he said that the burglar must have had to go really bad or was frightened by something shocking. I didn't think of it until he said that, but then, all the evidence clearly pointed to someone who wanted to stop me from competing in the contest—or even playing in the school orchestra. I also suspected that the ghost had come out of the closet and confronted this person as he or she stopped to read my diary. I couldn't wait to tell Jonah that he was right—that the ghost is here to protect me, not harm me.

The very next morning, the first really warm day of spring, I got the chance. I left for school early so I could stop at Jonah's house, and he greeted me at the front door with a cup of coffee in his hand and a book under his arm. I think the name of it was *Beloved*. I apologized for disturbing him so early in the morning.

"Not at all, child," he said.

"I know I don't like to be interrupted when I'm reading," I said. "I hope it's a good book."

"It is, and any good book deserves a second read. I don't have any problem putting it down for a while."

He opened the door wider and gave me a nod of his head to step inside. When he looked down, he noticed I did not have my violin. The look on his face got even more puzzled, so I told him what happened and that he was right about the ghost.

"That's very strange, child. Someone must have known you weren't at home. Do you know anyone who would have done such a thing?"

"I have my suspicions. Someone wanted to break my violin."

"Maybe. Or maybe they wanted to steal it but dropped it trying to get out of your house."

"It doesn't matter." The real reason someone broke into our house and broke my violin suddenly dawned on me. "It's me they wanted to hurt."

"I think you just need to let them know that no matter what they do, you are *not* going away. You will only get stronger. So we need to get you a violin to practice with," Jonah said.

"My mom said she'd take me to get a new violin when she can, or we can rent one."

"Well, that's no good," he said. "That contest is coming up fast, and you can't waste any more time. You need to be prepared."

"She said I might be able to borrow one at school. They might have extras."

"I wouldn't count on that," Jonah said. He started to sip from his coffee, then stopped. "Wait, I have an idea." I followed him to the music room where he pointed with his coffee mug to the corner. "Go get that box over there," he said.

I knew he was talking about one of his wife's violins. "No," I said. "I can't do that."

"Why not? Esther's violins deserve to be played, and I think you deserve to play them."

"But what if someone breaks into our house again and breaks this violin or steals it?"

"We won't let anyone find out," he said. The twinkle in his eye told me that he wasn't going to give in. "I tell you what. You go to the school and report what happened. See if you can borrow a violin. Then, after school, you can use Esther's violin to practice. If your mother gets you another one, you can use it. If not, I'll come with you to the contest, and I can hold Esther's violin when you're not playing it."

I opened the violin case to a beautiful maple-hued violin. "This looks like an antique, Jonah. It's not a student violin."

"Esther played that violin for many years. She loved it. It's a replica of a Guarneri."

"I know I'll be nervous playing this violin," I said.

Jonah was smiling pridefully. "Just treat it as your own. It has a nice sound, but it's not near as precious as Esther's Tartari violin. I'm sure you'll be very careful with it."

"Oh, I will," I said. "It might help if you accompany me on the piano."

"Oh no, Mary. Remember I told you I don't play anymore."

"I know what you said, but you are my grandpa and I have a right to tell you that I think it is silly to stop playing your music. That piano deserves to be played, and I think you deserve to play it."

Jonah laughed. "I should have known that you would use my argument against me. And I can't argue with that. I'll do it on one condition."

"What's that?" I was starting to sound defiant.

"I would like you to come with me to visit someone."

"Really? Who?"

"I'll tell you that when we get there. And you can bring your mother, if she's available."

"Deal," I said, feeling that was a small price to pay.

As I hurried down the sidewalk toward the bus stop, all I could think about was getting back to Jonah's house to practice with Esther's violin.

EIGHTEEN - RACHEL

HEND MOVED INTO THE HOUSE ON A DAY THAT FELT LIKE SUMMER. The pavement was warm, and the shade from Jonah's big oak tree was welcoming. Ari Perlin, the young doctor who helped Hend move from New York, drove her over from his parents' house and helped unload her bags and boxes. When Hend introduced us, she rolled her eyes, and said, "I told him he didn't need to bother, but he insisted."

"It wasn't hard to take a little time off work," he said. His smile was big and white, and with his golden, wavy hair, he appeared more like a California surfer than a Chicago doctor.

"Do you practice in Oak Park?" I asked.

"Yes," he said. "I joined my father's clinic here. It's sort of a family practice, and with my mother and sister, we almost have all the disciplines covered."

"Good to know," I said. "Between my daughter and me, we might find a reason to join your patient list if you have openings."

"We do," he said. "My dad is a pediatrician. I think you'd like him."

"She might actually need a gynecologist," I said.

"Oh, well that would be my sister, and I'm a GP, so I could see her for regular stuff. You too, of course."

"That's very kind of you," I said.

He looked embarrassed. "I'm beginning to sound more like a salesman, so I should probably go."

We shared a laugh, and Hend gave him a hug. When Ari left, Hend grabbed my hand and said, "I think he likes you."

"No," I scoffed. "It was nothing like that."

"Oh yes," she insisted. "He was definitely flirting with you."

"I'm going to have to ignore that," I said. "Even if it were true, I'm just not ready for anything like a serious relationship. I know this must sound strange, but I still love Jake. I didn't get to show him that as much as I wanted to. I didn't get to be with him long enough."

"I understand," Hend said. "When love is strong, it never goes away."

"So where is your son?" I asked.

"Harun wanted to go to school today. He's on the cross-country track team and wanted to practice for an upcoming meet. He has the address and should be getting here after that. We need to figure out the bus schedule for him."

"Of course. I don't know what I was thinking. Does he go to Oak Park High School?"

"No. He attends Frederick Douglas. Harun is somewhat sensitive. Not the gregarious type. I thought he might fit in at Frederick Douglas better. To my surprise, they have a principal who is a Muslim from Syria. I hope you don't think ill of me. My decision was not based on race or religion."

"I know exactly how you feel. Mary is very strong-willed, but she stands out as different, and in high school, that can be difficult. She has always found strength and solace in her music."

"Really? I would love to get Harun interested in music. He doesn't have many interests and is very much the loner."

"Sounds like he and Mary will get along just fine."

While we were standing on the sidewalk, a man with dirty hands and sleepy eyes appeared in the driveway of the house across the street and started toward us. He looked to be about the age Paul would have been. I didn't see where he came from, if he exited the house across the street or was just walking by. I assumed he might be needing directions. He walked right up to us without any indication of his intentions. He was dressed in khaki pants, a dark green t-shirt, heavy boots, and a camouflage baseball cap like he had either been working in the yard or hiking through heavy brush. He reeked of cigarette smoke.

Without any change in his solemn expression, he looked at me, then at Hend, and kept staring at her. "What are you doing here?" His voice had the inflection of a demand. He obviously didn't need or care about an answer.

"I beg your pardon," I said. "We live here."

"I know *you* live here," he said. "But not *her*. We don't want *her* here."

"That's ludicrous," I said. "Who are you?"

"You don't remember me?" he asked, his eyes burning through me. "I knew your brother. I live right there." He indicated the house across the street with a quick nod of his head in that direction. "Your brother used to come over and drink beer with us."

"Eddie?"

"Yep."

"I thought you moved away."

"I did. Came back after my dad died some years back."

"So it's just you living there?"

"None of your business. Anyway, I didn't come over here for small talk. You need to know that we don't want her kind in this country. It's bad enough we have a black family living right there." He glanced at Jonah's house.

"She has just as much right to be here as you do. She lives with me. You had your say, and now you can leave, or I'll call the police."

"You just bought a lot of trouble. I thought you would have learned your lesson with that black boyfriend you had."

I took Hend by the arm, and we headed toward the back of the house. The muscles in my hand were stiffening in anger, gripping Hend's arm. I felt her discomfort and loosened my grip. "I'm sorry," I said. "I can't believe that just happened. He got me so angry."

Hend leaned into me and whispered, "How can people be so evil?"

We made it inside and locked the doors before sitting down in the sunroom. I started shaking and then came the tears. "I don't know how you can stay so calm," I managed to say, choking out the words.

"I have lived with evil all of my life, but that doesn't make it any easier," she said. "I don't believe people like that man will ever change, so I try to focus all of my energy on good people, and I have learned to cherish good people like you."

Hend put her arms around me and held me until I stopped crying.

"I would certainly understand if you decided not to move in here."

"Nonsense. I am not going to let some evil man affect my decision. We can get through this together."

"I think I'm okay now," I said, chuckling as I wiped away the tears.

"How about you show me around your beautiful house," Hend said, tactfully changing the subject.

"Of course," I said. "Silly me. I already feel so comfortable with you, I forgot that this is your first day here."

Hend smiled as if examining me to make sure I was really okay. I took her hand, and we walked around as I introduced her to the house. "I want you to feel comfortable here too," I said.

"How much will you need for rent?" Hend asked. "Whatever you feel is appropriate."

Her practical formality surprised me. "I never had any intention of charging you rent," I said. "We're family, and I'm not going to charge family."

Hend squeezed my hand. "We are a family, aren't we?"

"A bit of a mixed salad." I laughed. "But somehow, it feels right."

"Like Mary said, all of our broken parts fit together and make us stronger."

We got to Paul's room, and I opened the door slowly. "This is your room."

Hend stood in the doorway, her hands clasped together over her heart. "So this was Paul's room before we met?" she asked.

I nodded.

She walked around the room slowly, occasionally touching a book or a trophy on a shelf, slipping her fingertips over the bed as she gazed into the past. She stopped in front of the dresser and picked up a photograph of Paul in his basketball jersey. "This may sound silly, but I wish I had known Paul when he was in school, free from the stress of war. I do feel his presence in this room. I will be comfortable here."

NINETEEN - JONAH

THE GREEN LINE WAS LESS THAN A MILE TO WALK from the house. I thought Mary might like the train ride, and it would help me because I hated driving in Chicago and paying for a parking spot if I was lucky enough to find one. I would rather walk the short distance to the hospital. Mary stared out the window the entire trip. She must have been thinking about something because the scenery was nothing to look at.

"What is it, child?" I finally asked.

"Nothing," was all she said.

"Really? Looks like you're thinking mighty hard about nothing."

"Not really thinking. Just wondering."

"Oh. So what were you wondering about then?"

"Being on this train is like when my mom and I were driving across the country from California. I look out the window and see all the people going somewhere, with something to do, and I wonder where life is taking me and if there's a purpose to my life."

"Now that's a big thing for a little girl to be wondering about. I can tell you what I think about that."

"What's that?"

"Well, I think that sometimes life comes easier for some folks, and not so easy for others. It all depends on what we are born into. Seems to me that the ones who end up with the better end of the stick are the ones who work the hardest at making their lives happen. We never know exactly what will happen. That sort of depends on what stands in our way. But I think you have a shot at having a great purpose in your life, if that's what you want. *You* are the one who needs to decide what that is."

"I'm not sure what that is. I like playing the violin, but what if I don't win that contest?"

"That contest is just an opportunity. It's not the end of the world. If you want to play the violin, then your goal should be to play the best violin you can. Other opportunities will come along. Life has a lot to offer. You should enjoy the ride, Mary. Esther used to quote this writer to me when I would get to feeling down. Her name was Ursula Le Guin. She said, 'It's good to have an end to journey toward, but it's the journey that matters, in the end.'"

I couldn't believe those words, which Esther had passed on to me, had stuck with me all these years. My life had been a good ride until it all went bad, so I guess, in a way, Esther was reminding me that I still had some life to live.

"A lot has happened since we moved here. Most of it so far has been good, so I think I'll enjoy the ride."

Mary raised her head back so I could see her big smile, and then she placed her head against my shoulder for the rest of the ride into town. It gave me time to think about my own words, Esther's words, and the realization that I had stopped thinking about the end of my road. I had made a pledge to help Mary as much as I could, and I was hoping that would end up being an honorable goal.

We got off at State Street and walked up to Erie through the neighborhood of all the jazz joints where I played years ago—almost the exact route Jake and Rachel walked from the movie theater that last night. Mary kept asking me when I was going to tell her who this person was that we were going to meet.

"A hospital?" Mary asked when we got there. "Hospitals are getting to be a regular thing for us."

"You're right," I said. "Didn't think about that before now, but at least we have come out better than we were going in."

"Are you going to tell me now?"

"We're almost there."

We went up to the ward labeled AMiCouS Program and stopped at the nurses' station where I signed in. A nurse came over and read the sign-in sheet before looking up at me over the top of her glasses. "It's nice to see you come back so soon, Mr. Culpepper."

"I brought a visitor," I said.

"And who is this?" The nurse gave Mary a half-smile.

"This is my granddaughter, Mary."

"Well, I'm sure you'll have a lot to talk about then. Tameka is in the day room. I'll walk you down there."

"Tameka?" Mary asked, somewhat stunned. "But I thought."

"Come on," I said. "I'll introduce you."

Tameka was in a wheelchair, her head tilted toward her right shoulder and leaning on the headrest. Her eyes stared out the large windows as if mesmerized by the glinting afternoon sun playing on the surface of Lake Michigan. Her eyes didn't move, not when shadows moved across the windows or when Mary and I moved in front of her. I reached down and took her hand, wondering if she could feel me, if she would be able to hear my voice, if she was trapped inside her body with no way to communicate what she needed.

I spoke as if to a sleeping baby, wanting my voice to wake her with a sweet, happy smile. "Tameka? It's your dad, baby. I brought someone to meet you. This is Mary. She's your niece."

I looked around at Mary to bring her closer. Her hands and arms were trembling, and her lower lip was quivering. I couldn't tell why, if she was frightened or simply moved by the injustice that life inflicts on some people. I asked Mary to take Tameka's hand, just for a moment, and hold it so Tameka would know she was there. Mary stepped closer, and I put Tameka's hand into Mary's. Together their hands trembled as one before Mary let Tameka's hand drop to her lap.

"What's wrong with her?" Mary asked.

We sat down in chairs facing Tameka, and for the next hour, I told Mary the story, how Tameka was such a playful, energetic, and caring child, how she had hopes and dreams just like her brother and sister, and how she wanted to be a doctor so she could help less fortunate people. Then I explained how it almost ended in that terrible car accident that took her sister, how she came back from that and fought hard to become the doctor she wanted to be, how the ice on the sidewalk had found Tameka's foot as she was leaving the hospital where she worked and she ended up hitting her head on the pavement, aggravating the same damage that lingered in her head from that car accident years before. I described how again Tameka didn't die because she got the care she needed right away and how all of her caregivers said she was lucky. I told Mary that I wondered what luck had to do with it when Tameka had been stalked by tragedy all her life.

"And here she sits where she has been since this past winter, watching but not seeing, seeing but not understanding, understanding but not able to respond to the life all around her."

I paused and shook my head. I saw tears in Mary's eyes.

"She was all I had left of the life I had before, and now all I can do is watch her fade away. I wanted to die first. I couldn't stand to see her existing in this shell with no hope."

"She can't speak, or move, or anything?" Mary asked.

"She can walk around with someone's help. I think that's how they keep her from having other problems with her muscles or circulation. But she doesn't seem to be aware of anything. They say she is in a semi-conscious or vegetative state."

"Isn't there always some hope though?" Mary said.

I reached over and took Tameka's hand again. "Tameka baby, I forgot to tell you. Mary is Jake's child. Jake's gift to us. He made me a grandpa—and made you an auntie." I squeezed her hand with both of my hands, but I couldn't even feel a twitch in Tameka's hand.

Mary stood and leaned over Tameka, holding Tameka's head in her hands and touching Tameka's forehead with her cheek. Her fluttering eyelids were full of intensity. Tears began to flow from her tight-shut eyes. Then with her left hand, Mary reached down and took Tameka's left hand and brought it up to her chest, pressing both of their hands to Mary's heart. She stood like that for what seemed like several minutes, but it might have been only moments before she started to slip or faint. I jumped up and grabbed Mary to keep her from falling as she released her hold on Tameka.

"I'm sorry," Mary whispered. "I'm so sorry."

Tameka was once again slumped in her wheelchair.

"I thought I could help," Mary said. "I thought I had a gift."

"I'm the one who should feel bad, Mary. It's my fault for bringing you here."

"No," Mary said. "I'm glad you did."

I gave Tameka a kiss on her forehead and whispered in her ear, "I love you, baby." I thought I detected a sound, a tiny squeak of a sound like a momentary turn of the bow on Esther's violin, a faint vibration of hope, but Tameka's eyes remained on that vast emptiness out the window. "We can come again another time," I told Mary. "But only if you want to."

"I would like that," Mary said.

As we walked down the hall, I was thinking how Mary was always ready to give everyone hope, except herself. She had not given up yet, and I knew I was going to need to be there for her to give her support. We were in the elevator watching the empty hallway through the closing doors when the nurse came running out of the dayroom, waving at us and calling me back. I reached between the doors just in time to stop them from closing, and we stepped back into the hall thinking that something terrible had happened to Tameka. The nurse ran up out of breath.

"It's your daughter, Mr. Culpepper," the nurse said between deep breaths. "She's calling for you!"

We ran back down the hall and into the dayroom. Tameka was still slumped in her wheelchair. My heart sank. But as I walked around to face her, I saw that her eyes followed me, and a slight smile broke across her lips.

"Daddy?" Her voice struggled to push the word through her still smiling lips.

I reached down and grabbed her trembling fingers. "Oh, baby. You're awake. I love you, baby." All this and more I muttered with my own trembling voice, rejoicing with flowing tears, kissing Tameka multiple times on the forehead, and grabbing Mary's hand to pull her closer.

"I saw what happened," the nurse said. "I was standing in the doorway. I've never seen this before. It is a miracle. *You* are a miracle," she said, looking at Mary.

Mary looked stunned. She had stepped closer to Tameka and was staring at her, watching every move, anticipating every move. I kept holding her hand as she reached across to smooth Tameka's hair off her face. I looked up, and by now, all the other nurses in the ward had come into the dayroom and were standing around with hands clutched over their hearts or pressing against their lips to stifle open, elated crying. The room was full of excitement and rejoicing and wonderment.

Twenty - Mary

Harun is quite handsome, Papa. You would like him. If he wasn't my cousin, I'd be attracted to him. He's the strong, silent type, and for some reason, that brings out a side of my personality I wasn't even aware existed. I must usually keep it bottled up inside.

Maybe this is what being in love would be like. I've never experienced that, as you well know. So I refuse to feel guilty that he is my cousin. After all, there is nothing serious between us. He's hardly said two words to me. He probably can't because it seems that I'm talking all the time when I'm around him. Sometimes I even feel giddy. I want to be with him all the time. I want to explore the world with him, not so much to find out about the world, but to know what he thinks, and to find out what he is all about. I want him to feel comfortable here—and comfortable with me, so the real Harun will come out.

I started with the house. That's where all things start in my life now. I introduced him to all of the rooms and explained where everything was like, "Here's the refrigerator. This is where we keep the food that needs to be cold," and then laughing until I turned red when I realized how dumb that was. I can tell when I am talking too much because he always looks at me with his head tilted just a tiny bit like a puppy does when it is trying to figure you out. So then I'll stop and apologize.

"I've never had a cousin before," I told him.

"Me neither," he said. "My mother told me I have cousins in Afghanistan, but it is too dangerous for us to go back there."

"Well, I don't care what anybody else says, you can feel safe here."

I was trying to console him and any fears he might have about being in a new place, then I showed him the dark and scary living room.

"Am I supposed to feel safe in here?" he asked.

There I was laughing again, uncontrollably this time, and of course, he tilted his head at me.

"What?" he said.

"I'm sorry. Sorry, sorry, sorry," I said. "It's just that I had the same reaction the first time I sat in this room. It's kind of growing on me, though."

"Next thing you're going to tell me is this house has ghosts."

"Oh, well, we can get to that later," I said.

This time he laughed. It was short and sweet, a kind of throaty under-the-breath laugh, which let me know it was going to take a lot to entertain Harun. I let the whole conversation about ghosts slide, hoping he wouldn't notice that I wanted to avoid the topic altogether. I took him to his room in the basement. I had been in the basement only once, never wanted to go into the basement, even the word basement made it sound like an upscale dungeon. Mama insisted I help her fix it up for Harun. I was surprised that there was already a bed and a night table with a lamp.

Mama had to take my hand and coax me down the stairs. "It's okay," she said. "My mother used to stay down here when she was feeling exceptionally low, and sometimes she stayed here for long periods until the depression passed."

"You sure it wasn't this room that made her feel that way?" I asked.

Mama laughed like I had just made a sad topic funny. "I never thought of that," she said. "You're probably right."

I tried not to think about that as we dusted, put fresh sheets on the bed, and carried down a table from Mama's bedroom, which she said she didn't need, but Harun could use as a desk. I never told Harun how the room had been used before. I never called it the basement either, preferring to say bedroom instead so he wouldn't feel that he was being shut away in a dungeon.

Harun looked around the room and nodded in approval without saying a word.

"You can fix it up if you want to make it feel more like your room. Posters on the wall, photographs, whatever. My mother won't mind."

"Nice."

I began to feel that he was uncomfortable with me in his room, so I started to leave. He grabbed my hand, and I felt something run up my arm, something electric that shocked me at first but also felt good.

"Thanks," he said, then let go of my hand.

For a moment, my hand stayed where it had been while he was holding it. When I realized that, I returned it to my side and smiled at Harun. "I was afraid you were going to feel that you and your mom were imposing on us, and I wanted you to know that isn't the case. We want you here. We're family, and we want you to feel like family. *I* want you to feel like family."

He smiled back at me and nodded shyly.

"Do you want to see my room?" I asked, quickly interjecting this question into the silence.

He smiled and held out his hand to signal that he would follow me.

I laughed. "I guess I talk enough for both of us."

Harun followed me up the stairs to my room. I cautiously opened the door as if something would escape if I opened it too quickly, and Harun stood back against the wall.

"You don't keep snakes in there do you, or lizards?" His eyes were posted on the floor at the small space of the opened door. "I hate creepy, crawly things."

I scrunched up my face at the thought. "Ewww, no. Nothing like that. It's just my ghost."

His lovely, dark eyes closed as his head tilted, this time against the wall. "Oh, I get it. I need to be more on my toes around you."

I smiled and stepped into my room. He wasn't ready to believe.

He saw my broken violin on a chair near the window where I had set it like it needed a period of lying in state for me to mourn. He seemed truly affected by its presence.

"What happened? Is this your violin?"

"Yes, it was."

I told him the story of how I found it broken at the bottom of the stairs. He thought it was quite hilarious that whoever broke my violin had peed on the floor. He kept saying, "That's so weird."

"Jonah let me use his wife's violin," I said, "so I can still practice for this competition I have coming up."

"That is so cool," he said.

"What?"

"That you play the violin and that you are good enough to perform and compete."

"I guess we'll find out," I said. "But I try not to think about it because then I get really nervous."

"But still, you have to be committed to get good at it."

"I never thought about it before. Maybe I am. My mother got me started. I guess I was too young to object. I do remember her telling me that playing the violin will make me disciplined not only about playing but about anything I might want to do. Being committed was easy because I don't have a social life, so I was never tempted to quit."

Harun lowered his head like I had hit a nerve. He was staring at the floor as he took a deep breath.

"That was supposed to be funny," I said. "Judging from your reaction, you must think I'm just sad."

"Not at all. It's just that we are so much alike in many ways, but you seem to have it together better than I do."

"Wow, no one has ever given me a compliment like that before. And since my life is a daily struggle, I'll assume that you're just delusional."

"No really. You play the violin, and you're good at it. I don't have a social life either, but all I can do is listen to music through my headphones to shut out the world."

I refused to believe that there was nothing more to Harun than a shell for absorbing digital sounds. I was at a total loss for how to motivate him, to explore what deep down he might be interested in, what might get him excited. I didn't want him to leave though. "Would you be my audience? I need to practice."

He agreed and stretched out on my bed with his legs crossed at the ankles and his hands folded in his lap. His comfort and familiarity were a little too comfortable for me. I was going to suggest we go downstairs, but I didn't want to insult him. I took out Esther's violin and took a few minutes to warm up and make sure it was properly tuned. Harun was wearing a smile that stretched from ear to ear. I narrowed my eyes at him, suspecting that his smile was an outer reflection of his inner laughter. The thought of that served to increase my determination to play perfectly. I settled the violin under my chin and began to play Paganini's *Caprice 24*, which almost explodes from the violin before it settles in a sweet and mournful transition to the powerful bowing between octaves, the galloping spiccato, and the fiery ending. Using Jonah's analogy of becoming a swan to play *The Swan*, I had decided to be a hare being chased by a fox. My fingers ran rapidly up and down the fingerboard. My bow arm changed quickly to keep the pace, up and down as if back and forth, then bouncing and jumping and finally running to safety at the abrupt ending. My concentration never left the music, focusing on each note as if that was the only way Esther's violin should be played. When I was done, with the bow raised above my head as if signaling success, I glanced at Harun.

The inner laughter was gone. His eyes were wide. His hands were palm down on the bed at his sides as if to hold him in place. He breathed deeply and on the exhale said, "Wow."

"Thank you," I said, lowering the bow to my side. "I'll take that."

"You are better than just good. That was amazing."

"Now you're embarrassing me," I said, putting the violin and bow away in the case. "I'll let you in on a secret. I learned to play that by watching a YouTube video of Hilary Hahn. She's so beautiful, and I can only hope that one day I will be at least half as good as she is."

Harun's brow slowly creased across the middle as if bewildered by something he was looking at on the wall behind me. "Not sure where that came from, but it seems to be a sign that you are going to win that competition."

I turned around and saw a perfect rainbow stretched across the wall, shimmering with the brilliance of each color. The end of the rainbow disappeared into the closet. I didn't want to point out that the sun was setting on the other side of the house and could not have put the rainbow on the wall. "That *is* beautiful," I said. "Must be from the ceiling light."

"Almost looks painted on the wall," Harun said. "Do you believe in magic?"

Before I could answer, he leaped off the bed and opened the closet door. I felt myself take in a sharp, deep breath, not so much at his lack of etiquette in a girl's bedroom, but more of a fear of what would be waiting for him inside the closet.

"What's that?" he asked, stooping down to reach behind the door.

I must have been walking in slow motion. By the time I reached the closet, Harun was holding up a small, copper object in front of his face. He held it out to me.

"What do you think?" he said.

He dropped it into the palm of my hand. "Well, it's certainly not gold," I said. "Feels kind of heavy, like lead."

"You mean lead like a fishing weight or a bullet?"

"I don't know. Why would that be in my closet though?"

We both stared at it for a long time without any new ideas about what it was or its origin. We decided to take it down to the kitchen and leave it on the table. It was perfect timing for our mothers to enter the back door. They were laughing at the tail end of whatever conversation they had been having.

TWENTY-ONE - RACHEL

WHEN HEND AND HARUN MOVED IN, I STOPPED CALLING MARY Peanut except when I was being affectionate with her, and that was usually when we were alone. I didn't want to embarrass her. I had gotten to the point of calling her Peanut even when I was referring to her in conversations with people she didn't know. I had to be careful not to let that slip out, like the day Hend and I arrived home together and were greeted by Mary and Harun in the kitchen. Mary was bursting to tell me something.

When Mary and I lived in California, I arrived home one day after a particularly difficult time at work with back-to-back depositions in the office, and I was beat. Mary was super excited about a field trip her class had taken to the Monterey Bay Aquarium, and she wanted to tell me every little detail about the sea otters, the African penguins, the sea horses, in fact, every mammal, fish, and the mysterious creature she had seen and touched. As soon as I stepped into the house, she confronted me with wide eyes and rapid, bubbling conversation, which hit my ears like a whistling teapot. I lost my composure immediately and yelled at her that I needed time to decompress. She started to cry, so I started to cry, which made me realize that I had broken my unwritten promise to myself that I would never approach our relationship in the same manner as my mother had done with me, and essentially destroyed ours. So I stopped, took a deep breath, and apologized. We sat down together and shared our days, which made both of us feel better, and ever since then, Mary has respected my need to relax, even if it is for only a few minutes at the end of my work day.

I could tell Mary was about to explode with the news she needed to tell me. Luckily, I had had a really good day. I had decompressed with Hend on the train home, and we were both in a good mood.

"It's all right, Mary," I said. "What is it?"

"You need you to look at something," she said, pointing to the table.

Harun was already pointing at the small copper object, almost touching it.

"What is it?" Hend asked.

"We think we know," Harun said, "but we wanted your opinion,"

I picked it up and held it in the palm of my hand. All four of us took turns leaning over for a close-up look at this small, crumpled piece of metal. "Did you find a gold nugget?" I asked. "Are we rich?"

"I have seen many of those back in Afghanistan," Hend said. "Bullets are everywhere, the ones that don't kill someone."

"Oh my God!" I felt the words fall out of my mouth full of fear. "Where did you find this?"

"In my closet," Mary said.

I don't know how much time passed where I was transfixed by what Mary said. I still held the bullet in the palm of my hand. I hadn't moved. I'm not sure I was even breathing. The sound of gunfire, breaking glass, and Jake hitting the floor filled my head.

"Mama?" I heard Mary calling me from far away.

Then I felt Hend's arm around my waist and saw her take the bullet from my hand and give it to Harun. "Sit. Sit," she said. "Let me get you something to drink. Please, Harun, get Rachel a glass of water."

We all sat at the table just staring at the bullet, which was now on display in the middle of the table like a museum exhibit. We stared in silence for a long time with Mary holding one of my hands and Hend holding the other. Harun sat opposite me at the table.

"I don't understand," Harun said.

Hend put her free hand on Harun's arm softly. "I'll tell you later," she said.

"It's all right," I said. "Harun should know. We shouldn't have any secrets about the past." I took a sip of water and placed the glass back on the table but held onto it to steady my hand. "About the same time that your dad, my brother, was killed in Afghanistan, Mary's father was killed here, in this house, in what is now Mary's bedroom. It happened before you and Mary were born. It was the best night of my life that turned out to be the worst night of my life."

"What happened?" Harun asked.

Hend gave Harun a side look that clearly said to not ask such questions.

"It's all right," I said. "I need to learn to talk about this. It was late at night. We just got back from seeing a movie. We were having fun. We were dancing, when suddenly someone fired a gun through the window and hit Jake in the back. The police suspected who did it, but they never proved it."

"This could be evidence then," Harun said, pointing to the bullet. "We should give it to the police."

"It was a long time ago," I said. "The police might not even care anymore."

"Or maybe there's a reason this bullet suddenly appeared now," Mary said. "Maybe it's a sign that we can find out what really happened that night."

"We should save it just in case," Hend said. She took a plastic sandwich bag from a drawer by the refrigerator and sealed the bullet inside.

"We should tell Jonah," I said.

"Why don't you and Mary go do that," Hend said. "Harun can stay here and help me prepare some dinner."

Hend was always doing nice things around the house without ever asking, or even volunteering. She just did things. I would find her cleaning the bathrooms or floors or tidying up the sunroom where we all gathered to relax and watch the television or read with snacks and books. She was always the first to get up from the table and start cleaning the dishes after every meal, where I was more inclined to leave the dishes until I had built up sufficient energy for another household task. I didn't blame Hend for making me look bad. I envied her boundless energy, and it was contagious. She refused to slow down or leave messes for another time, so I found myself joining her, which saved me from looking lazy and also cut the clean-up time in half.

I really enjoyed chatting with her, whether we were sitting over a meal or standing over dishes, and the topics could be anything but were usually in the form of venting our frustrations over the ways we were treated at work, mine because of being a woman, hers because of being a woman and a Muslim. Our bantering gave me great insight into Hend's personality, her concerns, her biases, which were only about food choices, and her desires to give Harun the best opportunities for the best possible life. We were alike in so many ways, it was uncanny.

Mary and I went to Jonah's house. We were surprised he was not sitting on the porch. It took him a while to answer the door, but we could hear noises so we knew he was home. He eventually opened the door while rubbing his brow with his shirtsleeve. He had something locked in his fist and in his other hand was a small book.

"Oh good, it's you," he said. "I thought it was going to be another salesman for a home security system or solar panels. I don't know why I get so mad. My own father used to sell Fuller Brush door to door."

"Did we interrupt something?" I asked.

Jonah stepped aside and waved us in. "Not at all. I was getting a room ready for Tameka."

"Tameka?" I must have looked shocked. "But I thought."

"Mary didn't tell you?"

"Tell me what?" I looked at Mary, and she was hiding behind this expression that children wear when they've been caught doing something they shouldn't be doing and they hope it will be laughed off with an 'Oopsie.'

"It happened again," Mary said. "The first time, I was happy and proud. This time, I'm a little scared. I don't know what it means."

"I don't follow," I said.

"Let's go sit down," Jonah said. "I'll explain."

We sat in the kitchen. Normally Mary would just tell me whatever was bothering her, but this time, she waited for Jonah. She seemed to need Jonah to explain it. Jonah set the book, which looked like a Moleskine agenda book, onto the table and unclenched his fist to reveal a knife, which he set next to the book. Without a word, he turned to the refrigerator where he took out a pitcher of iced tea and poured three glasses. As he brought the glasses to the table, he started to explain.

"You see I took Mary with me to visit Tameka at the hospital. I wasn't going to do that, at first. I didn't want to put any pressure on Mary, so we just went for a visit. Tameka was the same. The doctors had told me that she could function at a very minimal level. She can do a few things, not much, and she has to have help. Mostly she is in her own world, locked inside her body. After I saw what Mary did for you, I thought Mary could help Tameka. Nothing happened at first, so I was convinced that Tameka was going to be like that for the rest of her life. But Mary is Mary. We were leaving, and Mary gave Tameka a hug. Before we got on the elevator, they called us back because Tameka had come out of her coma. They'd never seen anything like it before. The nurses were saying it was a miracle."

I kept saying Oh my God over and over, but I'm not sure if they heard me because my hand was over my mouth.

"What is happening?" Mary asked. She looked frightened.

I felt frightened. I was afraid I had projected my feelings onto Mary. I was struggling to climb out of myself, to find the right words to make sense of it.

"We don't need to do anything," Jonah said. "In fact, the worst thing we could is to let anyone else know about this. It can just stay a secret right here with us. As far as we know, all of this has been a big, wonderful coincidence."

"You're right," I said. I reached across the table and took Mary's hand. "We can all just keep it a secret and see what happens."

"Should we show Jonah our secret?" Mary asked.

"Oh yes, I almost forgot." Mary put the baggie on the table, and Jonah looked down, completely confused. "Mary found it in her bedroom," I said.

"We think it's a bullet," Mary said, short and sweet like she knew to wait for Jonah's response.

"Mary's bedroom?" Jonah asked. "Is that the room that used to be your bedroom?"

"Yes."

Jonah put his fist up to his mouth and started tapping it against his lips. He never stopped staring at the bullet. "Do you think this is from that night?" he asked finally.

"Yes."

He was still tapping his fist to his mouth, thinking so hard I could feel it. "The police said that the one bullet they had was too messed up to be of any use. Why didn't they find this one?"

"I don't know. It might have been in the wall for the last fifteen years and finally just fell out."

"Or my ghost pushed it out."

Jonah and I both turned sharply toward Mary, not confused or angry or disturbed or concerned, but trying to absorb all the possibilities of what she had just said.

"Don't look at me like that," she said. "There's something very weird in my room. Call it a faulty lightbulb, or a ghost, or whatever you want, but it's there, and it scares the pee out of people, and it gave me the ability to heal people, and it put a rainbow on the wall to point to this bullet. It is trying to tell us something."

Jonah pushed the book across the table in front of us. "I think Jake's killer might still be out there," Jonah said.

TWENTY-TWO - JONAH

ESTHER, OUR BABY IS COMING HOME. TAMEKA WOKE UP, and the doctor at Shirley Ryan said she'd be able to leave the hospital soon. I told you there was something special about Mary. Well, it was Mary who brought Tameka back from wherever she has been trapped for the past year since she slipped on the ice. She must have some kind of life-giving spark or some other over-powering energy that eats away at cancer and whatever had Tameka locked inside her body.

Mary is such a simple child, and by that, I don't mean simple-minded. She's smart and talented, musically. I'm referring to her ability to see the good in people and her desire to help people see the good in themselves if they are trapped in a world of hate. She never said one unkind word about whoever broke into their house and smashed her violin. I told Mary how you used to quote the Bible and famous people like Dr. King and Ursula Le Guin. She likes hearing about that. She told me that she wants to model her life after Anne Frank who was able to express her belief in the goodness of man even when so much of her life was clouded by the hatred that forced her and her family into hiding. Mary knows that the time then was very different from today, but she also knows that the hatred is very much the same, that especially today, we constantly live on the brink of the world reliving those terrible times.

Mary told me that she cannot change the world, but she can try to help one person at a time and hope that this will make a difference. She quoted Anne Frank to me. "How wonderful it is that nobody need wait a single moment before starting to improve the world." I've started to see that difference in myself.

I've been preparing Jake's bedroom for Tameka because it has a bathroom with a walk-in shower, which will make it easier for Tameka. Am I just using that as an excuse? Maybe. I haven't been in Jake's room for fifteen years. I've never been able to put it behind me. I didn't want to, but it was wrong not to face it, to face Jake's death, and accept his memory. Tameka's coming home gave me the courage for that.

I was in there dusting and changing the sheets on the bed and boxing up Jake's trophies and clothes when I came across the knife I gave him all those years ago. I could've used it to cut that cigar I smoked. No matter now. That cigar made me sick, so I'm done with that. I might hold on to the knife, though. Just holding it makes me feel Jake. It's nice having something of his in my pocket. I didn't realize how it would make me feel.

I found something else, too. I was going through his desk, all of his books and schoolwork, and scraps of paper with to-do lists. I found this book in the bottom drawer. It looked like one of those diaries or planning calendars with a ribbon to mark an entry and a strap to hold the book closed. I was curious. I thought it might hold some of Jake's thoughts, his ideas, his feelings. It had more than that.

I started at the front where he had notes to himself as reminders to work on his passing, on his run game, his Hail Mary pass, and strength exercises. He had written down new plays with all the diagraming for field positions. There were pages mixed in between with lists of words with definitions like a vocabulary list he was working on. And there were pages very much like a diary talking about how he met Rachel, and how he felt about her, and his plans, their plans. He was quite the romantic, Esther. And he was quite the intellect, too. He would've been an inspiration to so many young kids growing up today who might not see the inside of hope unless someone is there to guide them in the right direction.

When I got to the page marked by the ribbon, my hands started shaking as I read his words. He said that Rachel's brother, Paul, came outside one day while he was shooting hoops in the driveway. Paul told Jake that he had joined the Army and would be leaving soon for training and probably the Middle East after that. He felt that this was the only way he could get away—the only way he could forget about what he had gotten involved in.

Paul told Jake to stay away from the neighbor across the street, said it was not right what was going on over there. He wouldn't say exactly what that was, but he did tell Jake what he had seen once, the last time he was over there. The only reason he had gone over there was because the old man saw him walking home and asked him to come over and have a beer with him. He went back that night, and there were already several boys from the high school sitting in the living room, drinking beer with the old man.

They were talking about Jake and what they could do to keep him from playing on the team. They were talking about everything from playing pranks on Jake, to threatening him, to starting a fight and beating him up, maybe breaking a bone or two. That was when the old man left the room and went to the back of the house, and when he returned, he was carrying an AR-15, an assault rifle he had slung at the ready like he was going to shoot everyone in the room. He slammed the magazine up into the rifle and told them that if they couldn't stop Jake, that he was going to do it.

They all had a big laugh about it like he was joking and really wouldn't do anything so stupid, but Paul apparently thought it was scary enough to take seriously. That's why he was warning Jake. The last thing Jake had written on the page was that if something happened to him, the house across the street was where we would find the person responsible.

I don't know why Jake didn't tell us about this, why he kept it a secret until it was too late. He didn't even tell Rachel about it. I found that out when Rachel and Mary came over to the house just about the time I had finished reading. This is the strangest part. They found a bullet in Mary's bedroom, what used to be Rachel's on the night Jake was killed.

I put the notebook on the table and opened it to the last page. Rachel read it as tears were streaming down her face. "Why didn't he tell me?"

"He didn't tell any of us," I said.

"I knew that old man over there was trouble. He gave me the creeps every time I would see him out in his yard. Mostly he would just stand around watching kids walk by on the sidewalk, or he would sit on his porch and smoke cigarette after cigarette. He would position himself so he could watch me and Jake whenever we were out in the driveway shooting baskets. Once I saw him out in the yard watering the plants in the flower bed, and he would turn and spray the kids walking by on his sidewalk, only the kids who weren't white, though. He was a scary, nasty old man. Paul never even told me about what he saw. Maybe they didn't want to scare me, but if they had said something, maybe we could have prevented what happened."

"Nothing we can do about it now," I said.

I tried to remember the detective's name from fifteen years ago but couldn't. I didn't want to turn over the bullet and maybe even the notebook to anyone else and have it get lost with mishandling and bureaucratic incompetence. They didn't seem to care fifteen years ago, so I figured they wouldn't care now.

TWENTY-THREE - MARY

I WAS READY TO GO, AND YET I SAT IN THE QUIET OF MY bedroom just staring at Esther's violin, focused on the connection I had with it. I hadn't thought about my dream or the ghost or the bullet or the pages of sorrow in Jake's Moleskine, which Mama had cried over, or the gift of healing I had been given, a gift which had filled me with pride at first, then fear. Esther's violin. The feeling I put into it through the hare scurrying across the strings to escape the fox. That was all that mattered.

We took an Uber into Chicago to the Symphony Center. The five of us just fit in the SUV. I was quiet the whole way except when Mama patted my knee and asked if I was okay, and I told her I hoped I wouldn't embarrass everyone. Jonah overheard us and put his hand on my shoulder and said, "Don't lose focus, and you'll be fine."

We were escorted to what appeared to be practice rooms with small stages for recital performances. Everyone sat behind the row of seats reserved for the judges, and I was escorted to another room where the performers, the contestants just like me, slowly filtered in and were instructed to wait. After waiting a while, I looked up and saw Camille sitting across the room. I was surprised that I hadn't seen her when I arrived. She was facing away from me and was holding her right hand in her left, cradling and rubbing it.

When all of the seats in the waiting room were filled, a young woman entered the room. Everything about her was elegant. She wore a black, silky dress that accentuated her slender frame and seemed to defy the smallest speck of dust or lint to settle upon it. Her hair was long and black and sparkled like a dark, flowing river. Her skin was smooth and unblemished. Her striking appearance was made even more prominent by her demeanor and the pleasant smile that greeted everyone in the room. I told myself at that moment that if she was an example of the musicians who represented the classical world of music, then that was my goal and I knew I was going in the right direction.

She introduced herself as Miss Jeong and said she was the Associate Concertmaster of the Chicago Symphony Orchestra and would be one of the three judges that day. She pointed to a room at the back of the waiting room and told us that was where we could tune our instruments and warm up. From there, we would be escorted to the performance stage, and the next in line could warm up. Each person would get fifteen minutes before the next person would be called.

Before she left, she called out the first two performers who took their places in or near the warm-up room. I started to get nervous and thought that I could calm my hands by focusing on Esther's violin. With the case on the floor, I pulled the violin to my lap. When I looked up, Camille was standing in front of me, much like the first day she introduced herself to me. She was still cradling her right hand in her left.

"I thought you said your violin was broken," she said. "That doesn't look like a school violin."

"It's my grandmother's violin."

"It must be special. Does it make you sound better?"

"I'm not competing with you, Camille. We just happen to be on the same path. You're a very good violinist, and I try to be."

Camille smiled like she had won a match of whatever game we were playing. "Today might be your lucky day," she said.

"Is something wrong with your hand?"

"I must have sprained it. Something doesn't feel right. I'm hoping maybe they'll let me play another day."

"Let me see," I said, and I set Esther's violin back in its case. I took Camille's hand in both of my hands and rubbed it gently.

Camille's eyes narrowed at me suspiciously. "What are you doing?"

"Focus on your music, Camille," I told her. "Not your hand. I think you'll be okay."

"Why are you doing that? It won't make me want to beat you any less."

"I want you to play your heart out, and I'll play my heart out, too. I want them to remember you because you're good, not because you injured your hand."

Camille pulled her hand back, moving her fingers gently. She stared at me like I was crazy. She started to walk back to where she had been sitting and turned back. "I thought you'd think I was the one who broke your violin."

"It doesn't matter," I said.

"Well, just for the record, it wasn't me. I felt bad for you. I really did."

Both of us went on to play that day. Ironically, she was right in front of me on the list. Mama told me later that she played *The Swan*. I suspected that was her sly way to intimidate me, thinking that I would perform the same piece. She must have forgotten to tell me. Just as well though because it might have worked, had I known.

When I went into the recital room, I tried not to look at the audience, which had filled the room with some standing in the back. The judges watched me as I took my place on stage. Miss Jeong had referred to them as the jury, which I immediately put out of my mind because it made me feel that I had done something wrong. Yes, they were going to judge me, but I was not going to let them or Camille intimidate me. Jonah told me I was there to make them feel the music as I feel it. I should only concentrate on expressing that feeling. I did smile at the judges as Jonah had instructed me to do, and Mama had agreed.

Miss Jeong announced my piece as she faced the audience. "Miss Mary Hester is here to perform Paganini's *Caprice 24*." She paused a moment, turned back to me, and smiled. "Quite a daunting piece. Good Luck." Then she took her seat in the front row.

That was the most nervous I have ever been performing in a recital. Performing for Mr. Drummond was a close second. All the other times were with fellow students of my violin teacher in California. There was a little bit of pressure, but nothing like this.

I positioned myself and nodded to Miss Jeong. She nodded back, and I began. I became so immersed in my story of the hare and the fox that all of the components of technique—posture, fingering, bowing, time signature, pauses and accents, and the worrisome spiccato section—all melded into the emotion of what I imagined Paganini must have felt when he composed *Caprice 24*. When I was finished, for a moment, I didn't even care what the judges thought. I was happy.

I wasn't expecting applause. It never occurred to me that anyone would applaud, and when it came, exploding into the air where the music had been, I bowed my head, hopefully in a humble manner, and covered my mouth with my right hand, still holding the bow, to conceal my not-so-humble smile.

There was more waiting. That was the excruciating part. We couldn't go into the recital room until everyone had performed. Eventually, Miss Jeong came back to the waiting room, thanked us for our performances, for allowing her to enjoy our performances, for being a part of a long history of classical music and performance. She encouraged all of us to continue with our study of music and perfecting our performance skills. She was sorry there could be only one winner of the competition because we were all deserving of recognition. The decision of the jury would take some time, and the winner would be notified in few days. We were all excused.

My family was waiting in the hall just outside the room and greeted me with hugs all around except Harun who held out his hand for me to high-five and said, "Good job."

Everyone laughed except Hend, who gave Harun a gentle shove on his back and said, "You can give her a hug, Harun. It's okay."

Harun rolled his eyes. "Thanks for embarrassing me, mom." He looked up at me with a half-smile like a wink and held out his arms. He made me laugh as we gave each other a quick pat-on-the-back hug.

"Thanks, cuz," I said.

We were in the car headed back home when Mama grabbed my hand, and I knew she had something to tell me. "I am so proud of you. You played beautifully. You looked beautiful. I am so, so proud of you."

"Thanks, Mama," I said. "I'm kind of glad it's over, though."

"It may not be," she said. "Miss Jeong came up to me as we were leaving the performance room. She told me that she was very impressed by your performance and that if you were serious about making music a career, she recommended I enroll you in Chicago Academy for the Arts. She has connections there and would be able to put in a good word. Many students from the Academy go on to Juilliard. She was very encouraging. Of course, it would mean a change of schools, but you haven't been at Oak Park very long so, I don't know, I guess I'm rambling now, but it all got me very excited for you. It's really up to you, though. I don't want to assume that this is what you want."

I was stunned. All I could say was, "Wow."

"You should do it," Harun said.

"We can go talk to them and check out the school, and then you can decide," Mama said.

"That is very exciting," Hend said.

I turned around to look at Jonah who had been silent through all of this. "What do you think?" I asked.

He was lightly tapping the violin case in his lap, and slowly, his smile emerged. "You are very talented at a lot of things, Mary. You shouldn't take any of them lightly. A good music school like the Chicago Academy would allow you to explore a life of music without leaving the rest of your talents behind."

"We can check it out," I said.

We weren't home long before my mother got a phone call from Miss Jeong to confirm that I had won the competition. It had been a unanimous decision with the judges. Mama handed me the phone so Miss Jeong could congratulate me personally. She looked forward to playing with me, and she would be in touch later with what the next steps would be.

I wasn't able to sleep that night. My heart was racing. My mind was racing. I started crying I was so happy.

Twenty-four - Rachel

A LOT HAS HAPPENED SINCE WE TALKED LAST. You would be very proud of Mary. She is apparently a prodigy on the violin. After winning the Chicago Symphony competition, she was accepted into the Academy of the Arts music program without an audition. Ms. Jeong put in a good word for her, and that was all it took. In all fairness, your dad actually had a lot to do with that too. He coached Mary on performing, and even though he never played the violin, he was able to teach her how to relate to the music better. That's the way I understand it anyway.

Mary starts at the Academy next week, and she's very excited about it. She probably won't have to practice her violin anymore after school because she'll get more than enough playing and private lessons at the Academy. She also starts rehearsals with the symphony soon. I was told she would be able to coordinate that with her Academy instructors. It's all such a whirlwind of good news for Mary. You're the only part that's missing.

That's what's so difficult about reading what you wrote in your notebook. I don't understand why you didn't tell me. We could've faced it together, and maybe none of it would've happened. You'd still be here with me. I feel so bad that I wasn't aware of any of it. Paul never told me what was going on either. He just left and joined the army so quickly. He must have been hiding something. There must be more to it than the warning he gave you. Now you're both gone, and it all seems so senseless. I keep telling myself that I have to focus on the good and not what could have been. The past is only a memory, and the future is yet to be, but I feel strongly that learning from the past will help me face whatever the future brings.

You'd also be happy to know that Tameka is now back home with your dad to recuperate from her head injury. She has basically defied death twice, and this second time seems to have something to do with Mary. I'm having a hard time understanding this part of Mary. She has never been a fake person, never pretended she's something that she's not. But we're talking about miracles here. First with my disappearing tumor, and now with Tameka waking up from a coma after Mary hugs her. I've always been a common-sense person, who helped in my career dealing with criminal cases and pleading with the jury about what would really make sense or no sense at all for my clients. But this thing with Mary is different. Common sense can't explain any of it.

Mary and I went over to your dad's house to bring some dinner and take some of the worry and burden off your dad. It was my first time seeing Tameka since she came home. Jonah took us back to the kitchen where Tameka was sitting at the table with her hands in her lap. Without hesitating, Mary stretched her arms across Tameka's shoulders, gave Tameka a big, cheery hug, and kissed her on the cheek.

"Is it okay if I call you Auntie Tameka?" Mary asked.

Tameka's face immediately sparkled with joy. She reached up and squeezed Mary's hand and said, "Yes, I would love that very much." The words came out slow and determined.

"We were just sitting here talking about family," Jonah said. "About Jake and Olivia and their mom, all the good times. I think it's good for Tameka to remember or be reminded about what she can't remember. She takes her time processing things, but it's getting better."

"There's no rush," I said.

"I don't know if I want to remember," Tameka said. "I forgot that Jake and Olivia are gone. It hurt a lot when dad reminded me what happened."

"It's true," Jonah said. "She asked me where they were, and I thought it best to tell her. We've been using up a lot of tissue to soak up our tears."

"That might be very normal," I said. "Blocking out a painful past probably helps with healing."

Tameka was staring at me. Her eyes narrowed and pushed together vertical lines of intense thought. She reached across the table, and I placed my hand on top of hers. Her eyes widened. "Rachel?" she said.

"Yes! I was afraid you wouldn't remember me." Our smiles emerged together. "We had some good times sitting on your bed, sharing our dreams. How you wanted to be a doctor and I wanted to be a lawyer. Mostly we just liked trying on clothes and make-up."

"And sharing stories about Jake."

"I especially liked the stories about Jake. I felt like I finally had a sister to share things with."

"You left, though. I didn't understand why you left."

"After Jake was gone, I couldn't stay. I should have told you. I'm sorry."

While we were talking, there was a knock at the back door. It was Hend and Harun.

"I hope it's all right if we join you," Hend said. "I took the liberty to order pizza for everyone, on me."

I heard Mary squeal, "Yay! I love pizza!"

"That sounds fun," I said. "And it's very nice of you to do that."

"Come in, come in," Jonah said. "Tameka is doing well, so the more the merrier. We're all family, right?"

"Right!" Everyone said in unison. We sat around the kitchen table, mostly talking to Tameka, sharing the stories of how we all found each other and came together.

Eventually, we heard another knock at the front door, which we thought was the pizza delivery. I told Jonah to relax and stay with Tameka. I opened the door, and the two women standing on the porch appeared puzzled. The older one said, "Not sure if we have the right house. We're looking for Jonah Culpepper."

"You have the right house," I said. "I'm a relative. I live next door."

"We're from Shirley Ryan Ability Lab," she said. "We came by to check on Tameka's progress."

"Of course," I said. "Please come in. I assume Jonah was expecting you?"

"Yes, he is," the young one said. "I talked to him this morning."

I guided them back to the kitchen where Jonah was preparing a pitcher of tea. An instant of surprise flashed across his face when he saw us, and he quickly shook it off and greeted the two women. The younger one, who said her name was Katy McGee, was the nurse Jonah recognized from the day he and Mary visited with Tameka. The older one introduced herself as Lori Doyle, Director of Pastoral Ministries at Holy Name Cathedral in Chicago. She worked with Katy McGee to assist with Tameka's care. They both kept smiling at Mary.

Finally, Katy McGee said, "You were with Jonah when Tameka regained consciousness, weren't you?"

"Yes," Mary said. "Tameka is my auntie."

"Oh, yes," Lori Doyle said. "I was told that Tameka woke up right after you gave her a hug. Is that true?"

"Not right away," Mary said. "We were about to leave."

"No need to be shy, Mary," Katy McGee said. "I was there. It was quite a miracle."

"A miracle indeed," Lori Doyle said. "In fact, I spoke with Reverend Carneli about you, and he agreed that I should come talk to you. Is that okay?"

"I guess," Mary said.

"What is this about?" I asked.

"We don't want to impose on you," Lori Doyle said. "It's just that the church is very interested in these special cases where it seems that some outside source has assisted in a cure or rehabilitation."

"You can use the living room," Jonah said. "I think I'll stay here with Tameka."

I sat next to Mary on the sofa, and Lori Doyle pulled up a chair opposite us. "Luckily, you were here today," she said.

"We live next door," I said. "We'll probably come over more often now that Tameka is living here."

"Of course," Lori Doyle said. "As you know, Tameka was a patient in the AmiCous Program at Shirley Ryan Ability Lab. That's a part of the hospital with special care for semi-conscious patients. Tameka was able to do many things, some rote memory skills and some autonomic skills, but she had very limited ability to speak or display any cognitive functions. She was in what is commonly referred to as a vegetative state. So to have such a remarkable recovery is quite astounding and probably why we jump to the conclusion of a miracle."

"She's not going back, is she?" Mary asked.

"Oh, no, no," Lori Doyle said. "Nurse McGee is here to examine Tameka to check on her progress and offer any assistance or advice. Nothing more. It's a service we provide, not as often as we would like, I'm afraid, but we are always willing and excited to help bring the patient back to a normal family living situation."

"Isn't there a chance that Tameka's recovery could be explained medically?" I was trying to point out alternate avenues of explanation because I didn't want Mary to be dragged into something she wasn't prepared to handle.

"You have to understand that Tameka suffered a severe brain injury when she fell on the ice and hit her head. This injury was compounded by the location of the injury, which was the same as the head injury she suffered in the car accident almost ten years ago. She was placed in a coma back then to facilitate her recovery. She went into a coma on her own the second time. The doctors examined and treated Tameka thoroughly. There are extensive medical records regarding her physical condition, EEGs, reactive therapy, REM measurements. Everything pointed to a long and extensive recovery, *if* there would be one at all. In short, no one expected this."

"I'm beginning to think that miracles happen more often than we realize."

"Has this ever happened before?" Lori Doyle was looking directly at Mary. "I mean, have you ever done something similar to what you did to Tameka and encountered the same type of results. A miraculous recovery?"

Mary looked at me, and we both shrugged at the obvious reply.

"Once," Mary said.

Lori Doyle was looking at both of us like a tennis match in front of her. "Did you do something to help your mother, Mary?"

"Yes."

"Very interesting. Would you tell me what that was?"

"This is getting scary," Mary said.

"I'm not here to scare you, Mary. Or hurt you. I promise I'll do everything to protect what you tell me."

"It's okay," I said. I grabbed Mary's hand.

"Mama was sick. She had cancer. She told me she was dying. I didn't want that to happen, but I didn't know what I could do. I just told the cancer to go away. I made a point to hold Mama every day and tell the cancer to go away, and it did."

"Is that true?" Lori Doyle asked me.

"Yes. We don't have any other explanation. Neither do the doctors. My oncologist lives with us. She can vouch for what Mary says."

"I also cured my friend's injured hand so she could play the violin."

"Really?" I asked.

"That's quite remarkable," Lori Doyle said. "Can you tell us about that?"

"Her name is Camille. She's not really my friend. We know each other, though. We both play the violin, and we compete against each other. Right before she was going to play, I noticed her hand was hurting. I didn't want her to say she had an excuse if I played better than her, so I held her hand, and she said it felt better."

"You didn't tell me about that," I said, a little shocked.

"I didn't want to gloat. This is all happening so fast. I didn't think any of it would work."

"But it did," Lori Doyle said. "And you have made many people happy. You seem to have a gift, Mary. And it needs to be protected."

"How?" I asked.

"We'll do whatever it takes to keep this out of the news. We don't really know what it is yet—or how big this might be. This is something where you have the opportunity to help many, many people. If you could do that, would you be willing to come to the hospital, let's say once a week, and spend some time with the patients?"

"We don't know," I said. "Mary is very busy right now with other commitments."

"I *would* like to help," Mary said. "But what if I can't? I'm scared. I never really asked for this."

Lori Doyle grasped her hands in front of her chest. "I understand, Mary," she said. "All of this is so new to you and can be quite scary, so take your time. Talk about it with your mother and contact us when it's a good time for you."

This day was special because I felt more like a family than I had ever felt, but already, Mary was having a very grown-up problem, which made my heart ache even more because you were not here to help. Mary needed guidance, and I needed guidance *for* her.

I tried to leave what I want for her out of it. I only focused on Mary's feelings. I know that playing the violin makes Mary feel good. This whole idea of helping people with miracles scares her. I had a talk with Mary about that. I could tell she was thinking about it very seriously. She needed time.

Mary told me, "There might be more than one path in life for me. Wherever life takes me, I will always want to give people hope for something better."

I asked her, "Did Anne Frank say that?"

Mary said, "No. I did."

TWENTY-FIVE - JONAH

THE FIRST PERSON TO SHOW UP WAS A YOUNG WOMAN about twenty years old, I would guess. She wore vintage or thrift store clothing, which looked too big on her body, and her tangled hair gave her a sad demeanor. She walked up and down the street ever narrowing the ends of her path until she was pacing back and forth like a caged cat directly in front of Mary's house.

A family came next, and they appeared to be homeless or lost, standing at the end of the front walk, not speaking to each other, the father standing resolute in one spot, staring at the house while the mother took turns breastfeeding two small children, leaving the other three children to run around dodging the caged cat as she shuffled by them.

The next day, more showed up, just milling around on the grass and in the street, not forming any line to determine who was first, next and, where the line ended. They occasionally talked to each other and asked questions, but no one seemed to know the answers.

I sat on the porch, pretending not to watch but still keeping an eye on those who stepped inside the yard and tried to look through the windows. I knew they had come to see Mary.

Eventually, Hend came out of the house and walked to the end of the front walk. I heard her talking to them as a few came over to her at first and then the rest when they realized what was happening. They were squinting in disbelief, doubting that they were in the right place, listening to Hend, stunned by her beauty, her big eyes and comforting smile, obviously a Muslim woman in her colorful hijab and not what they expected to come out of the house where they were told Mary lives. Hend spoke eloquently and with a helpful tone that elicited a care and concern for the people and what they were seeking.

First, she addressed the father who first showed up with his family. "Are you here to see Mary?" Hend asked.

"Yes," he said. "My child is not well. We heard that Mary can heal the sick."

The first young woman who came was standing only a few feet away from Hend with two tight fists crossed over her breast, listening intently but not saying a word. Others began to call out their various ailments and prayers that Mary might see them and heal them. They pushed in closer, and there was a shuffling of anguished bodies until Hend raised her hand, and silence spread over the small crowd.

"Mary knows you are here," she said. "But Mary is not feeling well herself. She needs her rest before she can greet you. Please understand that she cares about you and would like to meet with you, but you will have to wait, and I don't know how long that will be."

Someone in the back of the crowd in the street called out, "So it's true. She can heal people?"

There was a murmuring in the crowd that started to grow louder until once again, Hend raised her hand to hush the crowd. "I am curious where you heard that," she said.

A man in front responded, "Some of us have friends or relatives at the hospital, and they told us that Mary was there to heal people so they could speak and walk again."

"I heard from someone at my church," a woman near the front said.

"People are saying that Mary is a descendant of Jesus."

"How did you find out where she lives?" Hend asked.

"It was posted on the internet," the man said.

"There's a website for Mary the healer," a voice in the back said.

"I hope you can be patient," Hend said. "Mary will see you when she feels better. She will not see you if she is frightened of what you will do, so I ask that you remain calm and orderly. Thank you." And with that, Hend turned and started to go back into the house.

My concern was that there might be someone in the crowd of believers who might get impatient and try to stop Hend or force his way into the house. At about the same moment, I heard an angry voice from behind the crowd. Eddie was walking toward the crowd from his house across the street. Hend must have heard it too, as she stopped and turned back toward the noise.

"Are you people crazy?" Eddie was yelling and kept yelling. "You're blocking the street. You're disturbing this neighborhood. I'm calling the cops if you people don't leave!"

A man stepped out of the crowd. "Please remain calm. We are not doing anything wrong here."

Eddie walked up to the man, facing him nose to nose. "Oh yeah! You don't belong here, so get gone!" Eddie shoved the man in the chest with both hands, and the man stumbled backward and fell to the ground. A woman screamed and ran up to help the man on the ground.

I called the police from my cell phone and kept an eye on Eddie as I reported the disturbance.

Another woman who stepped up to help the first woman with aiding the man on the ground looked up at Eddie. "We're not doing anything wrong here, so go ahead and call the police."

"You're trespassing! You're loitering! You're talking to an Islamic terrorist! Her son is probably in his room right now plotting a mass shooting at his school!" Eddie continued to yell as he approached the woman and pointed to where Hend stood on the walkway. "You're all going to jail if you don't leave."

A white-haired older man stepped out of the crowd. He was wearing a black suit jacket and a black shirt with a white collar, like a priest. "We have a reason for being here. We have a purpose. We came to see Mary."

"You're wasting your time if you think some savior is living in that house! Mary is a fraud. She's just a kid. She thinks there's a ghost living in her bedroom. She's delusional, and she's not saving anyone."

I didn't realize that I had stepped out into the crowd, still holding my cell phone up so the dispatcher could hear what was being said. I had walked up behind Eddie. "The police are on their way, Eddie. You should probably go."

Eddie turned quickly, and when he recognized me, he took a step closer. "This doesn't concern you, old man. You're going to get hurt here."

The crowd started to circle around us. Eddie must have been getting nervous as he felt the people closing in.

"Are you going to fight all of us, Eddie?" I asked.

Eddie saw over my shoulder that a police car was turning onto our street. I saw over his shoulder that a police car was approaching from the opposite direction. Eddie turned away and pushed through the crowd, stepping across the street to the edge of his property. The crowd moved slowly to the side of the street in front of Mary's house. For some reason, I looked up and saw Mary standing in the window of her bedroom. She waved down at me with the fingers of her hand, which held the curtain up near her face. I felt a hand on my arm and noticed that Hend had stepped up beside me. She looked into my eyes, then looked down at my hand. I followed her gaze down to my hand, which was holding the open-bladed knife I had found in Jake's room. I quickly folded the knife and put it in my pocket.

"Maybe you should go back in the house," I told her. "I don't know what kind of cops these are."

They looked different than the Chicago Police I was used to. They didn't wear checkerboard trimmed hats, and they didn't wear the obvious bullet-proof vests over their uniforms. A very large white male stepped out of the first car. His partner was a small white woman who looked very young and was possibly a new recruit. She kept glancing at her partner as they approached. A tall young black male stepped out of the second car, and I felt myself sigh a bit of relief, but I was still skeptical. I held my phone up and stepped away from the crowd so they could see that I was the one who called.

Eddie stepped out in front of the male and female officers as they walked toward me. They both stopped suddenly, keeping their hands on their belts in front. I waved my phone over my head so they would see me. The large white male officer motioned to the curb where Eddie had been standing and told Eddie to wait there. The black officer had walked up by then and stood near where Eddie was told to wait. The large white officer walked up to me. His female partner walked over to where the small crowd was waiting.

"Are you the one who reported a problem?" the large white officer asked me.

"Yes," I said. "I called because it looked like things were escalating between this group of people and that man over there."

"In what way? What happened?"

"Well, the man lives right there. He came outside yelling at these people and telling them to leave. One man in the group tried to talk to him, but he wouldn't listen. He pushed the man to the ground."

"Did he do anything else to the man? I mean, could you tell if the man was hurt?"

"I couldn't tell. I live in that house right there. I was sitting on the porch the whole time. I came out here when that happened. I was able to see the man fall, but I didn't see if he hit his head or anything like that."

"What are these people doing here?"

"Nothing. Well, they're waiting to see someone who lives in that house, but they weren't doing anything wrong, as far as I could tell. I don't know if you were working fifteen years ago, but we had a problem here then. My son was killed."

"No, I'm sorry. I don't live here, so I don't remember that. Your son, you say."

"Yes. I don't want to see anything like that again."

"Of course not. I'm going to talk to this man over here now. Do you know him?"

"Not really. His name is Eddie."

The white officer and the black officer traded places, stopping halfway between me and Eddie to exchange a few words, which I couldn't hear. The black officer came over to where I was and shook my hand. He was very polite, called me sir, very respectful. Not that the other officer wasn't respectful, it's just that he didn't extend himself that extra step. I shouldn't judge. I remember that's what you always told me. He might have been feeling the same way I was, waiting to see how I felt about white cops if I was going to be a threat to him. That's something that needs to be worked on. Treat each other fairly and stop trying to second guess.

I didn't pay much attention to the white female cop until she walked back to where Eddie and the white male cop were standing. They stepped away from Eddie and closer to where I was standing. The white male cop said, "Does he want to do anything?"

"No," the female cop said. "He believes they weren't doing anything wrong, but he agreed to keep everyone out of the street and remain orderly. He wants this one to leave them alone."

"Remains to be seen," the male cop said. He went back to Eddie and seemed to be explaining what the female cop said.

Eddie said something to the white cop before turning to go back inside his house. The white cop came back over to where I was standing.

"The gentleman who was pushed to the ground doesn't want to file any charges, so we can't do anything about what happened," he said to me. "Is that all right with you? I mean do you think that will settle this?'"

"I hope so, officer," I said.

"We gave them warnings, so they know the next time we have to come out here, it might not go well."

"I'm not going to get involved," I said.

"Good," he said. "They told my partner here that they were waiting to see a young girl who lives there. They believe this girl has power to heal the sick. Do you know anything about that?"

"The girl they are talking about is my son's daughter. My son is the one who was killed in that house fifteen years ago. Her name is Mary. I'm her grandfather. She is very caring, and people benefit from her caring ways, but I don't think she claims to be a healer like Jesus. These people might be disappointed."

I sensed something wrong, or maybe I saw a movement or heard a noise behind me on my porch, so I turned around. Tameka was standing at the top of the stairs with her hands over her mouth and her eyes full of tears. She was looking across the street at Eddie who had come back out to the edge of the street. I excused myself to the police officers and hurried back to help Tameka. I was helping her back into the house, but I could still hear Eddie.

Eddie was pointing to Mary's house but yelling at the cops. "You should go talk to the people in that house. There's a couple of Arabs who live there. They could be Islamic terrorists. You know what I mean. Whenever I see the kid, he always glares at me like he hates me because I'm white. But I've lived here all my life. I'm an American. I don't know what they are. That family could be harboring terrorists."

That black police officer, Jerome Simons was his name, came back to the house later. Tameka was resting, so I let him in.

"I did some checking," he said. "After what you said about your son."

"Really?" I was surprised but still skeptical.

"Yeah, I read the reports. They were pretty thin."

"That doesn't surprise me. They didn't find much to go on back then. Blamed it on a boy who got into a fight with my son. Made my son sound guilty, too."

"Yeah, well, that might be what happened, but I have my suspicions. They may not have told you at the time, but they interviewed other boys who were in the car that night. Two of them talked about a weird old man who lived in the house where Eddie lives across the street. They said he was dangerous and threatened to kill Jake and threatened to kill them if they ever told anyone about what he was doing. They wouldn't say what that was. Another thing, the only bullet that was in evidence was never identified or matched with any weapon. I saw a photo of it, and from my army experience, it looked like it might have been fired from an assault rifle."

I went to the drawer in the kitchen where I had put Jake's notebook and the bullet Mary and Harun had found. I set them on the table in front of Officer Simons. "We just found these. I didn't know who to give them to until now. I didn't know who to trust."

TWENTY-SIX - MARY

Harun told me he wants to be a writer. We were sitting in the sunroom after dinner, and he was reading a book by Cormac McCarthy. He commented how he liked the way McCarthy wrote, simple and direct. Very much like Hemingway. He had to read Hemingway for school, but he didn't mind because he liked whatever Hemingway wrote. I felt I was really getting to know Harun, so I let him keep talking.

"Do you read a lot?" I asked.

"Yeah, I guess so," he said. "The more I read, the better I write. And you can get some insight into the way writers think, especially if you read some of their essays or memoirs." Harun chuckled as his eyes kind of rolled around in a circle.

"What?" I knew he was thinking something.

"I don't know if I should tell you this, but it's funny. It's in a book by Hemingway. *A Moveable Feast*. Have you read that?"

"No."

"Well, in this book Hemingway talks about a trip he took with F. Scott Fitzgerald and their wives. Do you know who F. Scott . . ."

"Of course I know who he is," I interrupted. "I had to read *The Great Gatsby* for school."

"Okay, so there are these two famous writers, and they stop at a restaurant or something when Hemingway and Fitzgerald go to the bathroom, and Fitzgerald asks Hemingway if his penis is too small."

"Oh my God!" I was shocked, but I started laughing and couldn't stop. "What did he say?"

"Hemingway told him that he was fine. He told Fitzgerald that he was just looking down on it, which made it look smaller. I guess that's a good example of how everything can appear different from a different perspective."

We were both laughing so hard our sides hurt.

I guess I'm a writer too, of sorts, since I write down everything that happens for you, Papa. I don't want to write the same way Harun wants to write, though. Harun said that writing, good writing, is an art form. I believe that, too. That's why I don't think that I will ever be good enough to make money at it. I do like to write down my thoughts, though, like Anne Frank did. Like she said, "Paper has more patience than people."

I feel like I'm getting old enough to think about what I'll do with my life. Maybe that's what Jonah was trying to get me to do when he asked me about playing the violin. I always thought I would play the violin in an orchestra—and maybe one day I could get a job doing that.

I told Harun, "I would like to read some of your writing one day, if it's okay with you."

"I haven't written much, a few short stories, some poetry," he said. "I think I need to experience something important to write about."

"You can write about us," I said. "We're not exactly dull here."

I had never shared important, personal thoughts before, and that is what I considered writing to be. It was more than the gossip I had shared with the only other friend I had, the girl back in California who ditched me. I was finally making a breakthrough with Harun.

"Anyway, I want to be able to say I read your stories before you became famous."

Harun laughed at that.

"I'm serious," I said. "It's important to know what you want to do with your life. I thought I knew, but I'm more confused than ever now. I believe the same as Anne Frank when she said, 'I don't want to have lived in vain like most people. I want to be useful or bring enjoyment to all people, even those I've never met. I want to go on living even after my death.' You will live forever through your writing, Harun."

"But you have your violin," Harun said. "Ever since I heard you, I knew that's what you were destined to do."

"Yeah, but then this miracle business came out of the blue. What do I do with that? Can you make money and support yourself by healing people?"

"Doctors do it all the time."

"I mean with miracles, you goof. Is that really a thing? And what if it stops? What if I can't do it anymore? Or maybe I really never could. I wanted to believe that I was the one who cured Mama and Tameka, but maybe it was just a coincidence that I had wished so hard for Mama's cancer to leave and that I was there when Tameka woke up. Why would the nurses talk about it though, like it was a miracle? And what if I really do have the power to heal people? It wouldn't be fair to cure only the people I care about. I can't go around and cure some people and not others. I can't play God like that. So what would I do if I had that power? There are so many questions I wish I had the answers for."

The next morning, people started showing up in front of our house.

+ + +

EDDIE IS THE ONE WHO BROKE MY VIOLIN. I know it now. Eddie is the creepy guy who lives across the street in the house Mama warned me about. There is no way he would know about the ghost in my bedroom unless he read my diary then peed his pants when he read it, or when the ghost appeared. I heard him tell the crowd of people in front of our house. I heard him tell them that I was crazy. But then, he let slip about the ghost. He as much as admitted to reading my diary. And if he knew about the ghost, that means he was the one who was in our house, and he was the one who broke my violin. There is no way to know if he meant to break it or if he wanted to steal it and just dropped it in his haste to get away? Why would he want to break my violin?

"You didn't tell me you really have a ghost in here." Harun was standing in the doorway to my bedroom.

"What?" I pretended it was all fiction.

"I heard that guy. My mother went out there to talk to the crowd, so I hid on the porch where they couldn't see me, but I heard the whole thing."

"I'm not crazy," I said.

"I didn't say you were. I've never seen a ghost. I'd love to see one. That's so cool."

"Really?"

"Yeah. There was nothing like this where we used to live."

"I don't really know if it is a ghost. It might be. I just know it's weird."

"Well duh. That's a given. But I'd still like to see it anyway."

"It doesn't always appear. In fact, it's been kind of rare lately. There's no rhyme or reason."

"Is it here now?"

"I don't know. It might be in the closet."

"Really? Where we found the bullet? Do you think it had something to do with that?"

"Yes, I do. That bullet has been in there for over fifteen years. Why would it just suddenly appear? I think someone wanted us to find it." I turned to look back out the window. "Why would the police be coming to our house?"

"What?" Harun came over to where I was standing at the window and looked down at the three police officers. "Maybe they want to see if you're who they say you are."

"I don't like this."

We went downstairs and tried to stay out of sight. Mama had answered the door and was talking to a large, white police officer. He kept apologizing and calling her ma'am. He asked if she knew how long the crowd of people was going to be sticking around out front. He asked if she knew the man who lived across the street. He asked if we had had any trouble with that man before. He said he didn't get a good feeling about that man. He apologized again for taking up her time, and then he asked about Hend and Harun. He didn't believe what that man was saying, but he had to check it out anyway.

Mama explained to the police officers that Hend and Harun were in fact of Arab descent, but they were not terrorists. "They are our family," she said.

"Do you mind if we come in and talk to them?"

"Yes, I do," Mama said. "I'm not hiding anything, but without cause to come into my house would be an invasion of our privacy. I understand that you are following up on what that man told you, but I happen to know him to be a racist and a troublemaker. He was telling you falsehoods just to get you to come over here and investigate us for something that doesn't exist. I don't want to be rude, officer, but you will have to take my word for it right now that we are peaceful here, and we are doing nothing to cause that man or anyone else trouble."

The officer stared at my mother for a long time. I thought he was going to push past her and take over our house, but instead, he smiled, nodded, and said, "All right, ma'am. No offense on our part either. Thank you for your time." He turned with the others to leave, then turned back suddenly. "Oh, but there is one thing, ma'am."

"What's that, officer?"

"Please do what you can so that crowd doesn't get out of control. They are here to see your daughter, I believe, so if things get worse, some of the responsibility could fall back on you."

"I'll do what I can, officer, but just for the record, we didn't invite them here."

I was afraid Mama was going to ask me to go outside and talk to the crowd, and I wasn't ready to do that. I grabbed Harun's hand and pulled him with me. "Come on. Let's go to Jonah's house. We can go in the back door."

The crowd was gathered at the end of our driveway, so we snuck around the back of the garage and climbed over the fence to the back of Jonah's garage. From there, it was easy to get to Jonah's backdoor, but we crept through his backyard like we were stepping on glass. I started to laugh, and thinking that someone in the crowd might hear me, we ran the rest of the way and tapped on Jonah's back door. He answered almost right away. He was in the kitchen with Tameka.

"Why are you creeping around in my backyard, child? That crowd out there is not here to steal you away. They want you to help them."

"I know. It's just that I'm not ready. I'm scared I can't do it. Help them that is."

"I've seen him before," Tameka said.

She looked frightened. I looked at Jonah, hoping he would know what she was talking about.

"She got out on the front porch," Jonah said. "I think she saw something and got frightened. It wasn't good for her, so I brought her back inside. It might have been the police. They were all standing in front of the house."

Tameka was twisting her hands and turning her head in anguish as if fighting with herself, trying to remember and yet also trying to push it all back out of her memory.

"The nurse said she shouldn't get too upset about anything. This doesn't look good. I don't want her to have a relapse and have to go back to the hospital."

Tameka was getting more agitated. She started to slam her fists down on her legs, and her eyes rolled back into her head.

Jonah looked at me. "Can't you help her, child?"

I held Tameka's head against my chest and stroked her hair.

"The nurse told me that Tameka might change, that her personality might be different than before her accident," Jonah said. "This isn't good for her, though. She either gets very angry or very frightened whenever she remembers something from the past."

Tameka began to paw at my arms, trying to pull them away. "Wait," I said. "I have a better idea. Bring her into the front room out of the light."

I ran ahead of Jonah and Harun as they picked up Tameka and carried her to the sofa in the music room. I started playing Esther's violin, a Mozart lullaby, which I had learned when I first started getting good on the violin. Almost immediately, Tameka relaxed and placed her head on the back of the sofa, her arms quietly at her sides.

"I remember this," Tameka said, smiling.

"I do too, baby," Jonah said. "Your momma used to play this for you to get you to go to bed."

"You too, Daddy," Tameka said. "You play, too."

Jonah sat at the piano and started to play the melody, so I switched to the accompaniment with long, relaxing legatos. Tameka closed her eyes, still smiling with a sweet memory on her lips, and nestled into the sofa. We let the music drift away softly as it carried Tameka gently into sleep.

"You did it again, child," Jonah said.

"Did I? I don't know. It didn't help when I held her."

"Well then, you have a magic touch with that violin. She felt it right away."

"I just remembered how music makes me feel. Something just clicked in my head. I knew that harsh light wasn't good for her either. I don't have any idea where all that came from."

"Whatever it was, child, you calmed her down. I was afraid we were going to lose Tameka again."

Harun whispered. "That was amazing. I never knew music could do that."

"Music is a very powerful thing," Jonah said. "My Esther said that we are closer to God through music. I think that's why she loved it so much."

"I'm glad you finally played the piano again," I said. "Tameka gave you a reason. I'm glad we both could help her."

Jonah gave me a hug. "We did, didn't we?" he said.

"I know I could never play the violin like Mary," Harun said. "But I might be able to play the piano."

"Jonah could teach you," I said.

Jonah scowled at me, then smiled. "I suppose I could."

"But I really like more upbeat music," Harun said. "Like jazz."

"Well, now that *is* interesting," Jonah said.

REVELATIONS

TWENTY-SEVEN - RACHEL

HEND WAS CARRYING A LETTER IN HER HAND. That was not the first thing I noticed about her, though. I was sitting in the sunroom where I could remove myself from the crowd in front of the house, but also keep an eye on the back of the house in case anyone got bold and nervy enough to come into our backyard. I had called out to Mary after talking with the police, but she didn't answer. When I sat down in the sunroom, I saw Mary and Harun scurry across Jonah's backyard to his back door. At least I knew she was safe.

I heard footsteps on the stairs and down the hall. When Hend entered the sunroom, she wasn't wearing her hijab. Her hair was long, falling over her shoulders to her back—thick, dark, and shimmery, reflecting the sun like silk around her wide, dark eyes and full lips. I could feel Paul next to me, punching my arm, laughing, "Ha, now you see why I fell in love with her."

Hend held out the letter. "I thought you might want this."

I sat up and took the letter. My name was handwritten on the front, and the envelope had been opened. "I don't understand. Where did you find this?"

"The table in my room. It was in a small box in the back of the drawer. It was already opened."

"How odd. I've never seen this before. It looks old."

"Do you think it's from Paul?"

"I don't know," I said. Considering where Hend found the letter, there was a good chance it could be from my mother. My hands started shaking. I pulled out the letter and unfolded it. There were three pages handwritten with only a date at the top with my name. The last page had Paul's signature. "You're right. It's dated shortly before he left home fifteen years ago."

"I wonder why he left it in the back of the drawer."

"That doesn't make any sense."

I read the letter at first eagerly wanting to hear Paul's voice even if it was only through the words he had written down fifteen years before. He began by telling me how much he loved me and didn't want to leave me but he was comfortable knowing that Jake would be with me and take good care of me. He felt he had to leave to start a new life and make a break from what had happened. He wanted to explain so I wouldn't think that he had abandoned me when our mother's condition was getting worse. He doubted that he could go through with it if he told me face to face, that I wouldn't let him leave. But why didn't I get his letter? And what did he mean by leaving because of what had happened? As I read further, all the nervousness came back to me, and I began to shake so much that Hend sat down next to me and put her arm around me. I could feel the anguish in the words Paul had written.

> I used to go to the house across the street with some of my friends because the old man who lives there would let us drink his beer. I began to notice that my friends would go off somewhere with the old man one at a time to another part of the house, and when I asked them what was going on, they didn't want to talk about it. The old man never asked me to go with him, so I never worried about it. One day, I was there by myself, and I fell asleep on the sofa after drinking a beer because I was tired from staying up late the night before to study for a test. I woke up when I felt something on top of me. The old man was kneeling on the floor in front of me, and when I tried to get up, my pants were down around my ankles.

I wanted to leave, but the old man wanted me to stay and kept asking me if I wanted another beer, and then he asked me if it felt good. I pushed past the old man, and as I was reaching for the door, Eddie stepped in front of me.

Eddie told me not to say anything. I told Eddie his father was sick, and Eddie said, "Yeah, but he ain't doing that to me anymore, so if you talk, I'll kill you."

I thought about it for a long time and almost felt sorry for Eddie, but I also hated and feared Eddie. I realized that the house across the street was a hornets' nest, and I didn't want to stir it up.

I gasped when I read that. The letter ended with Paul telling me not to say anything to our parents. He was ashamed and didn't want them to know what he had done. He included an address where I could send him mail if I wanted to. My tears were flowing so fast, I couldn't talk. I was sobbing, my chest heaving uncontrollably. Hend handed me a box of tissues, and I grabbed as many as I could to catch the tears. Hend pulled my head to her shoulder, and I felt her stroking my hair. She didn't need to say anything.

Finally, I was able to talk. "I never got this letter," I said. I handed the letter to Hend so she could read it.

"Paul never said a thing to me," Hend said.

"He must have thought I hated him because I never wrote, and then he was dead."

"He must have understood. He had nothing but kind words to say when he talked to me about you."

"My mother must have opened the letter and then never let me see it. I wish I could have helped him."

"Paul was a good man. He never talked about this. He only talked about getting married and returning to this country to start a family. I loved him very much, and this letter doesn't change that."

"That is so nice to hear," I said. "I never knew that Paul had met you until Paul's funeral. I wonder if he sent any letters to our parents telling them about his plans with you."

"I don't know. Maybe he never got a chance."

I didn't tell Hend that my mother had committed suicide in the chair next to the table where she found the letter. I felt my breathing get slower and more peaceful as thoughts of my family's tragedies drifted away. My breathing rose and fell with each stroke of Hend's hand over my hair. "Can I put my head in your lap for just a minute?" I asked.

"Of course," Hend said in almost a whisper. "I want you to."

I had never felt more relaxed. I could feel the warmth and softness of her skin through the fabric of her skirt and the mesmerizing touch of her fingers stroking my cheek and neck. It was a comfort I had never felt from my mother, and I welcomed it with years of longing satisfied in a few moments. "Are you happy here?" I asked, my voice muffled in the closeness of her lap.

"Yes," she said. "Very much so."

"I wanted you to know that in the short time we have known each other, I have come to feel very close to you. I enjoy your company. I'm glad that you're here, you and Harun. I feel like I have a big family again."

"Funny, but I have felt the same. And I can tell that Harun likes it here. He is becoming more defined as a person since we have been here. I think Mary draws that out of him."

"I'm glad," I said. "I'm so glad." I gave Hend's legs a hug from where I lay.

A punctuation of my feelings. I wanted to sit up and kiss her, but I didn't want her to feel incredulous or uncomfortable. I fought off the impulsive urge to display my emotions the way I was used to with Mary.

Instead, I sat up and smiled. "Thank you," I said. "I feel much better now. My eyes lowered to the letter that lay between us. "This letter feels like one more piece to the puzzle about that house across the street. We need to show this to Jonah. Maybe we can put the pieces together and make some sense of it."

I looked out one of the front windows. The crowd in front of the house was getting larger and spreading down the street. Hend and I went around the back of the houses, taking our chances crossing the driveways instead of climbing the fence behind the garages. I don't think we were seen. Mary answered the back door and said Jonah was in the music room with Tameka who was asleep. We walked softly down the hall and met Jonah as he stepped out, looking back to make sure Tameka had not stirred.

He could tell we were not there to visit. "Did something happen?"

"I guess you could say that," I said, handing him the letter. "More secrets revealed."

Jonah read the letter and stopped at the second page. "This confirms what Jake wrote in his notebook. All those boys that used to go to that house years ago. If one of them had stepped up and said something, maybe Jake would still be alive."

"They were afraid and embarrassed," I said. "It's obvious Paul was. He didn't know what was going to happen."

"He must have suspected something since he warned Jake."

"That's just it. He *did* tell Jake, but Jake didn't tell us. No one expected what happened. The question is what can we do now?"

"The old man died many years ago. There's nothing we can do about him or what he did."

"Maybe his son is no different, though."

"None of this is good for Tameka. She'll never get better with all of this going on," Jonah said.

"I need to go talk to the crowd," Mary said.

"I don't know if it's safe," I said.

"I can stand by her," Harun said. "We can go back to our house and go out through the front door. If there is any danger, we can run back inside."

"You and Hend go," Jonah said. "I should stay here with Tameka in case she wakes."

We all went back to the house through the backyard, and once inside the house, Mary walked straight to the front door then stopped.

"Have you thought about what you want to say?" I asked.

Mary turned around and almost fell into my arms. "I don't know," she said. "I didn't ask for any of this. I just wanted to help you and Tameka. Jonah made me think I could help Tameka. What if I can't help these people? I don't think I can save the world. I don't want to be a savior."

I was rubbing Mary's back. "You don't have to be, Peanut. You should just be yourself. Not someone they think you are."

Mary looked up at me with a look of determination in her eyes. "I think I know what to say," she said. And with that, she turned and opened the front door.

Harun went out onto the porch with Mary while Hend and I stayed in the doorway. Hend reached out and took my hand. I smiled at her, a worried smile but hopeful, and I squeezed her hand. When I turned back to look at the crowd, I noticed a man with a camera standing in the driveway, and over his head, I could see a van with a satellite dish on top parked several houses down the street.

"Someone must have called the local news station," I said. "There are reporters and cameras out there."

"That's okay," Mary said. "I've made a decision, so if they report this, then maybe I'll only have to say it once."

Mary was right. She was thinking quick on her feet. In the short time since we moved from California, Mary had grown up, and I didn't even notice. I realized that I would need to stop treating her as my little girl, but that was going to be hard.

TWENTY-EIGHT - JONAH

TAMEKA WAS CURLED UP UNDER A BLANKET ON THE SOFA. Her breathing was finally steady and peaceful. I looked out between curtains in the front window. The oak tree in the front yard was shimmering in a brisk breeze. The crowd in the street was turning, like a change in the surface current on a lake, toward Rachel and Mary's house. Mary was walking out to the front gate in her yard with Harun a step behind.

I slipped out the front door and stood in the shadows where I could see Mary, and hopefully, I would not be seen. I left the front door open so I could hear Tameka if she woke up disoriented or frightened. A hushed murmur stirred over the crowd like shallow waves sizzling over the rocky shore. Mary stood very close to the people pressed against the low fence in front of the house. Some reached out for Mary until she held up her hand to quiet the crowd. She seemed like a young lady, not the child I first saw pass in front of my house with her violin only a few months before, and she handled the crowd with a calm, commanding force in her voice.

"Please," she said, holding up her hand to silence the crowd. "Let me speak. Be kind to those standing with you so everyone can hear what I have to say."

She waited a moment while the crowd became completely silent.

"I am Mary Hester," she began again. "I want you to understand who I am and *what* I am. Only then will I be able to help you."

I was worried that she meant she was going to walk out in the crowd and touch each of them and let them touch her. I was worried that she was going to try to heal them. I saw that turning into a very dangerous mob scene where Mary could easily get hurt. I felt a touch on my arm and turned to see Tameka smiling up at me.

"Is everything okay?" she asked.

I put my arm around her. "I don't think you should be out here, baby. How are you feeling?"

"I'm okay, Daddy. What's happening?"

"Mary is going to talk to these people and hopefully get them to go back to their homes."

"Why are they here?"

"They need a miracle in their lives. They think Mary can give it to them."

"Can she?"

"I don't know, baby. I think she helped you, but I don't really know. You just might have been ready to come back. Your brain just needed a little rest. Time to heal. We could all use a little time to heal."

I turned to give Tameka a kiss on top of her head, and I noticed she was looking away, lost in thought, trancelike, mesmerized with a low moan coming from the bottom of her throat. It was like the coma still had a grip on part of her brain and was trying to draw her back. I needed to keep her here. I needed to help her fight it off.

"What is it, baby? Is something wrong? Talk to me."

"I remember now," she said.

"Remember? Remember what?"

"The night Jake was killed. That man was standing outside."

I looked up to see who she was talking about and saw Eddie across the street, on his porch, with his arms crossed in defiance on his chest, watching the crowd. "You mean that man at the house across the street? You mean Eddie?"

"Olivia and I heard the gunshots that night. We ran next door because we heard screaming. I think that's when I saw him outside. I must have thought that he had heard the gunshots too, and he came outside like we did. But I remember now. He was just standing there. He wasn't trying to help."

"What? Why didn't you say anything then?"

"Everyone was saying that it was a drive-by. That it was some guys from the high school in a black car. I forgot about that man. All I could think about was Jake. All I could think about was the hate that took my brother."

"You're right, baby. You didn't do anything wrong. We were all in shock that night."

"I saw him the next morning, too. He was putting something in his truck, and then he drove away. I must have forgotten about it because I never saw him again. Until now."

I looked back across the street, but Eddie was gone. I scanned the crowd and didn't see him. Quickly I looked toward Mary. She was facing the crowd with her hands held high above her head, palms out like a preacher embracing the congregation. Her head was tilted back, and her eyes were closed. Harun was standing behind her, watching the crowd. There was something wrong.

"Let's go inside," I said to Tameka. I kept my voice low and calm so she wouldn't pick up on any of the panic I was feeling.

We got inside, and I turned back as I closed the door. Eddie was in his front yard with a rifle. He pointed the rifle to the sky and fired one shot before lowering the rifle to the crowd. I crouched down, holding Tameka down too, as if expecting bullets to fly through the house. There was loud screaming and yelling in the street. I took Tameka behind the staircase to the door that led to the basement.

"Go to the bottom of the stairs," I told her, "and don't come out for any reason. I'm going to find out what's happening. I'll be right back to get you when I know it's safe."

She didn't say anything. She just nodded her head to let me know that she understood and she was all right. As she started down the stairs, I turned and ran to the back of the house.

Twenty-nine - Mary

IT COULD HAVE EASILY BEEN THE CRAZIEST THING I HAVE EVER DONE. I finally knew what Anne Frank meant when she said, "Although I'm only fourteen, I know quite well what I want. I know who is right and who is wrong. I have my opinions, my own ideas and principles, and although it may sound pretty mad from an adolescent, I feel more of a person than a child, I feel quite independent of anyone."

I, too, finally knew what I wanted. I knew what I *didn't* want. I knew what I wanted to say to express my beliefs to the people waiting in front of our house, but I didn't write down anything first, no outline, no summary, no rough draft—all the preparations I had learned in every English composition class I have ever taken. And I didn't practice either, first reading a script, then winging it in front of a mirror as taught in speech class. And of course, I knew that playing the violin with any skill at all required practice and preparation. I did none of that. I just opened the door and almost marched out to the gate to address the crowd. I could barely see anyone past the first or second row of faces staring back at me with impatience and longing. They needed help, if not for themselves, then for someone close, a friend, a spouse, a child. They were hurting with nowhere to turn for help. They were at a loss for where to find help to release the pain and suffering in their lives. They needed a miracle.

As I looked at their faces, I realized that they might receive what I was about to tell them as just one more rejection, one more empty speech to encourage them to hang on to what little they had left because life would get better if they just kept trying. Help was on its way. Something told me they wouldn't buy that. They had been told that before. Nothing had worked. No one had helped them. What they needed was a miracle. That was what I was going to offer them.

I held up my hand, hoping that would stop the murmuring so those in the back could hear me. As the noise subsided, there were a few voices that called out and quickly faded into the breeze that swept down the street.

"Help us!"

"Touch my baby, please!"

"Save my son from the devil!"

I waited until the last voice disappeared.

"Please," I said finally and kept my hand up to silence the crowd. "Let me speak. Be kind to those standing with you so everyone can hear what I have to say."

I waited another moment while the crowd became completely silent.

"I am Mary Hester," I began, hoping I would not falter. "I want you to understand who I am and *what* I am. Only then will I be able to help you. I don't know if I am what you are looking for. If I could give each of you what you need to make your life better, I would, but I'm just a girl. I'm only fourteen years old. I'm just learning about the world myself, so I don't have all the answers. I *do* know that we all need help in some form, a way out of the darkness that has shadowed our lives, the tragedy that has shattered what we had and turned our hopes and dreams to ashes and dust. We all want our happiness returned. We all want our dreams restored. We all want to feel blessed and needed and loved. I cannot help anyone who is not willing to help himself, though. I cannot help anyone who does not believe that *he* has a part in making his own life better. Man or woman, child or adult, this applies to all of us. We come from different backgrounds. We are born into different worlds, different religions, different politics, different economic statuses, different races or combinations of races, but we are all the same.

"We want the same happiness and comfort and love and security that will make our lives, however long or short, something that we feel was well-lived. We must first help our neighbors, friends, family, and even strangers before we can help ourselves. We cannot be selective or feel that we are better than anyone else in this world where we all want the same things. Only then, will we be able to leave this Earth with the peace of knowing that we gave ourselves to help others, and doing that, we helped ourselves, and doing that, we made this world a little better."

Some of those in the back of the crowd were yelling that they couldn't see me and were having trouble hearing me. It was all going to be for nothing. I feared they were going to get angry and turn on me. My message was going to be lost in their frustration.

I felt Harun brush against me on the side. "Get on my shoulders," he said as he bent down on one knee. I slipped my legs over his shoulders. He held my legs against his chest and lifted me up slowly. The crowd went wild with excitement.

I raised my hands to the crowd, feeling that something beyond me was controlling what I was doing and what I was saying. I began praying. I was praying for the crowd, but I was also praying for myself. I wanted them to know that I was one of them—I wasn't above them or better than them. I can't remember what I was saying. I *do* remember that I was trying to give them hope, trying to rise above their sadness and loss and accept that their lives, their world, can be beautiful if they look at it differently and cherish every moment with those they love—and even those they don't know.

I asked them to feel the power and blessings of their God, which comes from all of us and passes through each of us. I asked them to open their hearts and accept that power and that blessing and give it to others because that is love. Then and only then would the love they give erase the hate and make the love even stronger in others and in them. I wanted them to know that they can make this world a better place, that they have the power to make their own miracles.

I began to hear a few voices shouting Hallelujah and Praise God, and I was feeling good that they were accepting my message, that I might have been able to reach them, to change their lives, or at least change the way they look at their lives, when suddenly there was a loud bang, like fireworks, and another voice right as Harun lowered me off his shoulders and pulled me toward the house.

THIRTY - RACHEL

I DON'T KNOW WHERE HER COURAGE CAME FROM. Mary was suddenly so brave, so grown-up. Almost like a different child. I was very proud of her but also very frightened that she was going out to face a large crowd of people she knew nothing about.

The whole country has been so full of hate these past few years, so divisive over politics and religion and race relations that I feared there would be someone in the crowd who might want to hurt Mary just because others wanted her to be their savior.

And then there was Eddie. He had already confronted me and Hend because he didn't like a Muslim woman living in the neighborhood. He had already confronted the crowd outside and accused Mary of being a hack who believed in ghosts.

Hend and I went out on the front porch to keep an eye on Mary and Harun. Still holding hands, we shared a worried smile to acknowledge that our connection was welcomed and needed as a symbol of joining forces to protect our children. A premonition that something potentially tragic was about to happen made my hand tighten around hers until she placed her other hand over mine and gently massaged it. We both continued to scan the crowd as lookouts for any unusual movement.

"I don't like this," I said.

"Me neither," Hend said.

"That's not helpful."

"I know," she said, "but there's nothing we can do about that. It's part of being a mother. We are proud of them but always worried about them at the same time."

"I know, but this is different from her violin performances. She has never been in this situation before."

"You have to give her credit, though. Mary seems to know what she is doing, and Harun is there as a first-line of defense in case something *does* go wrong. I know he will protect her. He told me that she is the first person he ever really liked."

"I'll try to relax. Mary seems to be relaxed, and the crowd seems mesmerized by her. Still, I would rather be too cautious than too confident."

I heard a few voices in the crowd call out that they could not see Mary and some that were having trouble hearing her. Harun went around in front of Mary and stooped down to allow Mary to straddle his shoulders. He lifted her slowly, and as she rose above the crowd, there were gasps and crying as the voices called out.

"She is rising!"

"She is truly a child of God!"

"Mary is our savior!"

Those in front could see Harun holding Mary, but they too were stunned, poised, and possessed by the spiritual rapture flowing through the crowd. They gasped as Mary was lifted up. They seemed blinded to Harun standing beneath her. Mary raised her arms to the sky in a wide embrace as her words encircled the crowd and created a peaceful, trance-like state. Almost in unison, her audience raised their hands to the sky and closed their eyes to blindly and freely absorb the message and the energy. I was frightened for Mary. Something wasn't right. She was falling into a dangerous trap.

"I am here to give you whatever I have that can help you," Mary called out. "If you believe, you can feel the positive thoughts and blessings. You can transfer those positive thoughts to whatever is hurting you. But do not give up on those who love you and those who are trying to help you. Miracles come to those who accept the good and the bad that life offers, but never give up on giving others your love because whatever love you give, you will receive tenfold."

A deafening, sharp explosion echoed between the houses. Harun lowered Mary abruptly and pulled her even further down toward the ground. I looked across the sea of people. Eddie was in his front yard walking slowly toward the crowd, lowering his rifle. The crowd fell out of its trance and began looking around, confused, then startled and frightened as Eddie started shooting into the crowd.

I called out for Mary as I turned back and saw Harun already pulling Mary to the house. Hend and I both reached out to them as they got to the front steps.

We huddled them into the house and told them to run upstairs while I turned and locked the front door. After we all made it up the stairs, I heard banging at the door, something heavy, and wood cracking. Then I heard the door fling open and hit the wall.

"Get in the closet!" I whispered. "We have to be very still." We all huddled together in Mary's closet.

There was silence, then boards creaking on the stairs. Screaming in the street persisted, then sirens wailing. We shivered, stifled our cries, and prayed that the police would get to us before Eddie did. Footsteps down the hall, getting closer. The door to Mary's bedroom screeched as it opened slowly.

"I know you're in here, Rachel."

It was Eddie's voice calling out with a singular, sinister laugh in each word.

"I know this was your bedroom the night I killed your black boyfriend."

My jaw tightened when he said that, and I almost screamed when a shot rang out, deafening, echoing, shattering the plaster in the ceiling, raining it down softly to the floor.

"Did he die in your arms, Rachel? Come on out now. We're *all* going to die today."

The closet door opened swiftly, and there was Eddie, standing only a few feet away, the rifle slung over one arm and pointed into the closet. His eyes and his yellow teeth were glowing in the dark.

"You should have gone out with me, Rachel," he said. "I would've been much better for you than your black boyfriend ever could've been. But I guess it's too late now, huh? So this is it."

He paused and looked around as if listening for something. I think he was going to say something else. He wasn't ready to kill us yet. He never got the chance, though.

None of us saw what happened because the light got so bright, it blinded all of us. All we could hear were more gunshots and heavy thuds against the floor.

I screamed when I thought Mary was shot. I couldn't tell. I grabbed for Mary, trying to feel what happened. I waited for Eddie to shoot again, my whole body tensing in anticipation. There was only muffled crying.

The light finally dimmed and went out.

Only then could we see.

THIRTY-ONE - JONAH

OFFICER SIMONS WAS AT MY BACKDOOR. He had his gun in his hand but down at his side.

"Is everyone okay here?" he asked.

"Yes," I said. "Next door, I think he might be going next door."

We both charged over to Rachel's backdoor. He opened it slowly, which made me nervous because I wanted to get in there fast, but I also knew that his decision to enter quietly was strategically a better choice. He motioned for me to stay behind him as we slipped down the hall to the stairs. We heard a voice upstairs and then a gunshot.

All noise be damned, we ran up the stairs, and toward the top, I motioned toward Mary's room. The door was open. I could hear Eddie talking to Rachel. I heard him clearly say, "So this is it."

Officer Simons and I flew through the door and were immediately overwhelmed by an intense, bright light. I heard Officer Simons' gun go off right next to me, and I saw Eddie hit the floor near my feet, and I fell on top of him, grabbing for his rifle so he couldn't use it again. I couldn't see exactly what happened until the light was gone.

When Officer Simons helped me up off Eddie, I felt my hand release my knife, which had pierced Eddie's chest during my fall. Officer Simons and I looked at each other, sharing a moment of surprise.

Officer Simons nodded. "The coup de grâce," he said, then smiled at me and helped me up.

Officer Simons wanted to take me to the hospital to make sure I was going to be okay, or at least have a paramedic check me out and give me some oxygen. I kept telling him no, no, no. I was just a little light-headed that's all.

Eddie didn't make it, and that's okay. No one seemed to care much because he was a hopeless case, anyway. It's always a shame when someone dies, but he chose his path in life and death. An angry man will meet an angry death. My family was okay. That's all that mattered to me. He had come up there to kill all of them—I am sure.

That blinding light stopped him long enough for us to get to him. Harun had placed himself between Eddie and the others to make sure they were okay. We were all proud of that boy, and thankful.

When we got back to my house, Rachel and Hend helped me to the sofa in the music room. My breathing was getting steady and slower, but my arms were still shaking. Mary went down to the basement to tell Tameka she could come back upstairs. She rushed over and sat next to me. Rachel was on the other side.

Tameka took my hand in hers. "Are you okay, Daddy? Mary told me what happened." She looked around the room. "I hope everyone is okay."

"Yes, yes, we are okay now," I said. "But it's going to take a while to get the evil out of your house, Rachel, so everyone can stay here until you feel up to going back there."

"You're right," Rachel said. "I didn't even think about that."

"It was my room," Mary said. "I don't ever want to go back in there."

"That's very kind of you," Hend said. "It all could have turned out so much worse."

"Did anybody else notice that strange light?" Harun asked. "It was like someone turned on a strobe at just the right moment. I think it blinded that son of a bitch."

"Harun!" Hend reprimanded her son. "Don't talk that way."

"Sorry, mom," he said, "but he was *not* a nice guy. He was going to kill us. That light saved us."

"I think it's that faulty ceiling light," Rachel said.

"You better get that fixed before it starts a fire," I said.

"Just don't tell the police it was my ghost," Mary said.

We all had a laugh, which helped to relax the tension of coming down from the traumatic event. I wondered if anyone else except me thought that Mary's ghost really did spark that light into the room. The light was way too bright to have come from that 60-watt bulb in the ceiling, but that bulb was burned out after, and the fixture looked a little toasted. Stranger things have happened.

"I'm just glad you're all right, Daddy," Tameka said, giving my hand a squeeze in hers.

"I was worried too," Rachel said. "We were all worried. Before you got there, Eddie said something that surprised me. He said that *he* was the one who killed Jake. He confessed. Do you think it was Eddie who killed Jake?"

"I do. I wasn't sure until Tameka told me she saw him that night and later when she saw him leaving. He didn't come back here until his old man died, until he thought no one was going to look at him for murdering Jake. But that's not all. Stopping Eddie was necessary to protect my family. I wasn't able to do it before, but I could do it today. At least I had to try. That's why Eddie had to be stopped. He was going to kill all of you."

Rachel shifted on the sofa to face me and took my other hand. "Jonah, do you remember what you said right after it all happened?"

"I don't remember much. I could have been shot, and I wouldn't have known it."

"You said you hoped this would make up for all the wrong. You said it several times. What did you mean?"

"Oh, Lord, did I say that? I remember thinking it, but I didn't realize I had said it out loud. I guess, in the heat of the moment, we all do things we don't remember until later."

"We're you talking about Jake? Was Jake hiding something?"

"No. Jake did not deserve what happened to him. It was *me*. I felt that maybe it would make up for what I had done years ago. I have never told anyone before." I patted Tameka on the knee. "Not even your mother. I was too ashamed. What I did was out of anger for what happened to Jake."

So this is what I told them, Esther, and I'm telling you now because I can't live with it any longer. I thought it was those boys in that black car. I thought they drove by and shot up the house next door. I thought they had killed Jake, so I went after them. I gave you some excuse about needing to go back out after we got home from the hospital. I went looking for that black car, and when I found it, I found that kid with it. I was so angry, I could have killed him without a word. But he seemed to recognize me, and he didn't try to get away.

"You're Jake's dad, aren't you?" The look on his face changed. He didn't know why I was there.

I asked him, "What did you do with the gun?"

He looked even more puzzled and asked, "What gun?"

"The one you used to kill my son. Did you think you were just going to walk away and not pay the price?"

"What?" He was panicked. Stricken with fright. "What happened? Jake is dead?"

I thought he was playing me at first, but he started to shake and cry. "I didn't think he would really do it," the kid said.

I was still angry, though. I thought he was pretending not to know, scared because he got caught, and the first thing he could think of was to blame someone else.

"You're lying," I yelled. "You racist little punk. You know Jake's dead because you or one of your buddies killed him."

"It wasn't me," he said.

"Then who did it?" I screamed. "Tell me, now!"

He couldn't or wouldn't tell me who he was talking about, but something told me that this kid wasn't worth killing. Just as I felt my fists relax I watched the kid's jaw go from quivering to clinched.

"As much as I hated Jake," he said, "I didn't want him to die. It just wasn't right that Coach made him quarterback. That position was mine. I worked for it and waited my turn. Then, Jake just stepped in and took it all away."

I turned. I was going to walk away. I still had my anger. It had gripped me and wouldn't let go, but it wasn't worth releasing on that kid.

"Whatever," I said. "It wasn't his fault that he was better than you."

"Come to think of it. Jake got what he deserved," the kid replied.

I turned back around and stared at him.

"Yeah," he said. "You go talk to your neighbor if you want to know what happened to Jake. All I can say is none of this would have happened if you had never moved here, so you can just go back to where you came from!"

That's when he came at me, not in a rush, though. He just walked up to me like he had a perfect right, and he shoved me in the chest.

"You need to learn your place," he said.

I fell back a step or two, but I didn't fall down, so he came at me again. I guess he was feeling powerful like he could do whatever he pleased.

"You're out of line, boy," I said. "You need to let it go."

I was hoping he would back off, but instead, he got all red in the face and started yelling loud enough to wake the dead. "I ain't a boy. I'm a man—a white man, and your nigger boy wasn't better than me at anything."

He reached out to shove me again when I felt my foot plant behind me, and I swung my arm at him to slap him, to stun him, and put some sense into his head.

But it wasn't a slap. My anger had brought a fist back into my hand, and I hit him hard. I heard and felt the crack on the side of his head, and he fell to the ground without a sound, like he had fallen asleep and didn't even wake up when he hit the pavement and became a part of the grass and the gravel. I could see he was still breathing, but he was laying so still that I knew if anyone came up on us as I stood there over him, they'd think that I had come there to do exactly what it looked like. So I left. I found out the next day that the kid had died.

I've carried that secret all these years. I didn't mean to hurt him, certainly not kill him. That's not all, though.

I waited about a week, and then I went across the street to that old man's house. I didn't know what I was going to do. I didn't know who that kid was talking about, but I knew he meant that house because I had seen those boys going and coming at that house. I didn't know then what was happening there. I knew the cops were blaming that kid for Jake's death, and they weren't looking at anyone else, so I had to find out the truth.

When that old man answered the door, I was ready to confront him about what the kid had said. I was going to ask him why those boys were coming to his house. I was going to find out the truth. He turned the doorknob on the outer glass door and pushed it open slightly, then turned and walked back to where he had been sitting. I went on in, surprised that he was making this gesture to let me in his house since he hadn't spoken one word to me in all the time we lived across the street from him.

The whole house reeked of smoke and stale cigarette butts. The only noise was coming from a television across the room from where he sat. He immediately lit a cigarette from the pile of rolled ones next to the already full ashtray. He blew out the smoke along with a rattled spasm of coughs, which he ignored like they were just a part of his normal life.

"I heard about what happened to your boy," he said. "Shame."

"Really?" I said. "How did you hear?"

"Cops came around asking me if I saw anything. Told me what happened."

"What did you tell them?"

"Same as I'm going to tell you. I heard a car drive down the street about the same time as I heard some gunshots. Didn't see anything. Don't know anything else."

"Really?"

"Really. Isn't that why you're here?"

I noticed that after each word or few words he uttered, he had to draw in a deep breath, and he closed his eyes briefly as if to concentrate on the need to get that accomplished. His shortness of breath didn't keep him from the pleasure he received when next he inhaled long drags of smoke from his cigarette.

"I saw the car you're talking about," I said. "I was driving in when it was driving out. I know that car, and I know who it belongs to because I see them over here all the time."

I fudged a little on that last part to see if it would get a reaction from him. There was only a slight change in the lack of any expression on his face to a glimpse of anger in the narrowing of his eyes.

"Is that right?" he asked.

"Yes, and that tells me that you know more about what happened than what you told the cops and what you just told me."

"Those boys come over here just to visit. Nothing more. What they do when they're not at my house is none of my business."

"One of them told me that they didn't shoot Jake. He said I should talk to you about that, so I think he knew."

"He didn't know nothing." The old man's voice was getting as sharp as he could get it. Then he started coughing and took a while to stop. When he did stop, he snuffed out his cigarette in the ashtray and grabbed another one to light.

"You don't sound good," I said. "Don't you know those are going to kill you?"

"I got cancer and emphysema, so there's no reason to stop." He was looking at me like he wished he had the strength to get up out of his chair and push me out of his house.

"I know that those boys come over here to drink," I said. "I've seen them drunk, stumbling out of your house and down the street to that car. That's something you better stop because the next time I see it, I'm calling the police. I doubt that you want to spend your last days in jail, so you should think about that."

He reached beneath the cushion of the sofa with his free hand and kept it there. "I think you better leave now. You're lucky I even let you in here."

I didn't know if he had a gun hidden under that sofa cushion so I turned to leave, and as I walked to the door, I said a prayer that I would get out of his house before he decided to confirm my suspicions.

I realized that he wasn't worth my going to prison over, and I'm thankful that I'm not responsible for taking two innocent lives. God knows I *did* want to kill him before I got there but seeing him dying in such a wasted state was enough for me to believe that he had already received his judgment. I couldn't prove that he was the one who killed Jake anyway, and I couldn't even prove that he was buying beer for those boys. I didn't know what else was going on then. I knew the police couldn't prove any of it either, even if they were interested. They had already decided what had happened. Case closed.

As I sit here today, I don't think that old man killed Jake. He was too weak and feeble. He couldn't have held a rifle, much less aimed it with any accuracy. But his son could. The information from Paul that Jake wrote in his notebook and the letter Hend found both pointed our suspicions to that house across the street. Tameka's memory coming back to her sealed it up in a neat package for me.

I'm thankful that Officer Simons took the time to look back at the case they had fifteen years ago. Without him, they might not have looked at what happened when Eddie went on his killing spree and put two and two together. Eddie must have known he wasn't going to survive. Maybe he didn't want to survive, but I suspect he wanted to take all of us with him. Hate can destroy people. It changes people until they can't reason, can't find a way out of their misery, and lose all hope of a better life. Then hate forces people to place the blame on others instead of themselves. Reality is the enemy of hate's success, and love is the enemy of hate. I think that was what Mary was trying to tell those people, and she never knew Dr. King.

Thirty-two - Mary

TOMORROW IS MY BIRTHDAY. THERE HAVE BEEN a lot of changes since the shooting on our street. I feel guilty about it even though everyone in the family agrees it wasn't my fault, but I can't help but wonder. Had I talked to the crowd earlier, Eddie might not have done what he did.

Fifteen people shot, another ten injured including two children, trampled from the stampede to get away. One man sitting in his living room watching the television from his recliner was shot in the chest from a bullet that came down through his roof. He died because no one knew he was shot.

Jonah said he saw Eddie fire one shot into the air before he started shooting into the crowd. It must have been that bullet that came back down into that man's house.

There could have been more casualties, but the police drove onto our street blaring their sirens, which must have stopped Eddie from shooting at the crowd. Instead, he ran for our house to take shelter. He was never going to get away with what he did, so he must have wanted to take us along with him.

I'll never understand what must have been going through his mind. Anne Frank thought that all people were basically good. She never met Eddie. I don't know how she believed that, growing up in a world where there was so much open hatred for people just because of who they were.

We're experiencing that in this country now, and it's very real. My theory is that people are good *and* bad. They have to choose which one they want to be. Sometimes people are raised in a world that teaches them to hate others, and they think that's okay. Most of the time they keep that to themselves until they burst at the seams and strike out at those they hate, or when our leaders tell them that it's okay. Hate and violence go hand in hand. That's what happened to Eddie.

No one blamed me for what happened. They said it was just a terrible tragedy. The police reported that many people could have died. Some of the people in the crowd in front of my house were shot and received some serious wounds, but no one died from those wounds.

The police spokesperson behind the microphone told the group of reporters that he thought it nothing less than a miracle that none of those people died. Those reporters decided to make it a real story. They said the people came to see me looking for a miracle and that I had given them one by saving their lives that day.

Those same reporters wanted to interview me, wanted me to appear on their television shows. They came by the house, and Mama had to turn them away. Producers from talk shows and one from a show called the Ministry of Christ called. Mama canceled our home phone. She said no one ever called on that phone until now, so we didn't need it.

No one comes by the house anymore looking for a miracle since the shooting, even though it's safe now. Eddie died in my bedroom. I've been staying at Jonah's. I can't help but wonder if Eddie wanted to survive, to kill us, then give up to the police so he could be famous for what he did. But we survived, and he didn't. I don't feel blessed or lucky, but it was very fortunate that Jonah and that police officer found Eddie when they did.

The police searched Eddie's house for days. They found a manifesto handwritten in a tiny, scrawling, drunken print describing how the world is going to hell because of the people of color. I summarize that because the manifesto used disgusting racist words, which I cannot repeat. The police found more evidence on a computer, which Eddie was using to communicate with several hate groups he belonged to. These groups advocated starting a race war and urged their followers to cleanse their neighborhoods of undesirables. The police wouldn't identify the hate groups in Eddie's computer because the FBI was conducting further investigations.

The police also found photos on the computer that held evidence of child pornography. I didn't want to know anymore, but hopefully, that was being investigated too.

Everyone has been feeling sad and exhausted from the sadness. Our house was cleaned up, so Mama, Hend, and Harun moved back in. I stayed at Jonah's house, but I go to Mama's for dinner when I feel that Jonah and Tameka need some time alone. Most of the time we all eat dinner together, either at Mama's house or Jonah's. I went up to my bedroom once and stood in the doorway for a long time, but I didn't see the ghost. I didn't get any sense that the ghost is still there. I always thought you were the ghost. I thought you were protecting me. I thought you were responsible for the bright light that blinded Eddie, but no one mentioned the ghost again. Mama called an electrician who came by and repaired the ceiling light in my bedroom. It works fine now. I still don't want to stay there.

Mama and Hend have been very busy with their jobs, and Harun has been writing about what happened. We were able to laugh about him finally having something to write about. He won't let me read it yet. I've been practicing for my solo with the Chicago Symphony. Playing my violin helps me stay sane. It helps me feel the beauty in the world. I'd be happy if everyone felt that way. Passing that beauty on to others is what I want to do with my life. The performance is still a few weeks away.

✝ ✝ ✝

JONAH ANNOUNCED THAT HE GOT TICKETS TO A CUBS GAME.

"Esther and I used to go to Cubs games," he said, "because it was always fun to hope for victory even though it may never come. And it's a good way to take your mind off problems or worries or sadness."

"Perfect," Mama said. "We can make it a birthday party for Mary."

"My dad used to take me to Cubs games," Jonah said, "even though we lived down south, and it would have been easier to go see the White Sox. He liked cheering for the underdog and wanted to see them break the curse. He never lived to see it, but he instilled that in me, so Esther and I went to the games. She didn't get to see the Cubs break the curse either. We all know how hard it is to be without the one person we thought would be with us always. I've decided it's better to keep their memories alive as a family, sharing what we love to do."

We took the green line from Oak Park into Chicago and got off at Lake where we changed to the red line and took that all the way to Wrigley Field in Boystown. The stadium was huge, but we all held hands, except for Harun of course, so we wouldn't get lost.

Once inside, Jonah bought me a Cubs cap just like the one he always wears, and he bought Tameka one that was pink. Hend purchased a Cubs cap for Harun and a Cubs scarf for herself, which she wrapped around her hijab. Mama preferred a knit beanie cap. We were all being quite silly.

"It will keep my head warm," she said.

It did get cold up in the bleachers. And Jonah was right. The game really didn't matter that much, not that day, not for us. We relaxed, we laughed, we ate junk food until we felt sick, and we cheered for the Cubs even though half the time I wasn't sure what was happening. Once someone hit a home run, and I stood up and cheered, screaming with joy as loud as I could, but I was the only one, and everybody around us was staring at me. Harun grabbed my arm and pulled me back into my seat.

"That was the other team," he said.

They were all laughing at me.

I waved at the strangers around us and pointed to my cap. "Sorry, I just got excited."

"Wait until the centerfield fence lights up and makes a lot of noise," Harun said. "Then you'll know to cheer for the Cubs."

For the rest of the game, I waited for everyone else to stand up and cheer, and then I did. It was safer that way.

When the game was over, Jonah said, "I have another surprise for you, Mary. Well, it's actually for all of us."

We got back on the red line after a long wait to get on the train and headed south. This time, we got off at Grand in River North and walked a few blocks. Mama and Hend walked together, and when we crossed streets, they held each other's hand. Harun and I walked together looking down at the sidewalk. Jonah walked with his arm around Tameka. It was getting dark when Jonah stopped.

"Here it is," Jonah said. "A little birthday dinner along with some smooth jazz."

We were standing in front of Andy's Jazz Club.

"I remember this area," Mama said.

"Me too, Rachel," Jonah said. "That was a terrible night, but we're here to change that memory to a good one. We won't let bad memories be a curse to this family. Let's go celebrate."

"Are you sure it's okay to bring the kids in here?" Hend asked.

"It's a restaurant too, so it should be okay," Mama said.

"We got here before 7:00," Jonah said. "It doesn't become a nightclub until late."

I realized why Hend was so nervous when we got inside. It was noisy with table talk and bustling with waiters scurrying back and forth between tables and the kitchen. There was a stage with a trio of musicians who were playing soft jazz. We were seated by the hostess at a table against the wall opposite the stage. We had a great view, and I was surprised that Jonah was able to get such a good table.

Unfortunately, at the table next to ours was a man who was talking and laughing very loudly. It was hard not to notice. A waiter came to the table for our drinks order. I drank so much soda at the Cubs game that I just wanted water. Everyone else must have felt the same way because we all ordered water.

"You don't have to order water because of me," Hend said. "It doesn't bother me if other people are drinking alcohol."

Mama put her hand over Hend's hands in her lap. "I'm just trying to take better care of myself," she said.

"I've been in this country for fifteen years," Hend said. "When I first got here, some people didn't know I was Muslim. I was always having to explain myself to them. I'm glad I don't have to do that anymore."

"What do you mean?" I asked.

"Well, things like why I don't drink alcohol or eat certain foods," she said.

"That's why I don't mind if you do most of the cooking," Mama said. "That way, I don't have to worry if I'm cooking something wrong."

"I love to cook, though," Hend said.

"And I love to eat your cooking." Mama laughed.

"I am becoming more assimilated into the American culture."

"What's assimilated?" I asked.

"I don't feel so strict anymore about drinking and eating as I used to."

"Does that mean I can order a beer?" Harun asked.

"No, it does not," Hend said and pushed Harun playfully, but she caught him off guard, and he almost fell into my lap. Harun and Hend both apologized, but I didn't mind so much. I love feeling close and protected by Harun.

"I think you're already drunk," I said, pushing him back up.

"Apparently, I'll never get a chance to be drunk," Harun said.

"If you are going act like that loud, obnoxious man at the next table, then I hope I never see you drunk," I said.

Mama shushed me. "You want him to hear?" she said.

"I don't care," I said. "He is."

Behind me was a wall full of photographs under a big sign that said Wall of Fame. I was looking at the photographs when a man wearing a suit walked up to the table and pointed to a particular photo on the wall. "Do you recognize this guy?" he asked.

He was pointing to a young man sitting at a piano. I stared at the photo for a long time. "Wait! Is that you, Jonah?"

Jonah was getting up from the table to shake hands with the man in the suit. "I'm afraid so," he said. Jonah shook the man's hand and gave him a hug. "It's been a long time, Jeff." Jonah turned to all of us at the table. "This is Jeff Chisholm. He and his brothers own this joint. This is my family. We're celebrating Mary's birthday. Mary is my granddaughter."

"Happy birthday, Mary," Mr. Chisholm said. He pointed back to the photo of Jonah. "And yes, that's Jonah from the days when he played the piano here. We miss Jonah very much."

"I'm an old man now, Jeff," Jonah said. "Don't play so much anymore."

"We have a lot of new faces in the bands that play here now. Some are good, some not so much. No one can tickle those ivories like you did. It's good to see you again, Jonah," Mr. Chisholm said. They shook hands again. "Glad you're back and enjoy your celebration. We might have some surprises for you tonight."

"I love surprises," Tameka said. "As long as they're happy surprises."

And they were. It wasn't long before the band finished the song they were playing. Mr. Chisholm jumped up on the stage and took the microphone. "We have a special guest in the house tonight, folks. He was our favorite piano player here at Andy's a few years back. He's here with his family tonight, but I'm hoping he'll join the band up here for a song or two to entertain you just like the old days. Please give a warm welcome to Jonah Culpepper."

The whole restaurant started applauding.

"Oh no," Jonah said. He closed his eyes and shook his head with a smile.

"You have to play now, Jonah," I said.

"Yeah, go up and play, Daddy," Tameka said.

Jonah stood up and waved to the crowd. The applause got louder as he slowly started toward the stage. We were all applauding until my hands were hurting. Jonah sat down at the piano and said something to the drummer and the bass player that we couldn't hear. Jonah started playing a few notes on the piano like he was warming up, and then he stopped momentarily to speak into the microphone.

"This is a little something that has always been one of my favorites by a man I admire, *C Jam Blues* by Oscar Peterson."

Jonah immediately started playing and didn't stop for what seemed like ten or fifteen minutes. His fingers were moving across the keyboard like crickets on a hot sidewalk, jumping all over the place so quickly you couldn't keep up with them. No one in the restaurant was eating. They were all listening and moving in their chairs to the rhythm. A few women stood up at their tables and were dancing at their seats. Even the loud, obnoxious man at the next table was tapping his feet and strumming the tabletop. The whole place was jumping and mesmerized by Jonah's piano playing. I was crying and bursting at the seams with pride. Jonah was with us, and he was my grandpa.

When he was done, he made his way back to the table through thunderous applause from everyone who had come together in this restaurant, strangers who had become friends, united in their love of Jonah's music. We all got up from the table and gave Jonah hugs and kisses. The rest of the night was frequently interrupted by people in the restaurant coming by to shake Jonah's hand or to ask for an autograph. We didn't mind. It made the night special. The only time the attention was diverted from Jonah was when the waiters brought out a birthday cake for us and I had to blow out the candles.

"They even got the number of candles right," I said. "Someone must have told them."

"Don't look at me," Mama said.

I looked at Jonah, and he winked at me.

***

When we got back home, we were all exhausted from a wonderful day of fun and food. We were waddling around, looking ridiculous but too tired to laugh at each other. Mama and Hend said their good-nights, kissed me and Jonah and Tameka, then left hand in hand out the back door. Harun came up to me and gave me a big hug and kissed me on the cheek.

"Happy birthday, cuz," he said.

I kissed him back and blushed, hoping he wouldn't notice.

"If you two are done flirting," Jonah said, looking at me. "I need Mary to come with me for a minute."

Harun laughed. "I'm outta here."

"Me too, Daddy," Tameka said. "I'm going to bed."

Jonah gave Tameka a big hug and kissed her forehead. "Goodnight, baby." He waited until Tameka made her way up the stairs.

"Okay, birthday girl, let's go." Jonah took my hand and took me to the music room. He pulled out the violin case for Esther's Tartari violin and opened it. "I want you to play me something before you go to bed."

"With Esther's special violin? Are you sure?"

"No," he said. "With *your* violin. Happy birthday, my granddaughter."

"Oh my God! Really?"

"Really. It's time for you to have this violin so you can play it with the Chicago Symphony just like Esther did."

I wrapped my arms around Jonah and held on. I didn't think I would ever stop crying, and I didn't want to let go. I looked up at him. "What can I play for you?" I asked.

Jonah sat down in his reading chair. "Oh, I don't know. How about *Meditation*."

"I think that's my favorite," I said.

I made sure the violin was tuned and looked at Jonah before I started. His eyes were closed, and he was smiling. He must have sensed me looking at him. He said, "Esther and I will be listening."

I gave myself to the music so Jonah would know how much I

appreciated him giving me Esther's prize violin. And it was beautiful with a warm, sweet tone. I played as delicately as I could to give each note an ethereal sound, a feeling of an eagle floating with the clouds over meadows and mountains and cool ambling streams. I was almost crying as I felt the music giving me a feeling as close to anything religious as I have ever felt. When I was done, I held the violin over my heart and took a deep breath.

Jonah's eyes were still closed, his head tilted slightly toward one shoulder. He appeared to have fallen asleep with a tear still lingering in his eyelid. I put the violin back in its case and grabbed a pillow from the sofa to put next to Jonah's head. I thought he wouldn't mind if I snuck off to bed while he was still in his chair.

As I placed the pillow, I noticed his breathing was very shallow, even undetectable. My heart started beating rapidly again. I placed my hand on his chest. There was no movement. I placed my cheek near his nose. I felt nothing. His hands were cold. I shook his shoulders. Nothing. He was too heavy to move. I panicked. I tried pushing on his chest, but it wasn't working. He seemed to be gone. With tears streaming down my face, I held his head and wrapped my arm around him as tightly as I could.

"No, not now, Jonah," I cried through my tears. "Come back. I need you to come back. We all need you to come back. We just got started. Please come back."

I tried more than I tried with Mama. I tried more than I tried with Tameka. I tried harder and believed more than I have ever wanted anything before until I realized that it wasn't working. It had probably never worked. It had never been me. I needed a miracle, and I couldn't make one happen.

Jonah was gone.

THIRTY-THREE - RACHEL

THE DAY WE BURIED JONAH WAS THE SADDEST DAY I've had since Jake died. It was also one of the happiest. I knew Jonah would want all of us to be happy, to celebrate his life, and to keep his memory a happy one. This was the message he left with us.

I talked to Tameka about a service for Jonah.

"My Mama liked going to Calvary Memorial," Tameka said. "Not sure why I remember that. Maybe because Daddy never liked going to church. He went anyway 'cause he would do anything for Mama."

I didn't want Tameka to worry about the details, so I contacted Calvary Memorial, and as I was speaking to the receptionist, a man came on the line and identified himself as Pastor Eric Redmond.

"I understand you're calling about arranging a funeral and memorial service?" he asked. "Are you a member at Calvary?"

"I am not," I said, "but I'm calling about Jonah Culpepper, and he might have been."

"Oh, I am so sorry," he said. There was a definite sinking in his voice.

"Can you check?" I asked.

"There's no need for that," he said. "Jonah and Esther were loved very much here at Calvary. My wife and I were personal friends with them as well. Jonah hasn't been here much since Esther passed."

"He didn't get around much," I explained. "I'm sure he kept you in his heart, though."

"Of course we'll keep a place for a memorial service here. Our Senior Pastor Gerald Hiestand will want to participate as well, I am sure, as soon as he hears about Jonah. If you can come into my office, we can sit down and make arrangements."

"Of course," I said. "Can I give you my phone number now? When Jonah's obituary is printed, you might get some phone calls, and you can just refer them to me."

I wrote an obituary for the Chicago Tribune. Tameka found an old photo of Jonah, and we took it down to the Tribune offices. By some odd coincidence, the clerk in the obit office remembered going to see Jonah perform at Andy's Jazz Club. We ended up with a story about Jonah and his passing on the front page of the entertainment section and a small blurb on the front page referring to the main article.

By my best estimate, about five hundred people attended Jonah's memorial service at Calvary Memorial. There were congregants from Calvary, old neighbors from the South Side, friends, and music lovers, old and new, from Andy's Jazz Club.

As a last-minute act of salvation, Pastor Hiestand agreed to open the Fellowship Hall for the crowd after the service, and I hired a few food trucks to park in the adjacent parking lot with food and drink for all. There were sermons from Pastor Hiestand and Pastor Redmond, and there was music. Oh my was there music. A young woman in the choir stood up and sang *His Eye Is on the Sparrow* with piano accompaniment and backup voices from the choir. Her voice was reminiscent of Whitney Houston, and before she was done, there were Hallelujahs in the congregation as people closed their eyes and waved their arms overhead.

There was *Swing Low Sweet Chariot*, which started out slow and sweet but didn't take long to erupt into upbeat, happy rejoicing as a near frenzy rippled through the congregation with people standing and joining in with singing and clapping.

That was just the beginning.

There was *When We All Get to Heaven, God is Here*, and *Marvelous*, which was performed at Aretha Franklin's memorial. I'm sure that Jonah was thinking how marvelous it all was.

Pastor Redmond introduced Tameka and Mary. "Dr. Tameka Culpepper is Jonah's youngest child, and Mary is Jonah's granddaughter. They are here to give their voices to the celebration of Jonah Culpepper."

Mary didn't want to do it if they were going to call it a eulogy. "That sounds like a medical procedure," she said.

"I agree," I said, laughing inside. "Did you want to play a tribute on your violin?"

"Definitely not," she said. "This should be about Jonah, not me."

Mary always surprised me with her maturity.

Tameka and Mary walked up to the pulpit together. They had agreed to share the moment.

"We are here to share our love for Jonah Culpepper," Tameka said. "He would be touched by all the love in this church tonight."

"He loved his music and loved to make people happy with his music," Mary said. "Above all, though, he loved his family."

"Through all of the tragedy in our family," Tameka said, "my father never gave up on us, and near the end of his life, he was the happiest I had ever seen him."

"Jonah risked his life for his family," Mary said, "and would have given his life for his family. In a way, he did, because he has passed on to us his wisdom and the person he was."

Together they said, "It is with sweet sadness that we say we will miss you, Jonah. We will not say goodbye because you will be with us always."

Mary and Tameka continued to stay together. Tameka improved more each day and even talked about going back to work as soon as she could. She and Hend talked about medicine whenever they were together. This seemed to be Hend's way of checking Tameka's progress. Tameka wanted to pursue the dream she had before her accident and go to Africa with Doctors Without Borders to help with immunizing and researching some of the more deadly diseases in Central and East Africa. She planned to keep the house Jonah had willed to her and said Mary could live there as long as she wanted. Hend and Harun planned to stay with me.

The house across the street has a for sale sign in front now. Hopefully, a nice young family moves in. Right now, I can't bring myself to even look at that house. Mary's bedroom is still vacant. No one feels right about staying there. I'm thinking about renting it out to a student who would enjoy living here, but never tell her what happened in that room.

We all went together to see Mary play with the Chicago Symphony. She wore a long, silver gown that made her look tall and slender. Her dark hair was in the stylish French braid she loves to wear. She was very much a young woman in command of her presence on the stage. The audience applauded when she and the conductor came out and took their places. The conductor waited until Mary was ready. They looked at each other, and she smiled. She was nervous but still confident. I could feel it. The conductor turned to the orchestra, and a hush fell over the audience.

Mary told me that when she played Mendelssohn's *Violin Concerto in E minor*, she imagined life from birth to death, beginning with the discovery of the world around her, observing nature and people, questioning why things are the way they are, having conversations, arguing, agreeing, sharing, love-making, and finally celebrating the end. This is how she intended to play this very long concerto. "I think Jonah would be proud of me," she said. "It is my goal to play this evolution of life the way Jonah would have wanted me to - to bring a tear to his eye."

Her slender arms embraced the violin with tenderness. Her delicate fingers slipped effortlessly back and forth on the neck of the violin with graceful precision, and her control of the bow gave the music an ethereal feeling that captured the audience from the first note and did not let them go until the last. Even the expression on her face reflected her interpretation of the music as if she were passing through the evolution of the concerto. I felt what she was feeling—her peace, her bewilderment, her confusion, her anger, her ecstasy, and her joy. We were all mesmerized.

When the last note faded away, a thunderous applause erupted in the audience and didn't fade until Mary returned three times to take a bow. She held her violin and bow in one hand and blew kisses to the audience before placing both hands over her heart and bowing. She blew kisses to the orchestra who returned her gratitude with smiles, applause, and kisses. She was the sweetheart of the symphony that night.

The hugs I received from Hend and Tameka and even Harun told me they were feeling the same as me. As we waited in a ballroom set up as an after-party with VIPs and orchestra members, Hend and Tameka kept repeating how this was the beginning of Mary's career. When Mary appeared in the ballroom accompanied by the conductor and Miss Jeong, there was another resounding applause.

I almost gasped. This was the vision I had when I feared I was dying, and I longed to know what Mary would be like as an adult, when I saw her as so beautiful that I cried and my tears fell on her shoulder. My vision had come true, and I was here to witness it. Mary was still only fifteen, but I knew that this same vision would play out for her for many years. Mary saw us standing beside a table of hors d'oeuvres where we had decided to wait so we wouldn't lose Harun who was grazing at the table. Mary pointed to us, and Miss Jeong escorted her to where we were standing. Miss Jeong greeted us as if we were old friends. She introduced the conductor as Maestro Riccardo Muti.

"You really need no introduction," I said. "I am very honored to meet you."

He greeted us all around. "You have quite a beautiful prodigy here," he said. "I hope you enjoyed the concert as much as I enjoyed directing Mary with the orchestra. I think she might be headed toward a distinguished, solo career."

"I don't know what to say," I said. "Except thank you."

"As you can see," Miss Jeong said, "Mary is adored, and she deserves it. We are very proud of Mary. She is so adorable, but she is also a very beautiful young lady, and her playing was perfection."

"I wanted to thank you again for all you have done to help Mary. She is enjoying the Academy and has progressed with her playing immensely."

"Her performance tonight is certainly proof of that," Miss Jeong said. "I think Mary is going to have a charmed future. I'm sure our paths will cross again. I'm sorry, but Mary needs to greet her fans. All of these people in here are waiting to meet her."

"We'll be here," I said and gave Mary a hug.

Mary whispered in my ear, "I could feel Jonah with me here tonight. It was like he was watching me from heaven."

"You played like he taught you, so maybe he was," I said.

I gave her another hug, and Mary handed me her violin case. As she turned to walk away, Mary stopped and brushed something on her shoulder. She looked at her hand, then up to the ceiling, as if searching. I could see her whimsical smile emerge as she whispered, "Jonah?"

CPSIA information can be obtained
at www.ICGtesting.com
Printed in the USA
LVHW011106291021
701894LV00001B/6